OPERATION NAPOLEON

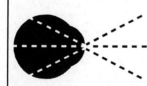

This Large Print Book carries the Seal of Approval of N.A.V.H.

OPERATION NAPOLEON

ARNALDUR INDRIÐASON

Translated from the Icelandic by Victoria Cribb

THORNDIKE PRESS
A part of Gale, Cengage Learning

Detroit • New York • San Francisco • New Haven, Conn • Waterville, Maine • London

GALE
CENGAGE Learning

Copyright © 1999 by Arnaldur Indriðason. English translation copyright © 2010 by Victoria Cribb.

First published in Iceland with the title *Napóleonsskjölin* by Vaka Helgafell, Reykjavík.

Thorndike Press, a part of Gale, Cengage Learning.

Thorndike Press® Large Print Thriller.

The text of this Large Print edition is unabridged.

Other aspects of the book may vary from the original edition.

Set in 16 pt. Plantin.

LIBRARY OF CONGRESS CATALOGING-IN-PUBLICATION DATA

Arnaldur Indriðason, 1961–
[Napóleonsskjölin. English]
   Operation napoleon / by Arnaldur Indriðason ; translated from the Icelandic by Victoria Cribb.
     p. cm. — (Thorndike Press large print thriller)
     ISBN-13: 978-1-4104-4446-2 (hardcover)
     ISBN-10: 1-4104-4446-5 (hardcover)
     1. Large type books. I. Cribb, Victoria. II. Title.
PT7511.A67N3713 2012
839'.6934—dc23   2011041061

Published in 2012 by arrangement with St. Martin's Press, LLC.

Operation Napoleon

■ ■ ■ ■

1945

■ ■ ■ ■

A blizzard raged on the glacier.

He could see nothing ahead, could barely make out the compass in his hand. He could not turn back even if he wanted to. There was nothing to go back to. The storm stung and lashed his face, hurling hard, cold flakes at him from every direction. Snow became encrusted in a thick layer on his clothes and with every step he sank to his knees. He had lost all sense of time and had no idea how long he had been walking. Still cloaked in the same impenetrable darkness as when he had begun his journey, he could not even tell whether it was day or night. All he knew was that he was on his last legs. He took a few steps at a time, rested, then carried on. A few steps. A rest. A few more steps. A rest. A step. Rest. Step.

He had escaped almost unscathed from the crash, though others had not been so lucky. In an eruption of noise, the plane had skimmed the surface of the glacier. One of its engines burst into flame, then vanished abruptly as the entire wing sheared off and whirled away into the snow-filled darkness. Almost immediately the other wing was torn away in a shower of sparks, and the wing-less fuselage went careering across the ice like a torpedo.

He, the pilot and three others had been belted into their seats when the plane went down but two of the passengers had been gripped with hysteria at the first sign of trouble, leaping up and trying to break into the cockpit in their panic. The impact sent them ricocheting like bullets off the sides of the cabin. He had ducked, watching them slam into the ceiling and bounce off the walls, before being catapulted past him and landing at the back of the plane where their cries were silenced.

The wreckage ploughed across the glacier, sending up clouds of snow and ice until it gradually lost momentum and ground to a halt. Then there was no sound but the howl-ing of the storm.

Alone of the passengers, he was deter-mined to brave the blizzard and make for civilisation. The others recommended wait-ing, in the hope that the storm would blow itself out. They thought everyone should stick together, but he was not to be stopped. He did not want to suffer being trapped in the plane; could not endure it becoming his coffin. With their help he wrapped himself up as well as possible for the journey, but he had not walked far in the relentless conditions before he realised he would have been better off inside the plane with the others. Now it was too late.

He tried to head south-east. For a split second before the bomber crashed he had glimpsed lights, as if from houses, and now he headed off in what he believed to be the right direction. He was chilled through and his footsteps grew heavier and heavier. If anything, the storm seemed to be growing more intense. He battled on, his strength failing with every step.

His thoughts turned to the plight of the others who had remained behind in the aircraft. When he had left them the snow had already begun to drift over the wreckage, and the scar left by its progress across the ice was filling up fast. They had oil lamps but the oil would not last long, and the cold on the glacier was unimaginable. If they kept the door of the plane open, the cabin would fill with snow. They were probably already trapped inside. They knew they would freeze to death whether they stayed

11

in the aircraft or ventured out on to the ice. They had discussed the limited options. He had told them he could not sit still and wait for death.

The chain rattled. The briefcase was weighing him down. It was handcuffed to his wrist. He no longer held the handle but let the case drag on its chain. The handcuff chafed his wrist but he did not care. He was past caring.

They heard it long before it swooped over them, heading west. Heard it approaching through the screaming of the storm, but when they looked up there was nothing to be seen but winter darkness and stinging, wind-driven flakes. It was just before eleven at night. A plane, was their immediate thought. War had brought a fair amount of air traffic to the area as the British had a base in Hornafjördur, so they knew most of the British and American aircraft by the sound of their engines. But they had never heard anything like this before. And never before had the roar been so close, as if the plane were diving straight for their farm.

They went out on to the front step and stood there for some time until the roar of the engines reached its height. With their hands over their ears they followed the

12

sound towards the glacier. For a split second its dark body could be glimpsed overhead, then it vanished again into the blackness. Its nose up, it looked to be trying to gain height. The roar gradually receded in the direction of the glacier, before finally dying away. They both had the same thought. The plane was going to crash. It was too low. Visibility was zero in the appalling weather and the glacier would claim the plane in a matter of minutes. Even if it managed to gain a little height, it would be too late. The ice cap was too close.

They remained standing on the step for several minutes after the noise had died away, peering through the blizzard and straining to listen. Not a sound. They went back inside. They could not alert the authorities to the course of the plane as the telephone had been out of order since the lines came down in another storm. There had not been time to reconnect it. A familiar nuisance. Now a second blizzard had blown up, twice as bad. As they got ready for bed, they discussed trying to get through to Höfn in Hornafjördur on horseback to report the plane once the weather had died down.

It was not until four days later that the conditions finally improved and they were able to set off for Höfn. The drifts were deep, making their progress slow. They were brothers and lived alone on the farm; their parents were dead and neither of them had married. They stopped to rest at a couple of farms on the way, spending the night at the second, where they related the story of the plane and their fear that it had almost certainly perished. None of the other farmers had heard anything.

When the brothers reached Höfn they reported the aircraft to the district official, who immediately contacted the Reykjavík authorities and informed them that a plane had been seen south of the Vatnajökull glacier and had almost certainly crashed on the ice. All flights over Iceland and the North Atlantic were monitored by air traffic control at the US army base in Reykjavík, but they had been unaware of any aircraft in the area at the time — the conditions had meant traffic had been at a minimum.

Later that day a telegram from the US military headquarters arrived at the office of the Höfn district official. The army would immediately take over investigation of the case and see to it that a rescue party was sent to the glacier. As far as the locals were concerned, the case was closed. Furthermore, the army banned all traffic on the glacier in the area where the plane was believed to have gone down. No explanations were offered.

Four days later, twelve military transport vehicles rumbled into Höfn with two hundred soldiers on board. They had not been able to use the airstrip in Hornafjördur, as it was closed during the darkest winter months, and Höfn was cut off from the capital to the west by the unbridged rivers of the Skeidará sands. The expedition force had had to circumnavigate the country in six-wheeled vehicles equipped with snow-chains, driving first north, then south along the East Fjords to reach Höfn. The journey north had been arduous, as the main road was little more than a dirt track, and the expedition had been forced to dig their way through heavy drifts all the way across the eastern desert of Mödrudalsöraefi.

The troops were soldiers of the 10th Infantry Regiment and 46th Field Artillery Battalion under General Charles H. Bone-steel, commander of the US occupying force. Some of the men had taken part in the army's winter exercises on the Eiríks-jökull glacier the previous year, but in practice few of them could even ski.

The expedition was led by one Colonel Miller. His men pitched camp just outside Höfn in barracks built by the British oc-

15

cupation force at the beginning of the war, from where they made their way to the glacier. By the time the soldiers arrived at the brothers' farm, almost ten days had elapsed since they had heard the plane, days in which it had snowed without respite. The soldiers set up their base at the farm and the brothers agreed to act as their guides on the ice cap. They spoke no English but with a combination of gestures and sign language were able to show Miller and his men the direction of the plane, warning that there was little chance of finding it on or near the glacier in the depths of winter.

'Vatnajökull is the biggest glacier in Europe,' they said, shaking their heads. 'It's like looking for a needle in a haystack.' It did not help that the snow would have obliterated all signs of a crash-landing.

Colonel Miller understood their gestures but ignored them. Despite the heavy going, there was a passable route to the glacier from the brothers' farm and in the circumstances the operation went smoothly. During the short winter days, when the sun was up only from eleven in the morning until half past five, there was little time for searching. Colonel Miller kept his men well in order, though the brothers quickly discovered that most of them had never set foot on a glacier and had scant experience of winter expeditions. They guided the soldiers safely past crevasses and gullies, and the men set up camp in a depression at the edge of the glacier, about 1,100 metres above sea level.

Miller's troops spent three weeks combing the slopes of the glacier and a five square kilometre area of the ice cap itself. For most of the time the soldiers were lucky with the weather and coordinated their searches well. They divided their efforts, one group searching in the foothills from a camp set up near the farm, while the other group camped on the glacier and scoured the ice for as long as daylight lasted. When darkness fell in the afternoon, the soldiers assembled back at the farm base camp where they ate, slept and sang songs familiar to the brothers from the radio. They slept in British-issue mountaineering tents, sewn from double layers of silk, and huddled for warmth around primuses and oil lamps. Their heavy leather coats reached below the knee and had fur-lined hoods. On their hands they wore thick, coarsely knitted gloves of Icelandic wool.

No sign of the aircraft was found on this first expedition apart from the rim of the tail wheel, of which Colonel Miller immediately took charge. It was the brothers who made the discovery, about two kilometres on to the ice cap. Beyond this fragment, the ice was smooth in every direction and there was no evidence that an aircraft had crashed or made a forced landing there. The brothers said that if the plane had gone down on that part of the ice cap, the snow had probably drifted over the wreckage already. The glacier had swallowed it up.

Colonel Miller was like a man possessed in his search for the plane. He appeared to feel no tiredness and won the admiration of the brothers, who treated him with a mixture of affection and respect and were eager to do anything for him. Miller consulted them a great deal for their local knowledge and they came to be on friendly terms. But eventually, after the expedition had twice been hampered by severe weather on the ice, the colonel was forced to abandon his search. In the second storm, tents and other equipment were buried in snow and lost for good.

There were two aspects of the expedition that puzzled the brothers.

One day they came upon Miller alone in the stable block, which adjoined the barn and cowshed, taking him by surprise as he stood by one of the horses in its stall, stroking its head. The colonel, whose courage and authority over his men was striking, had to all appearances taken himself quietly to one side to weep. He cradled the horse's head and they saw how his shoulders shook. When one of them cleared his throat, Miller started and glanced their way. They saw the tracks of tears on his dirty cheeks, but the colonel was quick to recover, drying his face and pretending nothing had happened. The brothers had often discussed Miller. They never asked him how old he was but guessed he could be no more than twenty-five.

'This is a handsome animal,' Miller said in his own language. The brothers did not understand him. He's probably homesick, they thought. But the incident stayed in their minds.

The other matter which aroused the brothers' interest was the wheel itself. They had had time to examine it before Colonel Miller found them and confiscated it. The tyre had been wrenched off the wheel so only the naked rim hung from the broken landing gear. For a long time afterwards they wondered about the fact that the wheel rim was inscribed with lettering in a language they understood even less than English.

KRUPPSTAHL.

■ ■ ■ ■

1999

■ ■ ■ ■

1

Control Room, Building 312, Washington DC,
Wednesday 27 January

The building stood not far from the Capitol in Washington DC. Originally a warehouse, it had undergone an elaborate conversion to house one of the capital's many clandestine organisations. No cost had been spared in the conversion, either inside or out. Now, giant computers hummed day and night, receiving information relayed from space. Satellite photographs belonging to the US military intelligence service were collected in a database, and there the information was processed, analysed and catalogued, and the alert raised if anything irregular came to light.

In official documents the warehouse was known simply as Building 312, but the organisation it housed had played a fundamental role in the US army's defence programme during the Cold War. Established shortly after 1960 during the most intense period of mutual suspicion, its chief role had been to analyse spy photographs taken of the Soviet Union, China and Cuba, and any other nations classed as enemies of the United States. After the end of the Cold War, its role included monitoring terrorist bases in the Middle East and conflicts in the Balkans. The organisation controlled a total of eight satellites in orbits ranging from 800 to 1,500 kilometres above Earth.

The director of the organisation was General Vytautas Carr, who stood now in front of a monitor which filled an entire wall of the first-floor control room, staring intently at a batch of images that had been drawn to his attention. It was cool in the room on account of the fans for the twelve powerful computer units which hummed ceaselessly in a cordoned-off section. Two armed guards stood at the doors. The room was intersected by four long banks of flickering screens and control panels.

Carr was not far off his seventieth birthday and ought to have taken retirement but for a special dispensation by the organisation. He was almost six foot five, his back ramrod straight, unbowed with age. He had been a soldier all his life, had served in Korea, and directed and shaped the operations of the organisation as one of its most dynamic chiefs. He was dressed in civilian clothes, a double-breasted dark suit. The monitor on the wall in front of him was reflected in his glasses, behind which a pair of small, shrewd eyes were concentrating on the two screens at the top left.

On one of the screens were images called up from the organisation's archives; these held tens of millions of satellite photographs taken over the last four decades. The other showed new pictures. The images Vytautas Carr was scrutinising were of a small section of south-east Iceland's Vatnajökull glacier, one taken about a year ago, the other earlier that day. The older image revealed nothing remarkable, just the pristine white expanse of the ice cap interrupted by the odd belt of crevasses, but in the new picture, down in the left-hand corner, a small mark was visible. The images were coarse and grainy but once touched up they would be sharp and clear. Carr requested a blow-up of the detail and the image magnified, then resolved itself until the black mark filled the entire screen.

'Who do we have in Keflavík?' Carr asked the man at the control panel as he enlarged the images.

'We don't have anyone in Keflavík, sir,'

he replied.

Carr considered this.

'Get Ratoff for me,' he said, adding: 'This had better not be another false alarm.'

'We have better satellite equipment these days, sir,' the other man said, holding the phone.

'We've never gotten such a clear picture of the glacier before. How many people know about the new images?'

'Only the rest of the eight watch, that's three people. Then you and me, of course.'

'Do they know the situation?'

'No, sir. They didn't show any interest in the pictures.'

'Keep it that way,' said Carr and left the room. He stalked down the long corridor to his office and shut the door behind him. A light was flashing on his telephone.

'Ratoff on line two,' said a disembodied voice. Carr frowned and punched the button.

'How long will it take for you to get to Keflavík?' Carr asked without preamble.

'What's Keflavík, sir?' queried the voice on the phone.

'Our base in Iceland,' answered Carr.

'Iceland? I could be there tomorrow evening. Why, what's going on?'

'We've received a clear image of the biggest glacier in the country. It seems to be returning an object to us which we lost there many years ago and we need a man in Keflavík to direct the operation. You will take two special forces squadrons and choose your own equipment. Call it a routine exercise. Direct the locals to the defense secretary if they're uncooperative. I'll talk to him. I'll also call a meeting with the Icelandic government to offer an explanation. The military base is a sensitive issue in Iceland. Immanuel Wesson will take over our embassy in Reykjavík and act as spokesman. You'll receive more detailed instructions on the way.'

'I presume this is a covert operation, sir?'

'I wouldn't have called you otherwise.'

'Keflavík. I remember now. Wasn't there some wild goose chase there in '67?'

'We have better satellites these days.'

'Are the coordinates the same?'

'No. This is a new location. That damn glacier keeps moving,' said Carr and cut short the conversation without saying goodbye. He did not like Ratoff. He stood up, walked over to a large glass cabinet and opened the door, taking out two small keys which he turned over in his palm. One was slightly larger than the other but both were finely scaled, clearly designed for small keyholes. He put them back in the cabinet.

It was many years since Carr had examined the wheel. He took it out now and weighed it in his hands. He reread the inscription: Kruppstahl. It, alone, had confirmed the crash-landing. Its make correlated with the type and size of the plane, its year of manufacture and capacity. This wheel was proof that it was up there on the glacier. After all these years it had at last been found.

2

Kristín closed her eyes. She felt the headache throbbing in her forehead. This was the third time the man had come to her office and launched into a diatribe against the ministry, blaming them for the fact that he had been cheated. On the first two occasions he had attempted to browbeat her, threatening that if he did not receive compensation for what he regarded as the ministry's mistake he would take the matter to court. Twice now she had listened to his tirade and twice struggled to keep herself under control, answering him clearly and objectively, but he did not seem to hear a word she said. Now he was sitting in her office once again, embarking on the same cycle of recriminations.

She guessed he was around forty, ten years or so older than her, and this age difference apparently licensed him to throw his weight about in her office, making threats and referring to her as 'a girl like you'. He made no attempt to hide his contempt for her, though whether for the sin of being a woman or a lawyer she could not tell. His name was Runólfur Zóphaníasson. He had a carefully cultivated three-day beard and thick, black hair, slicked back with gel. He wore a dark suit with a waistcoat, and a small silver chain attached to a watch. This he extracted from his waistcoat pocket every now and then with long, thin fingers, flicking it open self-importantly as if he did not have time to waste on 'this crap' — as he put it himself.

He's right about the crap, she thought. He sold mobile freezing plants to Russia, and both the ministry and the Icelandic Trade Council had assisted him in making business contacts. He had sent four units to Murmansk and Kamchatka, but had not received so much as a rouble in return and now claimed that the ministry's lawyer, who no longer worked there, had suggested he dispatch the units and charge for them later, in order to smooth the way for further contracts. He had done so, with the result that goods belonging to him to the tune of more than thirty million *krónur* had disappeared in Russia. He had tried in vain to trace them, and now looked to the Trade Council and trade department of the Foreign Ministry for support and compensation, if nothing else. 'What kind of idiot consultants does this ministry employ?' he asked repeatedly at his meetings with Kristín. She had contacted the lawyer who could not remember giving him any advice but warned her that the man had once threatened him.

'You must have realised that doing business with Russia these days is very risky,' she had said to him at their first meeting, and pointed out that although the ministry endeavoured to help Icelandic companies set up deals, the risk always lay with the companies themselves. The ministry regretted what had happened and would happily help him make contact with Russian buyers through the embassy in Moscow, but if he could not extract payment, there was little the ministry could do. She had repeated this message in different words at their next meeting and for a third time, now, as he sat before her with an expression of petulance and ill temper and that pretentious silver chain in his waistcoat pocket. The meeting was dragging on. It was late and she wanted to go home.

'You won't get off so easily,' he said. 'You trick people into doing business with the Russian mafia. You probably even take back-handers from them. What do I know? One hears things. I want my money back and if I don't get it . . .'

She knew his diatribe off by heart and decided to cut it short. She did not have time for this.

'We're sorry, naturally, that you've lost money in your dealings with Russia but it's not our problem,' she said coolly. 'We don't make decisions for people. It's up to them to evaluate the situation for themselves. If you're so stupid as to export goods worth tens of millions without any securities, you're even more of a fool than you look. I'm now asking you, please, to leave my office and not to bother me in future with any more rubbish about what you imagine to be the ministry's responsibilities.'

He gawped at her, the words 'stupid' and 'fool' echoing in his head. He opened his mouth to say something but she got in first.

'Out, now, if you please.'

She saw his face swell with rage.

He stood up slowly without taking his eyes off her, then suddenly seemed to lose control. Picking up the chair he had been sitting on, he hurled it at the wall behind him.

'This isn't finished!' he yelled. 'We'll meet again and then we'll see which of us is the fool. It's a conspiracy. A conspiracy, I tell you! And you'll suffer for it.'

'Yes, yes, dear, off you go now,' she said as if to a six-year-old. She knew she was goading him but could not resist it.

'You watch yourself! Don't think you can talk to me like that and get away with it!' he shouted and swept to the door, slamming it behind him so the walls shook.

Ministry employees had collected outside her office, drawn by the sound of the chair hitting the wall and the man shouting. They saw him emerge, purple in the face, and storm away. Kristín appeared in the doorway.

'It's all right,' she told her colleagues calmly, adding: 'he's got problems,' then shut the door carefully. Sitting down at her desk, she began to tremble and sat quietly until she had regained her composure. They did not teach you how to deal with this at law school.

Kristín was petite and dark, with short, black hair, strong features in a thin face and sharp brown eyes that shone with decisiveness and self-confidence. She had a reputation for firmness and obstinacy, and was known within the ministry for not suffering fools gladly.

The phone rang. It was her brother. He immediately felt her tension.

'Is everything okay?' he asked.

'Oh, it's nothing. There was a man in here just now. I thought he was going to throw a chair at me. Apart from that, everything's fine.'

'Throw a chair! What sort of lunatics are you dealing with?'

'The Russian mafia, or so I'm told. It's some kind of conspiracy, apparently. How are things with you?'

'Everything's great. I just bought this phone. Do I sound clear?'

'No different from usual.'

'No different from usual!' he mimicked. 'Do you know where I am?'

'No. Where?'

'Just outside Akureyri. The team's on its way to Vatnajökull.'

'Vatnajökull? In the middle of winter?'

'It's a winter exercise. I've already told you. We reach the glacier tomorrow and I'll call you again then. But you must tell me how the phone sounds. It's clear, isn't it?' he repeated.

'Great. You stick with the others. You hear

34

me? Don't attempt anything by yourself.'

'Sure. It cost seventy thousand *krónur,* you know.'

'What did?'

'The phone. It's got NMT's long-distance communication system.'

'NMT? What are you on about? Over and out.'

'You don't need to say over . . .'

She put down the receiver. Her brother Elías was ten years younger than her, forever immersed in one new hobby or another, mostly outdoor activities which involved travelling in the uninhabited interior. One year it had been hunting, when he filled her freezer with goose and reindeer meat. Another year it was skydiving, and he pestered her to jump with him, without success. The third year it was river rafting in rubber dinghies, then jeep trips across the highlands, glacier trips, skiing trips, snowmobiling — you name it. He was a member of the Reykjavík Air Ground Rescue Team. And it was just like him to buy a mobile phone for seventy thousand *krónur.* He was a technology junkie. His jeep looked like the flight deck of an aircraft.

In this respect brother and sister could not be more different. When winter arrived, her instinct was to crawl into hibernation and not emerge until spring. She never ventured into the highlands, and avoided travelling in Iceland altogether during winter. If she went for a summer holiday, she kept to the country's ring road and stayed at hotels. But generally she went abroad; to the US, where she had studied, or London, where she had friends. Sometimes, during the darkest period of the Icelandic winter, she would book a week's escape somewhere hot. She hated the cold and dark and had a tendency to suffer from depression during the blackest months when the sun rose at eleven and crawled along the horizon, to set after only five meagre hours of twilight. At this time of year she was overwhelmed by the realisation that she was trapped on a small island in the far north of the Atlantic, in cold, dark isolation.

But regardless of their differences, brother and sister got on very well. They were their parents' only children, and despite the ten-year age gap, or perhaps because of it, had always been extremely close. He worked for a large garage in Reykjavík, converting jeeps into customised off-roaders; she was a lawyer with a degree in international law from the University of California, had been working at the ministry for two years and was very happy to be doing a job which made use of her education. Fortunately, encounters like today's were the exception.

As long as he takes care up on the glacier, thought Kristín as she made her way home. The memory of her meeting with Runólfur would not go away. As she walked down Laugavegur shopping street, through the centre of Reykjavík and home to Tómasarhagi in the west of town, she had a prickling sensation of being watched. She had never experienced this before and told herself it was because she was still on edge. Looking around, she saw nothing to be concerned about and mocked herself for being so neurotic. But the feeling persisted. Come to think of it, she had never been accused of accepting bribes from the Russian mafia before either.

3

Keflavík Airport, Iceland,
Thursday 28 January, 2000 GMT

The giant C-17 US army transport plane landed at Keflavík Airport at around 8 p.m., local time. It was cold, several degrees below zero, but the forecast was for rising temperatures and snow. The massive bulk of the jet taxied through the winter darkness to the end of runway seven, which was reserved for the exclusive use of the NATO base on Midnesheidi moor. It was a remote, bleak location amidst the lava fields on the westernmost tip of the Reykjanes peninsula, lashed by constant gale-force winds, devoid of vegetation, barely fit for human habitation. Hangars large and small dotted the landscape, along with barracks, shops, a cinema and administration blocks. The naval air station had been a centre for reconnaissance flights at the height of the Cold War but these days the base's activities had been greatly curtailed.

Once the aircraft had come to a standstill, the aft door opened, releasing a stream of personnel who immediately began the task of unloading: powerful snowmobiles, tracked vehicles, skiing equipment, all the gear necessary for tackling the glacier. Fifteen minutes after the plane had touched down, the first transporter departed from Keflavík Airport with its cargo, bound for the Reykjanes highway and the south Iceland route to Vatnajökull.

The transporter was a German model, a Mercedes-Benz, its only marking Icelandic licence plates. It was no different from any other truck and trailer combo that plied the country's roads and as such drew no attention. In all, four trucks of varying models had pulled up to the C-17 when it came to a stop at the end of the runway. They departed from Keflavík Airport at half-hour intervals, mingling seamlessly with the civilian traffic.

Ratoff, the director of the operation, rode in the final vehicle. He had been met at the airport by the commander of the US military base on Midnesheidi, an admiral by rank, who had been forewarned of Ratoff's arrival and ordered to provide him with transport vehicles, no questions asked. The admiral, who had been exiled to this unpopular outpost after a scandal involving the large-scale embezzlement of supplies from a Florida base, had the good sense not to press for details, though he struggled to keep his curiosity in check. He had heard rumours about the commotion in the late sixties, and judging from the equipment being arranged in front of him, history was repeating itself: another glacier trip was planned.

'Don't you want our helicopters?' the admiral asked as he stood beside Ratoff, watching the cargo being unloaded. 'We have four new Pave Hawks in our fleet. They can move mountains.'

Ratoff was fiftyish, greying at the temples; a short, lean figure with Slavonic features and small, almost black eyes, clad in thick white cold-weather overalls and mountaineering boots. He did not so much as glance at the admiral.

'Just provide what we need and keep your distance,' he said curtly and walked off.

In the two days that had passed since the mark appeared on the satellite images, Carr had not been idle. The C-17 aircraft was scheduled to wait on standby at Keflavík Airport until the mission was accomplished, its huge bulk protected day and night by

40

eight armed guards. Its passengers had included General Immanuel Wesson and a ten-man team of Delta Force operators under his command, who were deployed to Reykjavík with orders to assume control of the embassy. The ambassador and his immediate staff were sent on leave without explanation or delay.

Snow had begun to fall in heavy, wet flakes, settling in a thick blanket over the south and east of the country, and overwhelming the trucks' windscreen wipers. There was a fair amount of traffic between Reykjavík and the small towns of Hveragerdi and Selfoss, but after that the road east was clear. The vehicles maintained a steady distance from one another as they drove through the impenetrable murk and falling snow, past the villages of Hella and Hvolsvöllur in their flat farmlands, to Vík í Mýrdal, huddled at the foot of its glacier, and on east past the settlement of Kirkjubaejarklaustur and over the bridges of the Skeidará sands, a vast outwash plain crossed by glacial rivers that were subject at times to devastating flash floods caused by eruptions under the inland ice cap. To their left, hidden by darkness, were mountains, glaciers and the barren interior; to their right, beyond the sands, lay the harbourless coastline of the Atlantic.

Nobody noticed them. Freight transport was common in the countryside where, in the absence of railways, goods of all kinds were transported by road: agricultural machinery, food supplies and fuel bound for Iceland's remote farms and villages.

Ratoff's briefing had included a detailed account of the military operation in 1967, the second major expedition mounted to search for the plane on Vatnajökull. Forced to circumnavigate the country on rough dirt roads, heading first north, then approaching the ice cap from the east, it had been difficult, then as now, to avoid attention. In the end they had been obliged to resort to drastic measures.

Ratoff's men travelled on under cover of darkness. In spite of the snow the roads were perfectly passable now that they had been asphalted. One by one they drove past the popular tourist destination of Skaftafell, making for Hornafjördur in the east. They passed through the lowland corridor of Öraefi, Sudursveit and Mýrar, between glacier and sea, then just before the town of Höfn turned left off the ring road, drove up into the farmlands at the foot of the glacier and stopped at the brothers' farm. By the time Ratoff's truck arrived, the soldiers were busy unloading the other transporters and the first snowmobiles were already on their way up to the ice cap.

The farmer stood at his door, watching the troops at work. He had seen it all before and though he did not know Ratoff, who now came walking towards him through the thickly falling snow, he had met others of his type. The farmer's name was Jón. He had lived alone on the farm since his brother's death several years earlier.

'Having another crack at the glacier?' he asked in Icelandic, shaking Ratoff's hand. Jón knew a smattering of English — he understood it better than he could speak it — but they still had need of the interpreter supplied by the base, a man who had been stationed in Iceland for several years.

Ratoff smiled at Jón. They kicked off the snow, went inside the warm, tidy house and sat down in the sitting room, Ratoff in his white overalls, the interpreter bundled up in a down jacket, and the farmer in a red-checked shirt, worn jeans and woollen socks. He was nearly eighty, his cranium completely bald, his face a mass of wrinkles, but he was still spry and straight-backed, still mentally and physically robust. Once the men had taken their seats he offered them strong black coffee and a pinch of

43

snuff taken from the back of his wrist. Unsure what it was, Ratoff and the interpreter shook their heads.

To Jón's knowledge it was the third time the army had mounted an expedition to the glacier, if you counted Miller's attempt at the end of the war. For some time afterwards, though, the colonel had returned every few years on his own, staying with the brothers for two to three weeks at a time while he scoured the ice cap with a small metal detector, before heading back to the States. He and the brothers were on friendly terms, but when they asked members of the 1967 expedition for news of Miller, they were informed that he was dead. That was the biggest expedition Jón had seen to date. As before, the brothers had acted as guides for the army, leading the soldiers up through the foothills and on to the ice sheet. They learnt that part of the wrecked aircraft had appeared on a satellite image — the military had stopped using spy planes by then. Over the years the brothers had sometimes been aware of the surveillance flights, but patrols of the area had ceased abruptly after the advent of the new technology.

The brothers had often asked themselves why the Americans were so obsessed with the German aircraft that they had the glacier monitored from space and turned up at the farm in force whenever they believed the wreckage was emerging from the ice. They had given Colonel Miller their word that they would never reveal the true purpose of the expeditions to their neighbours or anyone else; he had told them to dismiss the activity as military training exercises if the locals became curious, and they followed his advice. In private, however, they speculated endlessly, considering ever more wildly improbable theories: perhaps the plane was full of Jewish gold, or diamonds, or art treasures plundered by the Nazis from all over Europe. Perhaps there had been a high-ranking general on board, or a secret weapon from the war. Whatever it was, the US army was extremely keen both to lay hands on it and to do so without drawing attention to the fact. Every time a black mark appeared on their images of the glacier, the military authorities became very jittery indeed. It amused the old man.

'What did you see this time?' Jón asked, watching the interpreter relay his question to Ratoff.

'We believe we've finally located it,' the interpreter said, translating Ratoff's words. 'Better satellites.'

'Yes, better satellites,' Jón repeated. 'Do

you know what the plane contains? What it is that your people are so desperate to find?'

'No idea,' Ratoff replied. 'My job is merely to accomplish a specific task. It's nothing to do with me what the plane contains or where it comes from. My only concern is to follow my orders to the letter.'

Jón inspected Ratoff, sensing that he was a very different customer from the gentle Miller; there was something unclean, cunning even, about his expression; a hint of impatience, of an incalculable temper lurking beneath his outwardly calm demeanour.

'Well, I wouldn't be surprised if you found it,' Jón went on. 'There's been a warm spell since about 1960 and much of the ice in this area has melted.'

'According to our images, the nose is visible above the ice,' Ratoff told him. 'We have the coordinates. It shouldn't take us long.'

'So you know where you're going,' Jón said, taking a powerful sniff of the coarse tobacco. The snuff induced an overwhelming urge to sneeze in the uninitiated and was dismissed as a dirty habit by many, but the nicotine hit was every bit as strong as that from a cigarette.

'You don't need a guide any longer,' he added. 'Especially not a dinosaur like me. I'm no use to anyone these days.' He smiled.

'We're very familiar with the route by now,' Ratoff agreed, rising to his feet.

'Tourists use it a lot in the summer,' Jón said. 'They run glacier jeep tours from Höfn; I let them cross my land. There are more coming every year now.'

Shortly afterwards Ratoff emerged from the farmhouse with his interpreter. They strode over to a small vehicle with caterpillar tracks, climbed inside and set off without delay, past the farm in the direction of the foothills. There was no sign of the larger trucks now. The blizzard had grown ever more dense during the evening and visibility was poor. Their vehicle followed the trail left by the others in the newly fallen snow, its progress slow, crawling onwards through the drifts, its powerful headlights illuminating the way. By the time they reached the camp at the foot of the hills, brilliant floodlights had been erected within a rough circle of tents. Boxes of supplies lay scattered around and special forces soldiers in snow camouflage were working in an orderly, methodical fashion. Once the plane had been located, they would shift the camp on to the ice cap.

The outline of a large satellite dish loomed through the thick veil of snow outside the tent that acted as telecommunications centre. Ratoff went straight inside. Two men were busy setting up the radio system.

'How soon can we make contact?' Ratoff asked.

'In forty minutes at the outside, sir,' one of the men replied.

'Get Carr for me when you're done.'

Vytautas Carr was sitting in his office in Building 312 when the phone rang.

'Ratoff on line one,' his secretary announced. He pressed the button. It was 9 p.m. in the US capital, 2 a.m. in Iceland.

'Everything okay?' Carr asked.

'We're on schedule, sir. We'll head up to the glacier at first light tomorrow. It's snowing fairly heavily but nothing that will hold us up. As long as the coordinates are correct, it won't matter if the plane's been covered by drifts.'

'What about the locals?'

'Unsuspecting, and we plan to keep it that way, sir.'

'They keep a close eye on our military manoeuvres. We'll need to proceed with caution.'

'They'll keep their mouths shut as long as they're making money out of us.'

Carr ignored this. 'Is there any other traffic on the glacier?'

'We know about a rescue team on a training exercise but it's in a different sector and shouldn't cause us any problems, sir.'

'Fine. Get in touch when you find the plane.'

4

Tómasarhagi, Reykjavík,
Friday 29 January, 0600 GMT

Kristín woke up in the early hours with a sinking feeling about the day ahead. She knew the matter with the businessman was not over and that she was bound to encounter him again, maybe even later that day. Another source of worry was the knowledge that her brother was out on Vatnajökull in the middle of winter; he was experienced but you never knew how extreme the weather might become. After a bad night's sleep, she got up shortly before six, took a quick shower and put on the coffee. Sometimes she missed having someone there to share her worries with.

Not that she minded living alone. She had lived for three years with a man she met after coming home from university in the States, a lawyer like her. But once the honeymoon period was over he had become increasingly domineering and she was relieved not to have to put up with his overbearing behaviour any longer. He had been so different when they first met, so witty and entertaining. He used to make her laugh and spoiled her with gifts and surprises. But all that had gradually dried up once they had moved in together; he had landed his fish, and at times she felt as if he was tearing out the hook.

Although she had always been independent, she was by nature quiet, somewhat introverted, protective of her privacy, and did not mind the absence of a man about the house. The sex had been nothing to write home about either, so she did not miss that. If she felt the urge, she could satisfy herself and she enjoyed the freedom that gave her. Enjoyed having the flat on Tómasarhagi to herself; only one toothbrush in the bathroom; no need to tell anyone where she was going. She could go out whenever she liked and come home when it suited her. She loved being alone, not having to pander to anyone else's whims.

She had been so relieved when it was over that she was not sure she ever wanted to share her home again. Perhaps it was too great a sacrifice. Children had not crossed her mind. Maybe she was afraid of turning out like her parents. It had come as a surprise when, after they had lived together for a while, the lawyer had brought up the subject of children, saying they should think about starting a family. She had stared at him blankly and admitted that she had not given the matter much thought.

'Then maybe you could stop fussing over Elías all the time,' he said. 'He is not your child, after all.'

What an extraordinary statement. *Is not your child,* she thought. She had no idea what he was getting at.

'What do you mean?'

'I mean you treat him like a baby.'

'Like a *baby?*'

'You ring him ten times a day. He's forever round here. You've always got some reason to go to town together. He hangs out here in the evenings. Sleeps on the sofa.'

'He's my brother.'

'Exactly.'

'You're not jealous of Elías, are you?'

'Jealous!' he snorted. 'Of course not. But it's not natural, such an incredibly close relationship.'

'Not natural? There are only the two of us. We're close. What's unnatural about that?'

'Well, not unnatural exactly . . . it's just

he's your brother not your child. I know he's much younger than you but he's almost twenty, he's not a kid.'

She was silent for such a long time that he seized the chance to get up and claim he had some work to finish at the office.

Shortly afterwards, their relationship started to go downhill and by the end she had almost developed an aversion to him. Perhaps he had touched a nerve, opened her eyes to something she did not want to confront. She had met other men since but those had been nothing but brief flings and she had no regrets about any of them, with perhaps one exception. She regretted the way she had ended that relationship, the way they had parted. It was her fault and she knew it. Her sheer bloody ineptitude.

Just occasionally, when she was alone at home with time on her hands, she would have a vision of her future stretching out before her, saw herself growing older in lonely monotony, shrivelling up and dying; no children, no family, no nothing. Growing old in the oppressive silence of long summer evenings when she had nothing to do but read documents from the office. These moments tended to occur when she was disturbed by the shouts of children outside in the street or when she lay down in the evenings, feeling the weariness spreading through her body. Sometimes she thought the process was already happening, felt as if she were trapped inside time: all those long days, all those long, suffocating days, passed in solitary silence. At times she appreciated them, at others she wished her life were more eventful, presented more challenges, required more of her than merely sitting behind a desk all day and returning to an empty flat in the evenings.

Elías was her family. Their mother was dead, they had little contact with their father and few relatives to speak of. They had coped alone, she and Elías; taken care of one another. Perhaps the lawyer was right about him taking up too much of her time, but she had never minded.

She sat lost in a reverie over her coffee, leafing absently through the morning paper until it was time to leave for work. There was not much in the news. The national bank was in the process of being privatised and the minister for trade and industry was quoted as dismissing the need for legislation to diversify share ownership. The site of a Viking Age farm had been uncovered in the west of the country, and the Russian president Boris Yeltsin was due to celebrate his sixty-eighth birthday. It was quarter to nine when she left home. Sunrise was still nearly two hours off and the snow was falling thickly. She toiled slowly through the drifts. The traffic was heavy; people were in a hurry to get to work once they had dropped off their youngest children at the day nursery and seen the older ones off to school. The snow muffled the noise of the cars but a thick haze of exhaust fumes hung over the city. Kristín did not have a car; she preferred to walk, especially when the snow was deep like this. Distances were short in Reykjavík compared to California where she used to live; there you could talk about distance. Reykjavík had a population of only just over a hundred thousand but there were times when the locals behaved as if they lived in a giant metropolis, refusing to go anywhere without a car, even if it took only five minutes on foot.

On arriving at the office she was informed that the chairman of the Trade Council was waiting to see her, together with the foreign minister's aide. What now? she wondered, bracing herself for the worst. Once the men had taken a seat in her office, they explained to Kristín that the man with the portable freezing plants, Runólfur Zóphaníasson, had made threats against the chairman of the Trade Council, which were considered serious enough for the police to be notified. He had called the chairman late last night, apparently sober but raging about the advice he had received in connection with his dealings with Russia. During the call, he had threatened the chairman with physical violence and there was reason to believe he was in earnest.

'But what does this have to do with me?' Kristín asked, after they had filled her in.

'He mentioned you specifically by name,' explained the foreign minister's aide, a young party member with political ambitions. 'I gather he wasn't exactly in good humour when he stormed out of here yesterday.'

'He did nothing but hurl abuse as usual so I chucked him out. He threw a chair at the wall. I ignored his threats, and that made him even madder. What kind of headcase is he anyway? He thinks there's some kind of conspiracy going on. Here at the ministry.'

'I had the police run a check on him,' said the chairman, a plump man, with a small, kindly face. 'Runólfur has done a lot of wheeling and dealing in his time but nothing illegal, as far as they can tell. They went and had a word with him and he promised to behave, claimed he'd just lost his temper for a moment, but they warned us to be careful anyway. They don't put much faith in his word. I won't repeat the language he used about you in my hearing. Apparently he's furious about losing a large amount of money in Russia and he blames us for it.'

'I don't really know the ins and outs of the case,' Kristín said, 'though I can assure you that we never gave him any incorrect information.'

'Of course not,' the aide said. 'He alleges that we encouraged him to facilitate his business by sending over goods without any securities but that's utter nonsense. It's not our job to give out that sort of advice. How people conduct their business deals is entirely their own responsibility.'

'Of course,' Kristín agreed.

'Anyway,' the aide continued, glancing at his watch. 'We wanted you to be aware of developments and to warn you that it wouldn't hurt to keep your eyes open. If this Runólfur tries to intimidate you in any way, you're to call the police at once. They have been briefed about the case.'

The meeting ended soon afterwards and the day's business began. Kristín did not look up from her desk until midday when she went out with a couple of colleagues to a cosy little café near the ministry where she chatted and glanced through the afternoon paper over coffee and an omelette. When she returned to the office at one, there were a number of voicemail messages, including one from her brother saying he would ring back later. Otherwise the day was entirely uneventful.

She left work early. It had stopped snowing and turned into a beautiful, mild January evening. As it was Friday, she stopped off at a shop on the way home and bought some food for the weekend. She lived in the ground floor flat of a neat little two-storey maisonette built of whitewashed concrete, with a flat roof that had a tendency to leak. On entering the shared hall she heard the phone ringing inside her flat before she could even insert the key in the lock. She hastily opened the door, rushed over to the phone and snatched up the receiver.

'Hello,' said a voice that she immediately recognised as her brother's.

'Elías!'

'Hello,' her brother repeated. 'Can you hear me?'

'Loud and clear . . .'

But the connection was lost and she hung up. She waited beside the phone for a while in case Elías rang straight back but nothing happened, so she went and shut the front door, took off her coat and hung it in the cupboard. She had just sat down at the kitchen table when the phone rang again.

'Hello,' she said. 'Is that you, Elías?'

No answer.

'Are you on the glacier?'

No answer.

'Elías?'

Down the line she heard the faint sound of breathing and the suspicion flashed into her mind that it might be Runólfur. She stopped talking and listened intently.

'Who is this?' she asked eventually but there was no answer. 'Is that Runólfur?' she asked, adding after a moment's thought: 'Pervert!' and hung up.

She thought back over her meeting with the chairman and foreign minister's aide as she tucked into a sandwich and drank some orange juice. Later, she took a pile of documents out of her briefcase and tried to concentrate on work. Feeling sleepy, however, she lay down on the sofa in the sitting room and thought about making coffee, until she realised that she had forgotten to buy any milk. She ought to drag herself out to the shop before it closed, but could not be bothered and tiredness overtook her.

Kristín did not know how long she had been

asleep. She got up and put on her jacket and gloves. The local shop was only round the corner, she really ought to force herself out. Coffee was no good unless it was made with hot milk. She had just reached the door when the phone started ringing again, making her jump.

'What the hell is going on?' she asked, picking up the receiver.

'Hi, it's Elías. Can you hear me?'

'Elías!' Kristín exclaimed. 'Where are you?'

'I've . . . trying to get hold of you . . . day. I'm on the glacier . . .'

The connection was poor; her brother's voice kept breaking up.

'Is everything all right?' she asked, still groggy from her nap. She had got up far too early that morning.

'Everything's grea . . . Two of us . . . taken off on snowmobiles. Per . . . weather. It's . . . dark.'

'What do you mean, two of you? Where are the others?'

'We're . . . bit of a test drive . . . fine.'

'This is hopeless. I can only hear the odd word. Will you please go back and join the rest of the team.'

'We're turning round . . . lax. The phone

60

cost seven . . . thousand. Can't you hear
me?'

'Your phone's useless!'

'Don't be like that. When . . . you coming . . . glacier trip with me?'

'You'll never get me to set foot on any
bloody glacier.'

She heard her brother say something
unintelligible then call out to his companion.

'Jóhann!' she heard him shout. 'Jóhann,
what's that?' Kristín knew that Jóhann was
a good friend of her brother's; it was he who
had been responsible for getting him involved with the rescue team in the first
place.

'What are all those lights?' she heard Elías
shouting. 'Are they digging up the ice?'

'You should see this. There's something
happening up here,' he told his sister, the
pitch of his voice suddenly higher. She
heard him turn away from the phone and
shout something to his friend, then turn
back.

'Jóhann thinks . . . in the ice,' he said.

This was followed by a long pause.

'They're coming!' Elías exclaimed suddenly, the words sounding in fits and starts
over the poor connection. The excitement
had vanished and he sounded panic-

stricken, his breathing ragged.

'Who?' she asked in astonishment. 'Who's coming? What can you see?'

'Out of nowhere. We're . . . by snowmobiles. They're armed!'

'Who?'

'They look . . . soldiers . . .'

'Elías!'

'. . . a plane!'

But the connection was abruptly severed and however much she yelled down the phone, alarm now rising within her, all she could hear was the dialling tone. She set the receiver gently back into its cradle and stared blankly at the wall.

5

Washington DC,
Friday 29 January, 1500 EST

During a long military career that had taken him all over the world, Vytautas Carr had only once visited Iceland. He was aware that the US air base at Keflavík had been established after World War II on a wind-blasted site amid the lava fields known as Midnesheidi, about an hour's drive south-west of the capital, Reykjavík. In its time, the base had been one of the most vital strategic links in the West's chain of defences; the island's location in the middle of the North Atlantic proved ideal for a military superpower at the height of the Cold War, offering a superb vantage point for monitoring the movements of Soviet submarines, shipping and air traffic in the Arctic region.

He knew too that the British had occupied the country at the beginning of the war, before handing over their defence role to the Americans in 1941. The US headquarters had initially been in Reykjavík with the original detachment of troops later reinforced by the 5th Infantry Division under the command of Major General Cortlandt Parker, who had fought in Tunisia until the surrender of the Axis forces in Africa. The American occupying force had peaked at some 38,000 troops.

The presence of the US army had been a source of political friction in the country ever since the end of the war. The signing of the defence treaty in 1949 triggered a riot outside the Icelandic parliament and the left-wing political parties had been bitter in their opposition to the base over the years, though to little effect.

Government policy had always decreed that the nation should derive no profit from the NATO presence on its shores, and accordingly the military had never paid directly for their facilities at Keflavík Airport. Nevertheless, tens of millions of dollars had been poured into the pockets of the civilian contractors and service companies that carried out work on behalf of the military or held important contacts in favourably inclined political parties. In addition, the economies of the neighbouring villages had come to depend on the presence of the

Iceland Defense Force, which meant that the decision to scale down operations on Midnesheidi at the end of the Cold War was met by vociferous protests from the locals.

Carr rehearsed this background as he made his way to his weekly meeting with the US Secretary of Defense. He would be called upon to explain why a C-17, on loan from the Air Transport Division in Charleston, was standing idle in Iceland indefinitely in the middle of winter. He would also have to account for the presence of Delta Force operators. Carr experienced a wave of nostalgia for the days when covert operations were covert. Nowadays a crowd of politically elected officials had to be kept apprised of every last detail of military intelligence activities in every corner of the world.

The defense secretary kept Carr waiting outside his office for fifteen minutes — deliberately, Carr was certain — before calling him inside. Relations between the two had been less than cordial during the six years the secretary had held office and Carr was now aware of an even greater chill from that quarter. They exchanged the briefest of handshakes. The secretary had learnt of Carr's attempts to find compromising information on him — evidence of mistresses, a penchant for gambling or any other vice that could get him into trouble. Carr even went as far as to scrutinise his tax returns, bank accounts and credit card transactions. It was a precaution he took with every new defense secretary, and one which on occasion had proved useful when he needed leverage. But his luck was out this time: as far as he could establish, the secretary was as pure as the driven snow.

He was one of the Democrats' brightest stars, a youthful, reforming orator, with a wife and children and two pets; reminiscent of Carter in his prime. A forthright opponent of state secrecy, the secretary had made several speeches about the need for openness in relation to the operations of the secret service, which had acquired a new and more wide-ranging role after the end of the Cold War. What the secretary meant by 'new' and 'wide-ranging' was uncertain, but he was without doubt one of the most vocal advocates of cutting back expenditure on the secret services and of bringing their activities under scrutiny.

Carr could not stand the secretary's political posturing. It had pained him that he had failed to discover any disgrace in his past.

'What's this about a plane in Keflavík?' the secretary started before they had even sat down. 'What are you up to in Iceland? A C-17 costs $350,000 a day. Delta Force the same again. We cannot afford that kind of extravagance unless we're talking about a serious emergency. And Ratoff's a psychopath who in my opinion should not be on our payroll.'

Carr offered no answer. Under normal operational procedures, the secretary was not supposed to be aware of the existence of men like Ratoff. He reached into his briefcase for a sheaf of satellite images of Vatnajökull and handed them to the secretary.

'What have you got there?' the secretary asked. 'What are these?'

'Satellite images, Mr Secretary, of the south-eastern section of an Icelandic glacier known as Vatnajökull; the biggest glacier in Europe; a huge sheet of ice in a permanent state of flux. The enlarged image shows what we believe to be an aircraft that crashed on the glacier in the closing stages of World War II.'

'What kind of aircraft?'

'German transport, Mr Secretary. Most likely a Junkers.'

'And we've only just found it?'

We, thought Carr to himself. Who's *we?* Christ, politicians. They were always putting themselves centre-stage. Especially Democrats, with their demands for open government, for having everything transparent and above board.

He continued:

'As I said, Mr Secretary, it crashed during the closing stages of the war. An expedition was mounted from our HQ in Reykjavík a few days later. It was the middle of winter and visibility on the glacier was close to zero. The wreckage was buried in snow and eventually swallowed up by the glacier but it seems to be returning it to us now, a whole lifetime later.'

'Returning it? What are you talking about?'

'It's not unheard of. To reiterate, Vatnajökull is constantly on the move. It covers an area of 3,200 square miles, including several active volcanoes. It's composed of a number of smaller glacial tongues and its ice mass changes according to climatic variation. Anything that vanishes into the ice can resurface decades later. Which is apparently the case with the German aircraft.'

'But how do we know that a German plane crashed on the glacier if it was never found?'

'Two brothers living at the edge of the ice cap saw it fly past their farm at low altitude. And the first expedition found the plane's nose wheel.'

'The first expedition?'

'A two-hundred-man team searched the glacier shortly after the plane crashed but all they found was the wheel. We mounted a second, much larger, expedition in 1967 but were driven off the ice by more bad weather. This is the third expedition.'

'What on earth was the plane carrying?' the secretary asked.

'The wheel gave us an idea of the size and type of aircraft,' Carr continued. 'We've been keeping the glacier under close surveillance and I think it's safe to say that we've never been as near to finding the plane as now.'

'You don't seem very happy about it.'

'It might have been better if the glacier had held on to the plane for ever,' Carr replied. 'We're in no hurry to recover it, as long as it stays well hidden. In fact, it's so well hidden that we've been reluctant to go to the trouble of systematically searching the glacier and digging for it. Our main concern has been to check that it hasn't reappeared, which, as I say, seems to be the case now.'

'You mean we've been monitoring the glacier all these years?'

We. You would think the secretary had

been hunched over a screen scouring satellite images for the last forty years himself.

'The wheel gave a clue as to the plane's position,' Carr said, evading the question. 'Military intelligence has been monitoring changes in the ice in the specified area since the end of the war, first by aerial photography from spy planes, later from space after the advent of satellites.'

'Satellites? Spy planes? What the hell is this aircraft? Why are we so anxious to dig it up now that it's reappeared?'

Carr cleared his throat.

'I repeat: what the hell was the plane carrying? And why', the secretary added, 'is this a covert operation? Why involve Delta Force and that maniac Ratoff?'

Carr pretended to pause for thought.

'Are you familiar with the story of the Walchensee gold, Mr Secretary?' he asked.

'Gold?' the secretary responded, a mixture of suspicion and alarm crossing his telegenic face. 'Are you telling me there's gold on board? No, I've never heard of it.'

'It caused us one hell of a headache at the time. Shortly before the fall of Berlin, just before the Red Army took over the city and closed all routes in and out, it seems that a small freight train left for the Alps. On board were more than three hundred little bags, each containing a gold bar. The gold was being shipped out of the Reichsbank on Hitler's personal orders. It was the Third Reich's last remaining gold reserve.'

Carr gathered his thoughts briefly. He had the secretary's full attention.

'We don't know precisely where it was heading but in the event the gold got no further than the Bavarian town of Walchensee,' he continued, 'where it was buried in an undisclosed location near the Obernach power plant. Not long afterwards it was dug up by some of our troops, at which point it vanished. This was in February of '45. The war was ending. It is alleged that our men got wind of the gold by chance, dug it up and shipped it home to the States. The US government has always refused to comment on the story but it caused a political stink, and the German media resurrect the Walchensee gold story every few years. No one here knows what became of it but naturally the Germans don't believe us.'

'Christ, you mean to say it's inside the plane on the glacier?' the secretary said, aghast. He had swallowed it, hook, line and sinker.

'According to our best intelligence, American soldiers stole a Junkers from the Luftwaffe, painted it in our camouflage colours, filled it with gold and took off from Munich. They made a secret stopover at Prestwick in Scotland and were intending to make a similar refuelling stop in Reykjavík en route to the States but met a storm and crashed on the glacier. None of them ever made it off the ice alive so we assume there were no survivors. Our sources, however, are not wholly reliable. Understandably, none of the men involved in the theft has ever come forward and admitted it, but there is no specific reason to doubt the broad truth of the story.'

'How much bullion are we talking about here?'

'Six to eight tons.'

'That's a problem all right,' the secretary said, as if to himself. He was visibly shaken; the tables had been expertly turned on him by Carr, whom he had summoned for a tongue-lashing about the endless covert operations and private vendettas he was engaged in. He was not used to being so comprehensively wrong-footed but could not suppress a grudging respect for Carr's expertise.

'And that's not all, Mr Secretary,' Carr added.

'There's more?' There was no mistaking

the note of anxiety.

'It makes this gold story a very sensitive issue for us, politically speaking.'

'What? What is it?' the secretary asked. His progress to date had been assured and free from blemish, a spotless record which was now under threat.

'It concerns the origin of the gold.'

'What do you mean? What about its origin? What's so politically sensitive?'

'The bulk of the gold was acquired from concentration camps,' Carr replied.

The secretary took a moment to grasp the implications.

He groaned. 'You mean this is Jewish gold? Teeth? Jewellery? You are telling me that we have a plane which crashed under US command full of plundered Jewish gold?'

Carr drove home his advantage. 'If we said it was stolen by a handful of rogue American soldiers no one would believe us. The whole country would be under suspicion: the President, Congress, and of course the secret service organisations.'

'My God.'

'So as you see, Mr Secretary, it's a delicate matter.'

The secretary considered his non-existent options.

'You're right. Absolutely right,' he said finally.

'Mr Secretary?'

'That plane must never ever be found.'

'That's what the secret service is for, sir,' Carr concluded, the hint of a wry smile playing around his mouth.

6

Ratoff held the phone belonging to the boy who claimed his name was Elías and, as he walked into the communications tent that had been erected beside the aircraft, checked the last number he had dialled. According to the screen, the call had lasted long enough, Ratoff thought, for the boy to have described the area and their activities in detail. It was the only number that showed up on screen. Otherwise the phone appeared new and barely used.

'Have the embassy trace this number,' Ratoff ordered the chief communications officer. 'And I need to talk to Vytautas.'

'Vytautas, sir?' the officer asked.

'Carr,' Ratoff breathed. 'General Vytautas Carr.'

Ratoff left the tent again. The plane was now half clear of the ice. In the glare cast by four powerful floodlights a swarm of troops was busy digging it out with spades. The nose, which was relatively intact, jutted into the air like a raised fist. Ratoff could now confirm Carr's theory that it was a Junkers Ju 52, known familiarly to Allied troops during World War II as 'Iron Annie' or 'Auntie Ju'. The Ju 52s were Germany's principal transport aircraft, often used for carrying paratroopers and powered by three vast BMW engines, the third of which was situated on the nose. And there the propeller still hung, its blades mangled by their collision with the ice. Below the window of the cockpit the outline of a black swastika was just visible under the flaking camouflage paint, while two of the seven windows that lined the sides of the plane could now be seen above the ice. The tail-end was still buried but the wings had evidently been sheared off and would probably never be found.

Ratoff understood the urgency of the situation. If these hapless boys on snowmobiles had managed to alert people to the presence of armed troops and a plane on the glacier he would have to act decisively. He must establish whom they had called and try to prevent the information from spreading any further, from dividing and mutating like a virus. The leak must be plugged at all costs. He had begun to realise just what a major undertaking this was and how difficult it would be to keep it under wraps. Smaller-scale operations involving less equipment and manpower and set in an urban environment were more his style, whereas Arctic wildernesses with weather conditions that could change drastically in a matter of minutes were quite outside his area of expertise. Nevertheless, he believed they had a good chance of getting away with it if they played their cards right, if everyone concerned did what was expected of them. He had done his research: Iceland was the backend of beyond; if there was anywhere an old secret could be dug up without word getting out, then surely it was here.

He heard someone call his name from the communications tent and went back inside.

'It's a Reykjavík number, sir. Registered to a woman named Kristín. She has the same patronymic as the owner of the phone. His sister, maybe. Married women keep their father's name in Iceland. Here's the address. It looks as if she lives alone. I have the embassy on the line.'

'Get me Ripley.'

He was handed the receiver.

'Her name's Kristín,' Ratoff said and

dictated her address.

There was a silence while he listened intently.

'Suicide,' Ratoff said.

The man known as Ripley replaced the telephone. He and his colleague Bateman had arrived with the other Delta Force personnel, but Ratoff had sent them to the American embassy in Reykjavík with instructions simply to sit and await orders. To others, his ability to anticipate and plan for unforeseen contingencies was eerie.

Ripley relayed to Bateman the drift of the phone conversation. They were very similar in appearance, both tall, muscular and clean shaven, their fair hair combed into neat side partings. Over their neatly pressed, inconspicuous dark suits, smart ties and shiny shoes, they wore only waist-length blue raincoats. They could have been twins were it not for their contrasting features. One was more refined, with a narrow face and piercing blue eyes above a long, thin nose and a small, almost lipless mouth; the other somewhat coarser in appearance, with a square jaw, thick ripe lips, big chin and bull neck.

Having found the woman's address, they identified the shortest route through the streets of Reykjavík, then borrowed one of the staff cars, an unmarked white Ford Explorer SUV, and drove off into the snowstorm. Time was of the essence.

The journey took no more than five minutes despite the heavy going.

When they pulled up outside her house on Tómasarhagi, Kristín was trying to contact the Reykjavík Air Ground Rescue Team. She was still wearing her anorak as she stood by the phone, trying all the numbers listed for the organisation in the telephone directory, without success. No one answered. She dialled her brother's number again but there was still no reply. A recorded message announced that the phone was either switched off, out of range or all the lines were currently busy. Convinced now that he was in danger, she fought down the dread rising within her. She took a deep breath and tried to think clearly, tried to persuade herself that she was worrying unnecessarily, that her brother was fine and would phone her any minute to tell her what he had seen; that there was some perfectly reasonable explanation. She counted slowly up to ten, then up to twenty, and felt her heartbeat gradually steadying.

She was just about to ring the police when she heard a knock at the door. Dropping the telephone, she went and put her eye to the peephole.

'Jehovah's Witnesses,' she sighed. 'At a time like this!' She must be polite.

The instant she opened the door, two men barged inside. One clamped his hand over her mouth and forced her ahead of him into the living room. The other followed close behind, shut the door and conducted a swift search of the flat, checking the other rooms and kitchen to ensure she was alone. Meanwhile, the man who was holding Kristín pulled out a small revolver and put a finger to his lips to indicate that she should keep quiet. They were both wearing white rubber gloves. Their actions were methodical, calculated and practised, as if they had done this countless times before. Focused and purposeful, they got straight down to business.

Kristín could not make a sound. She stared at the two men in stunned bewilderment.

White rubber gloves?

Bateman found her passport in a drawer in the sideboard, walked over to Kristín and compared her face with the photo.

'Bingo,' he said, dropping the passport on the floor.

'Do exactly what I tell you,' Ripley said in

English as he levelled the revolver at her head, 'and sit down here at the desk.' He shoved her towards the desk and she sat down with the gun still wedged against her temple. She could feel its muzzle, cold, heavy and blunt, and her head hurt from the pressure.

Bateman came over and joined them. He switched on Kristín's computer, humming gently to himself as it warmed up, then created a new file and began quickly and methodically to copy something from a sheet of paper he had taken from his pocket. They conversed in English while this was going on, saying something she did not catch. Yet although they gave the impression of being American, to Kristín's astonishment the man was writing in Icelandic.

I can't go on living. It's over. I'm sorry.

She tried addressing them, first in Icelandic, then in English, but they did not answer. She knew that robberies had been on the increase lately but she had never heard of a burglary like this. At first she had taken it for some kind of joke. Now she was sure they were burglars. But why this unintelligible message on the computer?

'Take what you like,' she said in English. 'Take anything you like, then get out. Leave me alone.' She felt herself growing numb with terror at the thought that they might not be thieves, that they might have some other form of violence in mind for her. Later, when she replayed the events in her head, as she would again and again in the following days, she had difficulty remembering what thoughts had raced through her mind during those chaotic minutes. It all happened so fast that she never had time to take in the full implications of her situation. It was so absurd, so utterly incomprehensible. Things like this did not happen; not in Iceland, not in Reykjavík, not in her world.

'Take whatever you like,' she repeated.

The men did not answer.

'Do you mean me?' she asked, still speaking English, pointing at the computer screen. 'Is it me who can't go on living any longer?'

'Your brother's dead and you can't go on living any longer. Simple as that,' Bateman replied. He smiled as he added to himself sarcastically: 'What poets they are at the embassy.'

The embassy, Kristín noted.

'My brother? Elías? What do you mean, dead? Who are you? Are you friends of Elías? If this is supposed to be a joke . . .'

'Hush, Kristín. Don't alarm yourself,' Ripley said. The accent was definitely American.

'What's going on?' Kristín demanded to know, her terror suddenly giving way to blazing anger.

'A grand conspiracy involving the Reykjavík police, the Icelandic foreign ministry and the ministry of justice,' Bateman said gravely, catching Ripley's eye. He looked for all the world as though he was enjoying himself.

'A conspiracy?' Kristín repeated in Icelandic. 'The foreign ministry? Elías? What kind of joke is this? What kind of bullshit is this?' She was shouting now.

'She's lost it,' Bateman said, taking in her flushed face and heaving chest. 'Let her have it,' he added, and retreated a couple of steps.

Out of the corner of her eye Kristín saw the barrel of the gun and Ripley tightening his finger on the trigger. She closed her eyes. But instead of the shot she expected, there was a sudden violent banging on the door.

Ripley removed the revolver from her temple and clamped his gloved hand over Kristín's mouth. She struggled for air and could taste the plastic. Bateman went to the door and peered through the peephole, then returned to the living room.

'A male, fortyish, unaccompanied, medium height.'

'Let him in,' Ripley said. 'We'll take him too. Turn it into a murder. Ratoff needn't know.'

Ratoff, Kristín noted.

Bateman returned to the door. The banging resumed, even louder than before. A man was yelling Kristín's name. She recognised the voice and the hectoring tone but could not place them. In an instant, Bateman had opened the door, grabbed the man by the lapels and dragged him into the flat. As the door opened and Ripley's attention was momentarily distracted by the struggle in the hall, Kristín seized her chance. Leaping to her feet, she shoved Ripley away, sending him crashing into the table, and fled to the door. Now she could see who the visitor was: Runólfur.

'Look out!' she screamed. 'They're armed!'

Runólfur did not have time to reply. He saw Kristín rushing towards him, panic written on her face. Glancing beyond her into the living room he saw Ripley stagger into the table. There was a dull report and a tiny red hole appeared in Runólfur's forehead as Kristín dodged past him. She saw him collapse noiselessly into Bateman's arms. As she ran out of the flat, the next bullet tore past her ear and smacked into the door. She sped across the hall, through the front door, out into the snow and round the corner of the building with Ripley and Bateman hard on her heels.

Although Kristín had been on her way out when her brother called from the glacier, she had not got as far as putting on her shoes. She was wearing only thin socks, baggy tracksuit bottoms and a vest-top under her anorak as she hurtled across the back garden. The temperature had dropped below freezing and the snow was covered with a thin crust of ice that cracked beneath her weight, plunging her feet into soft wetness with every step. The cold was so painful that she wanted to cry out. Not daring to look back, she took a flying leap over the garden fence, sprinted across the road, into another garden, across it and over the next fence, vanishing into the darkness.

Later, when she had time to unravel the chaos in her mind, she would decide that her life had been saved by the fact that Ripley and Bateman were ill-equipped for running in snow. They never had a chance of catching her in their slippery, leather-soled shoes and by the time they had jettisoned them, she had disappeared. After observing where her tracks in the snow met and mingled with countless others, the two men turned and headed back to Kristín's flat. In spite of the gunfire and the commotion of the chase there was no sign of the occupants of the flat upstairs.

Bateman and Ripley shut the door behind them, re-emerged from the flat five minutes later and climbed wordlessly into the Explorer.

7

Vatnajökull Glacier,
Friday 29 January, 1930 GMT

Ratoff advanced towards the boys from the Icelandic rescue team. They were barely out of their teens, both dressed in the rescue team's uniform of orange cold-weather overalls, with its logo emblazoned on breast and shoulder. They looked petrified. When the soldiers had swiftly borne down on them they had tried to make a break for it but after a brief pursuit had been headed off and brought to Ratoff. The men had found the phone on the boy who said his name was Elías. The other, Jóhann, had no phone or other transmitter. The boys were both tall, blond and good-looking. Ratoff, short and unremarkable himself, assumed that all Icelanders looked like this.

Their snowmobiles had been picked up on the little Delta Force radar screen, and Ratoff had watched as they broke away from their main party and branched out on their own. They maintained a course directly towards the plane and he had been unable to think of a plan to deflect them. At least the main rescue team, located some forty-five miles away, posed no immediate danger; the only members to leave the party were these two boys.

The Icelanders were escorted to Ratoff's tent where they waited, flanked by armed guards. They had seen the plane, the swastika below the cockpit, the team digging the wreckage out of the ice; they had seen upwards of a hundred armed soldiers moving about the area, and although they could not have any understanding of what was going on, they had seen too much. Ratoff would have to conduct his interrogation with care; there must be no visible signs of violence, yet neither could it take too long. Above all, it was imperative to prevent the rescue team from searching for them in this sector. Ratoff was up against the clock, but it was how he worked best.

Elías and Jóhann were too frightened to feign ignorance of English. In fact, like most Icelanders they spoke the language remarkably well. And they were too naive to dream that they had anything to hide.

'Kristín,' Ratoff said in a dry, rasping

voice, walking up to Elías. 'She is your sister?'

'How did you know that?' Elías asked in surprise, glancing from Ratoff to the armed guards and back again. It was barely fifteen minutes since his phone had been confiscated.

'Did you call anyone else?' Ratoff asked, ignoring his question.

'No, no one.'

'You weren't in contact with your team at all?'

'My team? Why? How did you know about my sister? How do you know her name's Kristín?'

'Questions, questions,' Ratoff sighed. He looked into the middle distance as if lost in thought, then backed away from the boys, glancing around until his gaze alighted on a tool box which stood on a trestle-table at the back of the tent. He went over to the box, opened it and nonchalantly rummaged inside with one hand, first taking out a screwdriver and contemplating it thoughtfully before replacing it in the box. Next he took out a hammer and weighed it in his hand before returning that too. Elías spotted a pair of pincers. The boys were staring at the little man with blank incomprehension. He gave the impression of being very composed, almost polite: his manner was cool, calm and deliberate. They had no idea what a dangerous scenario they had stumbled upon. Closing the tool box, Ratoff turned back to face them.

'How about I promise not to stab your friend, would that put an end to your questions, I wonder?' he asked Elías, as if weighing up the possibility. His hoarse voice was soft enough for Elías to miss the violence of his threat at first.

'Stab?' Elías repeated in shock, his eyes on his friend. 'Why would you do that? Who are you? And what's that plane with the swastika?'

He hardly saw the movement. All he knew was that Jóhann shrieked, clutched his right eye and fell on the ice where he lay writhing in agony at his friend's feet.

'If I promise not to stab him again, would that encourage you to stop wasting our time?' Ratoff asked Elías. His voice was difficult to hear over Jóhann's screams. In one hand he was holding a small metal awl.

'What have you done?' Elías gasped. 'Jóhann, can you see? Talk to me.' He tried to bend down to tend to his friend but Ratoff seized him by the hair, dragged him upright and pushed his own face close to Elías's.

'Let's try again. What coordinates did you give your team before you set off?'

'None,' Elías stammered, dazed with shock. 'We said we were going to test-drive our snowmobiles and might be away for four to five hours.'

'Did they know where you were headed?'

'We didn't give them an itinerary. We were only going to try out the snowmobiles. They're new. We never meant to wander far from the team.'

'How long have you been away?'

'About half that time. Maybe three hours.'

'When will they start looking for you?' The questions came one after another, he was disorientated by them and by his bleeding, sobbing friend; he had no sense of what he should or should not be saying, and this was precisely what Ratoff intended.

'Very soon if we don't turn up on time. They've probably started looking already. How do you know about Kristín?' It was beginning to come home to Elías that his life was in danger but he was more worried by the fact that this man knew his sister's name.

'What did you tell your sister on the phone?'

'Only that I was trying out a new snowmo-bile. That's all, I swear,' he said.

'No more than twelve minutes had elapsed from when you talked to her to when I got hold of your phone. Which means that you would have been quite close to here when you called her. What does she know, Elías? Do remember that your friend's sight is at stake. Perhaps you described what you saw? It is out of the ordinary. Why wouldn't you?'

'Nothing. I didn't tell her anything. I ended the call when I saw the soldiers coming towards us and we tried to escape.'

Ratoff sighed once again.

His attention turned to Jóhann who had been helped to his feet by two of the guards. Ratoff stepped up close to him and stared into his good eye. The awl flashed and screams rang out from the tent again, carrying a long way through the still air on the ice cap. The men by the plane paused briefly in their digging and looked up, before resuming their work without comment.

Ratoff emerged from the tent with a thin spattering of blood on his face. He walked rapidly to the communications tent where he found two messages waiting for him. He would talk to Ripley first. Finding a cloth, he dried his face deliberately and thoughtfully, as if he had just washed.

'A regrettable suicide?' he asked when Ripley came on the line.

'I'm afraid not, sir,' Ripley replied. 'The target escaped and we were forced to leave a body behind in her apartment.'

There was nothing but static from Ratoff's end of the line.

'She had a visitor, sir, whilst we were with her. An unforeseen eventuality. Our orders were to move in directly and we had no time to prepare.'

'So what now?' Ratoff asked eventually.

'We find her, sir.'

'Do you need more men?'

'I don't think so, sir.'

'And how do you propose to find her?'

'Is her brother still alive?'

'More or less.'

'We need any available information, sir. Does she have a boyfriend, any friends — old or new — or family? Anything we could use. Did he manage to pass on anything?'

'Only to his sister. She knows the glacier is swarming with armed soldiers, she knows there's an airplane in the ice, she knows her brother's disappeared and I'm reasonably sure she knows where Elvis is hiding. If you imbeciles hadn't let her give you the run-around, we'd be in the clear.' Throughout this speech, one of Ratoff's longest in days, neither the tone nor the volume of his voice changed in the slightest.

'We'll find her, sir. We'll track down her family. We have her credit and debit card numbers and can monitor any use of them. She'll turn up and when she does, we'll be waiting.'

8

General Vytautas Carr was sitting in his office when a call came through on his private line. His thoughts had been wandering while he waited for Ratoff to make contact. Carr had parted from the defense secretary having given an assurance that no news about the plane in the ice would ever reach the public domain. The young Democrat had pronounced with great solemnity that the operation was to remain clandestine and that he did not want to know the details; in fact, he did not want to hear another word about it until it had been successfully concluded. Then, and only then, would he apprise the President of the essential facts. That way, if anything went wrong, the President would not have to tell any lies but could claim in all honesty that he had had no idea about any plane full of Jewish gold stolen by the US army. Nevertheless, the secretary could not restrain himself from asking for clarification of a few points.

'What are you planning to do with the plane?' he asked as they wrapped up the meeting.

Carr was prepared for the question, as well as the inevitable follow-up.

'We'll remove it from the glacier along with any wreckage we find, including bodies and other contents, and bring it back to the States. That's what the C-17's for, Mr Secretary. It has unlimited weight-bearing capacity. It'll depart from Keflavík and fly without refuelling stops to our facility at Roswell, where the Nazi plane will disappear permanently.'

'Roswell?' the secretary queried. 'Isn't that the alien town?'

'I can't think of any better hiding place. After all that alien nonsense anything reported about Roswell and what goes on there is dismissed as bullshit, except by a tiny minority of UFO nuts. If the news gets out that we're hiding a Nazi plane at Roswell, it'll raise an even bigger laugh.'

'And the gold?' the secretary asked.

'No need to waste it. I imagine it'll disappear into the Federal Reserve Bank, unless you have another suggestion.'

96

They had parted on better terms than before. The defense secretary's appreciation of the role of the secret service had improved dramatically, creating a new degree of understanding between them. Not that that mattered a damn to Carr, though he did derive a private satisfaction from having brought the secretary to heel. By the end of their meeting Carr could have ordered him to stand on one leg and stick out his tongue and he would have obeyed without hesitation.

Carr had come a long way from his Lithuanian origins. His original surname had been Karilius but in an attempt to integrate into his adopted country he had shortened it to Carr. His parents had emigrated to the US in the 1920s and he was their only child; he was eleven years old when the US entered the Second World War and used to follow the news reports from the frontlines avidly. As soon as he was old enough, he joined the army and was rapidly promoted through the ranks, being appointed US army liaison officer to NATO. But desk work did not suit him and he had himself transferred to active duty when the Korean War broke out, going on to set up the covert operations service there, and undertaking numerous missions behind enemy lines. After Korea, he joined the army intelligence corps.

Carr inherited the aircraft on Vatnajökull in the early seventies when he took over as chief of the organisation, and during the five years it took him to learn his role fully, his predecessor gradually filled him in on the background to the presence of a German plane in the ice. By the end of that time, Carr knew all about the plane and what it was carrying and how to act if the plane was ever found. What they were following now was a prearranged procedure that Carr reviewed every few years. Only a handful of individuals in the highest echelons of the army were aware of the plane's existence or the procedure for dealing with it. For fifty-four years the knowledge had been kept strictly confidential, successfully limited to this tiny group, passed down from generation to generation, from one incumbent of office to the next. Even Carr did not know the whole story, though he knew enough. Enough not to want to imagine the fallout if news about what the plane was carrying ever got out.

The phone on his desk purred and he picked up the receiver.

'We're on schedule, sir,' Ratoff announced.

'No trouble locating it?'

'It was buried but the coordinates were correct. We've already uncovered half the fuselage. I estimate that we'll have it in Keflavík in three to four days at the outside.'

'No hitches?'

'Nothing significant. There's a rescue team from Reykjavík conducting a training exercise on the glacier. It's located some distance away but two of its members managed to stray into our area.'

Carr tensed: 'And?'

'They lost their lives in an accident about thirty-five miles from here. Drove their snowmobiles into a deep crevasse. We'll ensure they're found quickly so the team doesn't wander into our area looking for them.'

'Were they young?'

'Young? I don't understand the relevance, sir. They were old enough to see us and the plane.'

'So everything's in hand then?' Carr concluded.

'One of them had a sister in Reykjavík.'

Carr's disappointment was impossible to conceal.

'He made contact with her by phone after he entered the area. We know who she is but she gave us the slip. We're tracing her now.'

'Who's *we?*'

'Ripley and Bateman. The best available option in the circumstances.'

'For Christ's sake, Ratoff, try to control yourself. The Icelanders are our allies.'

Carr put down the receiver, picked it up again immediately and started dialling. It was time to put phase two of the operation in motion. The defense secretary had been concerned about Ratoff's involvement and now even Carr was beginning to have his doubts about his choice of mission director. Carr knew the alarming details of his army career better than anyone. Ratoff undeniably delivered results but he tended to be over-zealous.

He had to wait a good while for his call to be answered, and spent the time mapping out his next moves. He would have to fly to Iceland. But first he would honour an old promise.

'Miller?' he said. 'It's Vytautas. The plane's turned up. We need to meet.'

9

Kristín ran blindly towards the coast road at Aegisída, then veered west, her instincts keeping her as far as possible to the dark gardens. Her only thought was to flee; she never once looked back.

A succession of terrible images flashed through her mind. She saw the light going out in Runólfur's eyes as the bullet entered his forehead, heard the whine of a second bullet and saw it thud into the door. Her ear hurt; it was bleeding. Her thoughts darted to her brother on the glacier: they had said he was dead. She remembered his last words: armed soldiers, a plane. A few minutes later two men had forced their way into her flat and tried to kill her. They had mentioned a name — Ratoff — and a conspiracy involving the Reykjavík police, the foreign ministry and the ministry of

101

justice. It had seemed preposterous at first but any illusion had been dispelled as Runólfur crumpled to the floor in front of her.

The cold soon began to make her bones ache. She psyched herself up to look over her shoulder as she ran but could see no sign of the two men. Dropping her pace, she took a better look around and finally slowed to a standstill. She was surrounded by apartment blocks. Noticing that the door to the basement of one building was ajar, she slipped inside, pulling the door to behind her. It was pitch black inside and she was met by a stench of refuse. She made her way to the back and crouched down in the dark like an animal.

She lost track of time. Eventually, hearing no sound of movement, she crept forwards, cautiously pushed at the door and peered out through the crack, surveying her surroundings. There was nobody about; they had not followed her. Not far off was a small estate of terraced houses, their lights shining cosily through the icy darkness. What should she do? Knock at one of the doors and tell them everything? About the men and the body in her flat and the police complicity? But if the police were involved, who could she notify about the murder, about her brother on the glacier and the two killers? And what if the ministry she worked for was also implicated in the murder? She fumbled at her jacket, feeling for the wallet in her pocket.

What if they had killed Elías the way they had killed Runólfur right in front of her eyes? she thought. What kind of men were they?

Gradually anger got the better of her fear, allowing her to think more logically. She must find shelter somewhere; acquire clothes, information, maybe even go to the glacier herself and try to help her brother, if he was still alive. She did not dare contact the authorities; not as things stood, not until she knew more, until she was sure it was safe. But where was she to go? If they knew about her, surely they would know about her father too, in which case she could not go to him. The thought suddenly struck her: should she not warn him in case they paid him a visit next?

She dashed out of the rubbish store and over to the terraced houses where she hammered on the door of the nearest and leaned on the doorbell. The man of the house answered quickly, his wife and two children hovering behind his shoulder. They had been watching television and had evidently sprung to their feet when they heard the banging and ringing. Kristín barged her way inside the moment the door opened.

'I have to make a phone call,' she cried. 'Where's the phone?'

'Just a minute, miss,' the man said, looking at her in horror. She was sweating in spite of the cold, her chest was heaving, her face a mask of terror, her clothes soaking wet and blood was oozing from one ear, caking the right side of her head.

'I asked you, where's the phone?' she repeated as he staggered back before her into the little kitchen, where he pointed dumbly to the telephone. His family clustered around him.

Three rings, six. He did not answer. She tried to think clearly: where could he be? His answering machine kicked in and she waited impatiently for the tone, then spoke hurriedly.

'Dad? You've got to hide. The moment you hear this, disappear. I don't know what's going on but they've killed a man and tried to kill me, and they'll almost certainly come after you. Elías may be dead. There are two of them, dressed like Jehovah's Witnesses. I know this sounds insane but please do as I say and go into hiding. Don't worry about me, just hide! And don't try to make contact with me.'

The little family were gaping at her. The man exchanged alarmed glances with his wife and both looked down at the children, huddling closer together, their eyes fixed on this wild woman as she ended her message. When Kristín put down the receiver and turned to face them, they all stepped back simultaneously.

'I'm sorry,' she said, seeing the terror on the children's faces. 'It's all true, I swear to God. They were going to kill me. Can you lend me some clothes? But please don't ring the police — they may be involved. Try to forget this happened.' She shivered involuntarily as the adrenalin began to ebb from her body, her teeth chattering together. 'Do you have any clothes you could lend me? God, I'm so cold. Do you have any shoes and socks?'

'If we give you some clothes,' the woman said, speaking as calmly as she could, 'will you leave?'

'I'll leave right away,' Kristín assured her. 'Just please don't call the police.'

A few minutes later she emerged from the house dressed in an outfit belonging to the woman: a pair of jeans, a thick jumper and winter boots. Under normal circumstances she would have found it odd and uncomfortable to be wearing someone else's clothes which smelt of a strange, alien perfume, but there was no time for such thoughts now. The door slammed behind her. They had given her a plaster for her ear as well. As she walked slowly out of the culde-sac and on to the main road, the occasional car drove past cautiously in the snow. Kristín loathed snow; it reminded her of nothing more than Icelandic winters and the inner darkness they brought with them. She walked along the pavement, wondering what to do, before eventually deciding to head back in the direction of Tómasarhagi, looking round warily all the while. She had come up with a plan of sorts, though she doubted that she was in any fit state to think rationally or to work out the simplest solution.

She would handle this alone, at least to begin with. She did not dare to go to her friends or family for fear that her pursuers or their henchmen would be waiting. Only a few minutes had elapsed between her conversation with her brother and their appearance on her doorstep. Perhaps they were tapping her phone. But why? Did it have something to do with Runólfur? They had killed him, after all, and he had been raging about a conspiracy; about the Russian mafia.

She knew only one man who could tell her about soldiers.

Taking care to keep out of sight, she peered over at her own house. There was no sign of the police or anyone else; everything looked quiet, domestic, unremarkable. When she reached the main road she hailed a taxi, one which fortunately accepted cards.

'Where to?' he asked.

'Keflavík Airport,' she replied, casting a nervous glance out of the rear window.

10

Ratoff did not see them land but heard the thuds as they collided with the ice on their headlong descent into the crevasse. It was pitch dark on the glacier, the moon hidden behind thick clouds, the only light emanating from the headlamps on Ratoff's tracked vehicle and the snowmobiles. By the time they had reached the crevasse, one of the young men was unconscious, the other dead. Ratoff ordered his soldiers to push their snowmobiles into the chasm on top of them, after which his men set to work obliterating their tracks. Once this was done, Ratoff dropped Elías's phone into the crevasse after him.

In the end he had forced Elías to give up the salient facts about Kristín, information which he duly passed on to Ripley and Bateman. Elías had held out for a long time but

Ratoff was good at his job. The boy had surrendered everything about his sister's friends and colleagues, where their father lived and how he often made long trips abroad, and about Kristín's ex-boyfriends, the lawyer and his circle; even about their mother's death a few years earlier in a car crash. He revealed how his sister had taken a postgraduate degree in California and how, despite sometimes visiting friends abroad, she hated travelling in Iceland and that trips into the interior were her idea of hell. Elías had told Ratoff everything he wanted to know, before finally begging for mercy. But by then his friend Jóhann was dead. The last thing Elías heard before he lost consciousness was Ratoff whispering the news in his ear that his sister was dead too.

Ratoff's men laboured away at clearing the ice from the German aircraft, working in four-hour shifts, sixty men to a shift. They were well on schedule; more and more of the fuselage had been uncovered until they could now see into the passenger cabin through the first of the side windows. When Ratoff returned to camp, he walked over to the German plane and spent a long time peering through the window. He could dimly make out shapes on the floor that might have been bodies. He was summoned to the communications tent and straightened up. Ripley was on the line.

'She used her debit card to pay for a taxi to Keflavík, sir,' Ripley informed him. 'Did her brother say anything about Keflavík?'

'Why the hell is she going to Keflavík?' Ratoff asked. 'What happened at her place? How much does she know? Surely the logical move would be to go to the Reykjavík police?'

There was a short pause on the line.

'She knows there's a strong possibility that her brother's dead,' Ripley admitted hesitantly. 'She may also be under the impression that someone's trying to murder her because of a conspiracy involving the Reykjavík police, the Icelandic foreign ministry and the ministry of justice.'

'Are you out of your goddamn minds?'

'We underestimated the job, sir. It won't happen again.'

'Won't happen again?' Ratoff hissed. 'It should never have happened in the first place!'

'We're just leaving her father's apartment now. He's not at home. She left a message on his answering machine and we're taking it down to the embassy to get it translated.'

'She knows too much. Far too much.'

'What about Keflavík?' Ripley asked again.

'She may be on her way to the base. Her brother mentioned an ex-boyfriend there. She ditched him suddenly and they haven't met in a while, but it's possible she will look to him for help or information now.'

'Understood, sir,' Ripley said.

'Don't screw up again.'

'Understood,' Ripley repeated.

Ratoff gave him the man's name and hung up, then stepped out of the communications tent and looked over at the plane. Like other members of Delta Force, he was dressed in thick, white camouflage and snow goggles which he had pushed up on his forehead, warm gloves and a balaclava. There were no names or ranks, no indications of any affiliation or any other markings on their clothes, nothing to connect them to the unit.

Carr had not told him exactly what the plane contained and he burned to know more. He knew something of its history, knew that it had taken off from Germany at the end of the war, heading for Reykjavík, and had hit bad weather and crashed. But he had no idea whether Reykjavík had been the intended destination or if the plane had been scheduled to continue, perhaps all the way to the States. Nor did he know the identity of her passengers.

He returned thoughtfully to the wreck and peered into the passenger cabin again. Ratoff had been trying to fill in the blanks by guesswork but knew it was futile; he would not be able to satisfy his curiosity until he could get inside. Turning away, he went back to his tent. An image floated into his mind of the boy's face as he told him his sister was dead, of the torment in his eyes before he darkened them for ever. But the young men's deaths had no impact on Ratoff. He calculated for collateral damage in all his assignments and in his view they amounted to nothing more. He would complete this job to his full satisfaction and any obstacles would have to be eliminated. Carr had asked if they were young — he was obviously getting soft in his old age. No doubt he would ask the same thing when he was informed of the woman's death.

He gave orders to be put through to Carr.

'We believe she's on her way to the US base in Keflavík, sir,' he said when Carr came on the line, 'and I have a good idea who she's going to meet.'

11

Central Reykjavík,
Friday 29 January, 2100 GMT

The meeting was extremely formal, despite the choice of venue. By special request of the US military authorities, the prime minister and foreign minister of Iceland were now seated face to face with the admiral from Keflavík air base, in his capacity as the most senior officer in the Defense Force, and the general, who was temporarily discharging the office of US ambassador to Iceland during the abrupt and unexpected absence of the regular incumbent. The ministers had been summoned to the meeting with an unceremonious haste that might be interpreted as high-handedness if the circumstances did not turn out to be exceptional. The Icelanders had been given no information about the reason for the summons and discussed a number of possible scenarios as they travelled in the prime minister's car to the city centre hotel suite where the meeting was to be held. They were inclined to believe that it heralded an unexpected presidential visit, remembering that they had been given practically no warning when the summit meeting between Reagan and Gorbachev was held in Reykjavík in 1986.

On arrival they were greeted by the admiral, a casual acquaintance from various official receptions. He introduced them in turn to the general, a short, pugnacious-looking man whose name, the Icelanders learnt, was Immanuel Wesson; he was pudgy, red-faced and buck-toothed, and walked with a slight limp due to the fact that one of his legs was shorter than the other. The prime minister eyed him sceptically, wondering whether he had ever been on active duty or had enjoyed a lifetime's service behind a desk and in the officers' mess.

It was about nine in the evening, the streets were quiet and there were few guests in evidence at the hotel. The suite had been the foreign minister's idea; he often held meetings there with overseas guests on unofficial visits who wished to keep their names out of the press. As a setting it had that bland yet expensive anonymity characteristic of hotel rooms: white leather furniture, tasteful paintings by Icelandic artists on the walls, thick white carpets on the floors and a full-size bar. The Americans surveyed the opulent surroundings and nodded to the Icelanders as if in approval of the venue. There was an atmosphere of quiet expectation.

Formalities concluded, they took their seats on the room's ostentatious three-piece suite and the prime minister addressed the Americans:

'Perhaps you would be kind enough to tell us what's going on?' he suggested, loosening the knot of his tie.

'We would like to begin by thanking you, gentlemen, for agreeing to this emergency meeting,' the admiral commenced, regarding each of them in turn, 'and by apologising for the short notice. Once we've explained the matter, you will understand why it was unavoidable. It is absolutely vital, and I cannot emphasise this enough, that nothing said in this meeting leaves these four walls.'

The ministers nodded and waited. The general now cleared his throat.

'As you are naturally aware, according to the terms of the defence treaty between our nations, we monitor everything that happens within and around Iceland's borders for military purposes, using a combination of submarines, reconnaissance planes and satellites. In particular, we have in recent years been closely monitoring a section of the Vatnajökull glacier.'

'I'm sorry, did you say Vatnajökull?' the foreign minister interrupted, looking disconcerted.

'Allow me to explain, gentlemen,' the general said. 'We can answer any questions afterwards. In the past we operated surveillance flights over this area of the glacier but since we acquired satellite capabilities the process of monitoring has become much easier. Our interest in the glacier is historical but at the same time presents something of an embarrassment for us. In the closing stages of World War II one of our aircraft crashed on the glacier and was lost in the ice. We know more or less exactly where it went down but adverse weather conditions prevented us from reaching it until too late. By the time a search party from our Defense Force in Reykjavík finally made it to the glacier, there was no trace of the plane. As I said, the glacier had swallowed it up.'

The general paused and the prime minister seized the opening this offered.

'What's so special about this plane?'

116

'Recently, the aircraft turned up on satellite images of the glacier taken by military intelligence,' the general continued, ignoring the interruption. 'Having confirmed our original suspicions with the help of these images and others of the same area taken subsequently, we decided to send an expedition to the glacier to excavate the plane and transfer it to the base prior to repatriating it to the States. This will inevitably necessitate the movement of considerable numbers of military personnel and equipment through Icelandic territory.'

'And you require the Icelandic government's permission for this operation,' the foreign minister concluded.

'It has never been our wish to act against your will,' the admiral interjected.

'Naturally we will travel through the country as inconspicuously as possible,' the general resumed, 'taking the utmost care not to cause any alarm. We have drawn up plans which we will review with you in greater detail later. We know how the army is viewed by many Icelanders and we are aware that military manoeuvres on Icelandic soil are frowned on by the public, but this is an emergency and if the expedition is to be successful, we must proceed in absolute secrecy. But, needless to say, we wouldn't want to act without your full cooperation. I'd like to make that absolutely clear from the outset and stress that this is above all a scientific expedition. The military personnel will be accompanied by some of our most senior scientists.'

'What's so special about this plane?' the prime minister asked again.

'I think we had better leave it at that for the moment. We wanted to inform you in case anything went wrong — and of course in a spirit of mutual cooperation.'

'Went wrong?' the foreign minister echoed him. 'How do you mean?'

'In the event that news of the operation leaks out,' the admiral replied, 'we would like you to be ready with an explanation about the troop movements and our presence on the glacier.'

'And what, General, do you suggest?' the prime minister enquired.

'Small-scale winter exercises. It would probably be best to describe deployments of small Belgian and Dutch NATO forces in collaboration with the US Defense Force. That should take off most of the heat.'

'Is that all you're prepared to tell us?' the foreign minister asked.

'We regard this as the best way.'

'Best way? Why all the secrecy? Why can't

we simply announce that you're mounting an expedition to the glacier to recover a plane? Just what exactly is going on here?'

'It's a sensitive issue, that's all I can tell you at the present time,' the general replied. 'I hope to be able to provide you with a fuller explanation in due course.'

'General, the issue is extremely sensitive for us too,' the prime minister pointed out. 'I advise you to be straight with us, otherwise I fail to see how this can work. What is this plane and why does it pose a problem?'

'With all due respect, it's not your concern,' the general answered, abruptly abandoning any attempt at politeness.

'And with all due respect to you, we're not accustomed to such lack of courtesy in our dealings with the Defense Force. You have not requested permission to carry out the operation, merely told us what you are planning to do. Does that mean you've already set an operation in motion? May I remind you that such an act would represent a serious violation of the defence treaty, something the Icelandic media would be very dismayed to learn. Hitherto we have been prepared to accommodate American interests in any way we can and while we're grateful that you've seen fit to inform us of this operation, I'm afraid the feeble excuses you are proposing will prove inadequate if we are compelled to account for our actions.'

'Please excuse us if we come across as disrespectful,' the admiral intervened in a placatory tone. 'Of course we value your contribution to the West's efforts for peace and international stability but in this case I think the general is right. This matter is best resolved without any external involvement, and then forgotten.'

'I'm afraid that won't do,' the foreign minister replied. 'A plane from the Second World War? How do we know that's true? For all we know, it could have crashed yesterday. Who's to say it even exists? Frankly, I find the whole thing extremely far-fetched.'

'We could have passed it off as a routine exercise,' the admiral replied, 'but the matter is so serious that we can't afford to be disingenuous. You will simply have to trust us. If questions are asked, it's important that the answers given by all sides are consistent. It's imperative that we keep the existence of the plane secret.'

'I repeat: what is so special about this plane?' the prime minister asked.

'I'm afraid we can't answer that question,' the admiral replied.

'Then I'm afraid this meeting is over,' countered the prime minister, tightening the knot of his tie and standing up.

The Americans watched the ministers get ready to depart. They had been prepared for the fact that the Icelanders might not buy the half-baked story about a plane and Belgian troop movements, but had felt obliged to mount this as a first line of defence.

'Are you familiar with the Manhattan Project?' the general asked, rising to his feet.

'The Manhattan Project? Vaguely,' said the foreign minister.

'It was the codename for our nuclear testing programme in the 1940s. At the end of the war a considerable number of German scientists who had been involved in the Nazis' nuclear experiments were invited to America and employed on the Manhattan Project. It became a source of major embarrassment to us after news broke about the Holocaust. The Jews claimed that some of these scientists had worked in the death camps, carrying out experiments on the prisoners.'

The general allowed the ministers a chance to absorb the implications. This was the story he had been instructed to feed them if the meeting failed to go according to plan, a contingency he now judged necessary. The ministers observed him with quizzical expressions.

'We were engaged in a race against the Russians, as on all fronts in those days. They managed to recruit far more German scientists than we ever did, though no one criticised them, of course. But that's another story. The plane took off from Hamburg with four German nuclear scientists on board. It made a refuelling stop in Scotland and was scheduled to land again in Reykjavík en route for New York but was damaged in a storm and crashed on the glacier. Since no sign of them or the plane has ever been found, we believe everyone on board was killed. Now, however, we have a chance to retrieve the wreckage from the glacier and take it home.'

'But I still can't see why the discovery of the plane should be kept so clandestine,' the foreign minister interrupted.

'If news of the plane and its mission is made public, it will reignite the whole debate about German scientists working in America, coverage that we could well do without and which would risk jeopardising relations between the US and Europe. That's all there is to it. Now, gentlemen, you are in possession of all the facts. May I take it you are willing to cooperate?'

The ministers looked at one another, then back at the Americans.

'I think you have a lot more explaining to do,' the prime minister said.

12

Ever since the Icelanders had taken over the international airport at Keflavík in the 1980s with the construction of their own civil aviation terminal, public access to the military zone had been severely restricted. Local dealings with the army had always been kept to a minimum but now the base became more isolated than ever. Standing among the bleak lava fields, the military zone was demarcated by a high fence, pierced by only two gates which were guarded at all times. Although it was not considered necessary to mount a guard on the fence itself, the military police monitored it during their regular patrols of the residential area.

Kristín directed the taxi driver to a new housing estate which lay adjacent to the perimeter fence. After waiting for the cab to disappear down the street, she set off at a run in the direction of the military zone. The fence soon loomed out of the darkness and after a hasty glance around she started to climb it. There was barbed wire along the top and she had to ease her way over it with extreme care to avoid the spikes which nevertheless ripped at her clothes and scratched her hands. Finally, she was over and jumped down the other side; it was a drop of about three metres but the snow was soft and absorbed most of the impact. Rising to her feet, she brushed down her borrowed clothes and assessed the damage. Her ankle ached from the fall but the injury did not seem serious, so after a brief pause to recover, she set off, limping a little.

During the drive she had forced herself to take stock of her situation, to impose some sort of order on her chaotic thoughts. Runólfur had been involved in business with the Russians; he had spoken of a conspiracy when he visited her office at the ministry; he had made threats against the chairman of the Trade Council and now he was lying dead in her flat with a bullet in his head. He had mentioned the Russian mafia. Yet *she* had been the killers' intended target. They had referred to a conspiracy as well, but they were American. How did that fit?

And how was it connected to what her brother had seen on the glacier? Was he actually dead, as they had claimed — was Elías really gone? It was more than she could bear to follow the thought through.

Soon she came to a block of flats and pressed one of the doorbells. The building was three storeys high with two cold, empty stairwells. It contained twelve apartments in all. Like the other military accommodation blocks on the base, it had been built by Icelandic contractors in the style of a massive bunker, with thick concrete walls designed to withstand major earthquakes as well as a relentless battering from the Icelandic climate which was particularly savage here on the exposed Reykjanes peninsula. The windows were suitably small and thickly glazed.

After a while, a voice said 'Yes?' over the entry-phone.

'Steve?'

'Yes.'

'It's Kristín,' she said in English. 'I have to talk to you.'

'Kristín? Kristín! Just a minute.'

He buzzed her into the dark stairwell where she groped for a light switch. A cigarette machine stood on one wall and another sold chocolate and nuts. The cheap

126

floor tiles were plastic. She climbed up to the top floor where she found Steve's door open but knocked anyway.

'Come in,' he called from inside the flat.

She entered, closing the door behind her.

'Hi,' Steve said, his arms full of newspapers and magazines that he had picked up off the floor and sofa, something he plainly did not do very often. 'Sorry about the mess. I wasn't expecting you. In fact you were the last person I expected to see.'

'It's okay,' Kristín replied.

'I dozed off. But what are you doing here? It must be a year . . .' He trailed off in midsentence.

She had been here once before and nothing had changed. The apartment was small, consisting of a kitchen, a living room, one bedroom and a cramped bathroom. The place was a tip, littered with piles of newspapers, fast-food packaging and dirty dishes cluttering up the sideboard. The walls were covered with photos and posters: James Dean in a long coat, standing on a New York street in the rain; Che Guevara, outlined in black on a red background — nothing you would not find in any left-leaning movie buff's home.

'I didn't know where else to turn,' Kristín said, trying to choke back the tears that, despite herself, threatened to come.

'What's the matter?' he asked, sensing her agitation and putting down the bundle of papers.

'I didn't know where else to turn,' Kristín repeated. 'You have to help me. Something terrible has happened to my brother.'

'Your brother? Elías? What's happened to him?'

'Two men just tried to kill me in my apartment. Americans.'

'Kill you? No . . .'

'They killed Runólfur.'

'Runólfur?' Steve had difficulty pronouncing the name but even more in understanding Kristín. 'What are you talking about? What's going on?'

'I didn't know where else to turn,' Kristín said a third time, as if stuck on repeat. She was pale. Her chin trembled and she chewed at her fingernails as she tried to control herself.

Perplexed but troubled by her distress, Steve went slowly over, put a tentative arm around her and led her into the living room.

'They were going to kill me,' she choked. 'I don't know why. They claimed the police and ministry were involved. Elías phoned from the glacier saying he'd seen soldiers and a plane, then we were cut off. I was just

128

trying to get hold of the rescue service when these men turned up. They said I was going to commit suicide, then Runólfur knocked on the door and they shot him. I managed to get away. They said Elías was dead.'

Steve took care not to interrupt her. Clearly something traumatic had happened but he could make little of this incoherent monologue. He had never expected to see Kristín again, so her appearance now was inexplicable. Had she gone mad in the meantime? He wondered how long it would take for a doctor from the base to get to his flat.

'Elías saw some soldiers on the glacier,' Kristín tried again. 'They must have been American soldiers. That was the last thing he said before we were cut off. Do you know what American troops could be doing on the glacier?'

'The glacier?'

'Vatnajökull. I can tell you think I'm talking nonsense. I keep thinking I'm dreaming, that this is a nightmare and I'll wake up. But I'm not going to wake up. I'm never going to find that everything's all right. It's all true.'

He searched her face, as if it would give a clue to what chaos raged in her mind.

'And then there are the Russians,' she

added hesitantly.

'The Russians?'

'The man they killed in my flat was doing business with Russia. The Americans shot him in the head. When he came to the ministry he was ranting about a conspiracy against him. His killers mentioned a conspiracy too. I don't know what to believe. I've got to find out what happened to Elías. I tried to phone the rescue service but they didn't answer and then these Jehovah's Witnesses turned up.'

'Jehovah's Witnesses?'

'The men who tried to kill me. There were two of them, dressed like Jehovah's Witnesses — you know, dark suits and ties, neat hair, like the Jehovah's Witnesses who go from door to door with pamphlets. That's why I opened the door. I thought they were Jehovah's Witnesses. I'm such a fool!'

'Okay, it's okay,' Steve said soothingly, aware that none of this was okay. 'What the hell have you been doing at the ministry that could lead to this?'

'Nothing. Just my job. I haven't done anything. It's not my fault. I've done nothing to cause any of this. Nor has Elías.'

'No, of course not. But it sounds like two completely unrelated matters. American soldiers on Vatnajökull on the one hand,

and a conspiracy linked to doing business with Russia on the other.'

Kristín took a deep breath and wiped her eyes. Her cheeks were streaked with mascara. 'I know. I can't make any sense of it.'

She was calmer now. Steve was glad to have dispelled the tension inside her by accepting what she said without casting doubt on her bizarre story. Whatever her real state of mind, she was at her wits' end and it would be wrong to argue with anything she said. Her sobs gradually subsided and she was able to speak with more composure.

'Can you check this stuff about soldiers on the glacier for me? Ask around? Talk to people?' she asked.

'I'll see what I can do,' Steve replied. 'What exactly did your brother say?'

'That there was a plane in the ice and soldiers on the glacier.'

'Did he say "*in* the ice"? Doesn't that strike you as odd?'

'What?'

'As if it was buried in the ice. Is that what he said?'

'In the ice, on the ice — what the hell's the difference? He mentioned a plane and soldiers.'

'Is it possible that there's a plane in the ice?'

'For Christ's sake, Steve, I can't remember if he said *in* the ice or *on* the ice. It doesn't matter. I just need to know what's happening up there.'

Steve nodded. He had been stationed on the base for three years, employed by the press office to liaise with those Icelandic government ministries that dealt with the US military, chiefly the foreign ministry. He lived alone; he and his wife had divorced back in America. Of Irish extraction, he was dark, with an unruly mane of black hair. Although a few years older than Kristín at thirty-five, he was about her height, lean and strongly built. He used to make her laugh. They had met in an official capacity and eventually he had willed himself to ask her out to dinner.

On their first couple of dates at restaurants in Reykjavík, he had told her all about himself and his family. His people had always been in retailing but, having not the slightest interest in business, he had broken the mould by studying politics at university, followed by a stint working for the US defense department. But his real love was travelling, so when the opportunity to work in Iceland came up, he seized it.

For their third date he had invited her to the officers' mess at the base, followed by a drink at his place. Once they got back to his apartment he had been considerate but her confidence had evaporated without warning and she had panicked, unable to face the prospect of getting into bed with an American on the base. The stories about Icelandic women and GIs were ugly: 'Yankee whores' they called them. The public had always taken a harsh view of Icelandic women who got involved with American servicemen, a throwback to the Second World War when the girls had welcomed the first foreign soldiers to arrive on these shores, seeing them as an escape route to a brighter future, a new life overseas, or else admiring their uniforms and foreign manners, so familiar from the movies, and seeing them as providers of cigarettes, nylons and good times. 'The situation', as it was known, was a source of shame in Iceland and women who slept with the army were branded as sluts, an attitude Kristín felt had changed little over the years.

When she tried to explain, however, he was hurt that she saw him in those terms, so she left and after that they gradually saw less and less of each other until their relationship simply petered out. It was a senseless, silent drawing away from each other; they had not spoken for six months but had never really ended it definitively.

'Why don't we start by calling the rescue service?' he suggested in an attempt to placate her. 'Find out about your brother.'

He stood up, found the number and rang it. No one answered. He tried another number; no answer there either. He tried the third number, then beckoned her over to take the phone: someone had answered at last. She sprang up.

'My name's Kristín,' she said, 'is that the Reykjavík Air Ground Rescue Team?'

'Yes.'

'How can I get hold of your team on Vatnajökull?'

'We have several contact numbers for mobile phones and walkie-talkies. Can I help at all?'

'Has there been an accident on the glacier? Is anyone missing?'

'May I ask who you are?'

'Kristín. My brother's with the team. Elías.'

'I'll put you through to the leader of the team on Vatnajökull. Please hold the line.'

Kristín waited. She watched Steve pacing back and forth in his small living room; stared unseeingly at James Dean in the New York rain, at the face of revolution.

'Hello,' she heard a voice say at the other

end. 'Is that Kristín? This is Júlíus. I'm in charge of the team here on Vatnajökull. Can you hear me okay?'

'Loud and clear,' Kristín said hurriedly. 'Is Elías with you? Is he all right?'

'I'm afraid Elías is missing.'

'He's missing? How come? Where is he?'

'He and Jóhann left camp about seven hours ago and haven't returned yet. But we've traced a signal from Elías's phone and expect to find them as soon as it gets light. They may have got lost — it's very dark here. But I can't rule out the possibility that they've had an accident. Elías has plenty of experience on glaciers though, so there's no need to panic.'

'Have you noticed any soldiers in the area?' Kristín asked.

'Soldiers? No. What do you mean, soldiers?'

'Elías phoned me from the glacier and said there were soldiers coming towards him.'

'When did Elías call you?'

'It must have been about three or four hours ago. We were cut off seconds after he saw the soldiers.'

'No, we haven't noticed any movements up here. The boys were test-driving our new snowmobiles and could have covered quite a distance in that time, but there's no one around except us.'

'Didn't they give you any idea of where they were going? Do you think Elías could be in danger?'

'They didn't, and I can't imagine so, not unless he's travelling in the dark. There's a large belt of crevasses several hours to the west of us, but he's careful, and so's Jóhann. I expect they've stopped somewhere and their phone's out of range. If they stay where they are, we'll find them quickly once it gets light. What on earth made you call about Elías? Did you have some kind of premonition?'

'I was informed that Elías was dead,' Kristín said, 'and that it was connected somehow to the soldiers he saw on the glacier.'

'Elías isn't dead. He's missing but he's alive.'

'Kristín.' Steve was looking out of the living room window, the curtain pushed to one side. He was staring down at the car park in front of the building.

'Can I get hold of you on this number later?' Kristín asked, ignoring Steve.

'Who told you Elías was dead? Who would do a thing like that?'

'It's too complicated to explain now. I'll talk to you later.'

She took down his number and rang off. Júlíus had a manner of natural authority that in any other context would have been reassuring, she thought; he spoke confidently and precisely. But the conversation had done nothing to allay her fears.

'How did you get here?' Steve asked.

'By taxi.'

'Did anyone else know you were coming here?'

'No, no one.'

'Did you pay using cash?'

'No, by debit card.'

'Those men, did they have fair hair?' Steve asked in a level voice.

'Why do you ask?'

'Actually, it can't be, these guys aren't wearing jackets and ties, they're in ski-suits and boots.'

'Steve, what the hell are you on about?'

'There are two men standing outside, staring up at my window.'

'What do you mean?' Kristín said, the colour draining from her face.

She ran to the window, peered down at the car park and gasped in horror.

'Jesus, it's them. How the hell did they find me here?'

Steve leapt back from the window as if he

had been struck. 'They've seen us. Come on!'

Kristín was still wearing her coat. Steve yanked on boots and a thick down jacket; seconds later they were outside on the landing. Peering down the stairwell, they saw Ripley and Bateman entering the hall below and running towards the stairs.

'Shit,' muttered Steve.

'Have you got a gun?' Kristín asked.

'Why would I have a gun?'

'Just my luck to meet the only bloody American who doesn't carry a gun,' she swore in Icelandic.

'Come on,' he cried, running back into the apartment and locking the door behind them. They dashed out on to the little balcony. It was a six-metre drop to the ground — too high. Nor could they swing down to the balcony below, but there was a chance they could jump on to the one next door. From the front door to the apartment came the sound of hammering. Steve helped Kristín climb on to the rail and, grasping the ice-cold metal, she pushed herself up, almost succumbing to vertigo when she looked down, convinced for a moment that she was going to fall. Large lumps of snow slithered off the balcony, vanishing into the darkness below. Conquering her dizziness and ignoring the pain from her hands as the cold bit into them, she jumped over to the next balcony, dropping to the cement floor with a thud and a gasp. Steve followed just as the door to his apartment burst open.

He snatched up a heavy plant pot from the floor of his neighbour's balcony and used it to smash the glass of the veranda door, before opening it from the inside. They hurried in, straight through the apartment, kicking children's toys out of the way and almost falling over a vacuum cleaner, and out on to the landing, then raced down the stairs.

Ripley and Bateman ran through Steve's apartment and, hearing the sound of smashing glass, out on to the balcony where they saw that the veranda door of the neighbouring apartment was open. Spinning round, they rushed back through the apartment, only to spot Steve and Kristín vanishing into the stairwell. A fat man wearing nothing but his underpants emerged from the neighbouring flat and walked straight into Ripley and Bateman's path. They collided with him, knocking him to the ground where Ripley tripped over him.

Steve and Kristín made the most of their head-start, hurtling out of the front door of the building as the two men regained their feet. Steve ran to his car, Kristín following close behind. It was unlocked and Steve got behind the wheel, Kristín jumping in beside him.

'Keys . . . keys!' Steve shouted, slapping his jeans frantically, then digging his hand into a pocket.

'Where are the keys?' Kristín shouted back.

'Got them!' Steve replied, extracting a bunch from his pocket and shoving the correct key in the ignition. He pressed the accelerator to the floor as he turned the key. Nothing happened. The ignition hissed but the engine failed to catch.

'Jesus!' Steve swore between clenched teeth.

He tried again, thumping the steering wheel, stamping his foot down and switching on the ignition. The engine coughed for a few long seconds, then roared into life. He rammed it into drive and the car took a bound, hurling Kristín back in her seat. The stench of petrol filled her nose as the wheels spun in the snow, the engine screeching as the tyres tried to get a purchase, the back of the car skidding sideways, but just as the two men raced out of the building the wheels caught, the car jumped forwards and they were away.

Looking back, Kristín saw them chase the car briefly before giving up and standing at a loss, watching the vehicle disappear from view.

Steve turned his eyes from the road to look at Kristín. 'I thought you were crazy when you arrived at my place. Out of your mind.'

'Thanks, I noticed.'

'I don't think so any more. Sorry.'

He drove on, checking the mirrors every few seconds. Kristín noticed that he was gripping the steering wheel hard to stop his hands from shaking.

'There's only one way they could know about you,' Kristín said after a minute's silence.

'What's that?'

'Elías. They're connected to what's happening on the glacier. They've got your name from Elías. That has to be it. They must think he's told me something; that he's told me about them. And about the plane, whatever it's doing up there. The men are in contact with the soldiers and they got my phone number from Elías's mobile. That's how they knew. They know I'm his sister. And they think I know something; that Elías told me something. That's why they're after me.'

'But who are they? Who are they working for?'

'I almost forgot. One of them mentioned a name when they attacked me. I wasn't supposed to have heard. Something about "Ratoff". Do you recognise the name?'

'Ratoff? Never heard of him.'

'Oh God, Elías!' Kristín sighed. She slumped deep into the passenger seat, raking her hand through her hair. 'What's happened to him? They said he was dead.'

Steve drove grimly on, marvelling at the extraordinary turn the evening had taken. To think that he had come to this frozen island for a quiet life.

'Kristín, I'm going to make a few calls and try to find out what's going on. Do they actually know who you are?'

'They knew where I lived. They knew about Elías. They seem to know everything I do before I do it. Yes, Steve, I'd say they know who I am.'

Kristín looked at him, then out of the rear window again. She thought about Elías, and about her father who must have gone abroad; he was forever travelling — not that they had ever had foreign holidays as children — and did not always bother to mention when it was for short trips. They did not have much contact; a phone call every month or two, a stilted conversation and some bland expression of hope that all was well. Kristín felt sad that she could never go to her father about anything, that she always had to cope on her own. And the worst of it was that he would probably blame her for what had happened to her brother. He always had done.

13

Miller answered the door himself and invited Carr inside. He lived in a two-storey wooden house with a tidy garden, situated in quiet, forested countryside now covered with a light dusting of snow, not far from Washington DC. Miller shuffled along in his worn-down felt slippers; he was around eighty now with a pronounced stoop, his remaining wisps of hair completely white, his face dotted with liver spots. His wife had died twenty years earlier and though they had never had any children he was well looked after, receiving home help three times a week and meals on wheels at lunchtime and in the evenings. On the face of it, Miller was nothing but a useless old husk waiting to die, his many years of service behind him, but the fragile, elderly exterior disguised a mind as lively and resourceful as ever.

After the two men shook hands at the door, Miller showed Carr into his ground floor study which was filled with mementoes of a long life, predominantly photographs of his military service: World War II comrades, scenes from Korea and Vietnam, but there were pictures from peace time as well. Everything inside the house was as neat as a pin. The walls were lined with books, mostly about war.

'Are you sure it's the plane?' Miller asked, taking out two small tumblers and filling them with brandy. It was far too early for Carr but he said nothing; the time of day had obviously ceased to have any meaning for Miller.

'No question,' Carr replied, sipping.

'Are they inside yet?'

'Not yet. Ratoff's in charge.'

Miller frowned. 'Was that really necessary?'

'In my estimation the operation needs a man like Ratoff. It's as simple as that.'

'Are you still planning to fly it over the Atlantic? To Argentina?'

'Yup, Argentina.'

'So the procedure hasn't changed?'

'No. Everything's going to plan. Though they were spotted with the plane. By locals

— two of them. I'm afraid they saw too much, but according to Ratoff everything else is under control.'

'I don't suppose he spared them.'

Carr turned away and looked out of the window.

'And the brothers?'

Carr shrugged.

Miller closed his eyes. He remembered the brothers as they had been when he first met them at the foot of the glacier all those years ago: friendly, hospitable, cooperative and, most important of all, discreet. They had never asked questions, simply invited him into their home and acted as guides on the glacier. They had been more or less the same age as him.

'Ratoff hasn't been briefed on what the plane contains, has he?' he asked.

'He'll soon find out. But I'm confident we can trust him, at least to bring us the documents. We have trucks on the spot to transport the dismantled plane to Keflavík. The bodies will accompany the wreckage. I've given Ratoff instructions about what to do with any papers he finds. No doubt he'll read them but it's an unavoidable risk and in any case, he's stuck on an island — where can he go? All being well, this chapter of the war will be closed in a few days' time and we'll finally be able to breathe easier. *They'll* be able to breathe easier.'

'And what about Ratoff?'

'We're keeping our options open.'

'If he reads the documents, he'll think he's in danger.'

'Let's just wait and see how he plays it. Ratoff's not a very complicated man.'

Miller swirled the brandy in his glass.

'Do the others know the situation?'

'The few who are left.'

'And the politicians?'

'I'm confident I've managed to frighten them off. I gave them the Walchensee gold story. Our young secretary of defense didn't know whether to cry or piss himself when I told him. You only have to mention the Jews and they start shitting themselves.'

'But something's wrong.' It was a statement, not a question. Miller knew his successor; he had guessed from Carr's expression and the way he talked that all was not well. It would not be the first time Carr had come to him for guidance or support but he was a man who could not bear to admit to mistakes.

Carr spoke crisply and precisely. 'There's a young woman in Reykjavík, the sister of one of the boys who disturbed the excavation. Apparently the boy told her over the phone that there were armed troops and a plane on the glacier — Ratoff extracted that much from him. She's given our men the slip twice now, and is being assisted by an American from the base, an ex-boyfriend. Presumably she went to him because of what her brother said about soldiers. They're currently somewhere on the base but I'm assured that the area has been secured and the base commander is cooperating. They won't get far.'

Neither man spoke for a while.

'The operation was a necessity of war,' Miller said at last. 'We had to clean up after the politicians. Always have done.'

'I know — though I'm more inclined to put it down to temporary insanity. It was bedlam in the last months of the war.'

'That's not to say that we shouldn't have gone into Russia. Patton was right about that.'

'They hesitated.'

'And we lost half of Europe.'

Miller topped up their glasses. Brandy was one of the few luxuries he still permitted himself. The doctors had told him he did not have long. Not that he cared; he had reconciled himself to dying a long time ago and would welcome it when the time came.

'It's not our job to write history; that's for

others to do,' he said.

'No, our job has always been to wipe the slate clean and rewrite it,' Carr replied. 'History's all lies — you know that and I know that. There have been so many cover-ups, so many fabrications; we've told the truth about lies and lied about the truth, taken out one thing and substituted another. That's our job. You told me once that the history of mankind was nothing more than a register of crimes and misfortunes. Well, it's also a register of carefully constructed lies.'

'You sound tired, Vytautas.'

'I *am* tired. When this is over I'm going to retire.'

Miller took another sip of brandy. It was his favourite label, an exclusive French cognac, and he savoured it lingeringly before letting it slip down his throat.

'The brothers told me that the winter of '45 was unusually hard,' he remarked. 'The snow didn't melt on the slopes above the farm until July. I searched the area with a small party at the time but we found no trace of a crash. The fuselage must be fairly intact under the ice, which means the bodies must be too. They've been deep frozen for more than half a century.'

He paused.

'I envy that animal Ratoff. I've been looking for that plane all my life and now that
it's finally been found I'm too old to see it.
When will it reach Argentina?'

'Ratoff says four days, though that could
change. There's bad weather forecast for
the area — a storm's expected within the
next twenty-four hours. You can always
come to South America if you feel up to it.'

But Miller was far away. He was thinking
of the layers upon layers of snow and ice he
had spent so many years fruitlessly probing.
The glacial accumulations, winter after
winter, blizzard after blizzard, burying the
frozen casket ever further from the world.

'I've often thought it would probably be
best for us if the glacier held on to the plane
for ever, so we wouldn't have to worry about
it any more. It would be best for everyone.'

'Maybe. Sometimes I think that damn
plane is the only reason we established a
base in Iceland. Sometimes it seems that
important.'

Silence fell on the small room again.

'About the sister? Can't we let it go?' Miller asked eventually.

'Not until the transport's airborne. After
that it won't matter.'

'So all she need do is lie low for a few days
and she'll be out of danger?'

'Something like that.'

Miller took another mouthful of brandy.

'Who over here knows about the discovery then?' he asked.

'You and me. The defense secretary who's under the impression that the matter involves Jewish gold. A handful of individuals at the company. The others are all dead and buried.'

'And soon we'll be joining them.'

'It's ancient history; few people apart from us know what the plane really contains. These new young men don't appreciate the situation. They're too naive to understand the need for secrecy. They don't care if the plane's story gets out. They might even try to exploit it for other purposes, God help us. They're fanatics. We mustn't drag this out — the longer the recovery takes, the more likely it is there'll be a leak.'

'When you talk of fanatics . . .'

'I mean I can't be sure what they'd do if they knew the role the plane played.'

'It's too bad we don't have the astronauts to deflect the world's attention this time around.' Miller smiled wryly.

'Poor Armstrong. He never had a clue what he was doing in Iceland,' Carr remarked.

'He took another giant step for mankind there.'

Miller abruptly changed the subject. Carr had checked his watch and he had the sense that he would soon be leaving.

'I got to know the Icelanders a little when I was stationed over there in '45. A baffling nation. They live on this rocky outpost of Europe in the far north of the Atlantic. It's dark most of the year round and for centuries they lived in dwellings little better than holes in the ground; rocks and peat sods were the only building materials they had to hand. When I was there they were just beginning to emerge from the ground, just starting to build themselves proper houses. Yet despite all that they were a cultured people. Take those brothers, for example — they'd read Milton in Icelandic translation. Knew every word. They'd learnt long passages of *Paradise Lost* by heart.'

'What's your point?'

'There aren't that many Icelanders in the world. Let's not reduce their numbers unnecessarily.'

'I assure you we won't.'

Miller looked down at the glass in his hand.

'If I can't make it to Argentina, will you send him home to me?'

'As I see it, nothing has changed since we last went over the procedure. It's only right that he should come back to you.'

'I keep thinking about the temperatures. It can't have got above freezing up there in fifty years. If he wasn't badly injured, he ought to look just as he did. Strange how I can't stop thinking about it. More as the years go by. It would be like going back in time.'

14

Vatnajökull Glacier,
Saturday 30 January

The Delta operators worked tirelessly at clearing away the snow. They were digging from both sides of the wreck simultaneously, throwing up great mounds, and in the growing light the plane became steadily more distinct. The nose now jutted up at a twenty-degree angle, though the tail was still buried in dense, hard-packed ice on which it was difficult to make any impact. The door, which was supposed to be located on the left-hand side behind the row of windows, had yet to be uncovered. From what they could tell, the fuselage was largely intact and not much snow appeared to have penetrated inside.

Powerful floodlights shed a yellowish glow over the scene during the night, but as the daylight grew stronger they were switched off, their hot surfaces sending a fine vapour rising and curling over the crust of the glacier. A number of white tents stood huddled on the ice, each containing a gas lamp that burned night and day for warmth. Largest of all was the communications tent. Electricity was provided by portable oil-powered generators, and the surrounding area was littered with oil barrels, snowmobiles, tracked vehicles, and beyond them large pallets for transporting the wreckage.

The work was progressing well. The wind was light and the temperature on the glacier hovered at around $-15°C$. Some of the men had been detailed to work with pickaxes to break up the hard surface, while another small group was busy cutting the plane in half with powerful blowtorches. The sections would then be loaded on to the pallets and towed down to where the trucks were waiting to drive them west to Keflavík Airport. Ratoff stood outside the communications tent, watching the blue flare of the oxyacetylene and the showers of sparks which flew from the metal carcass. By his reckoning, the job was on schedule. A storm was forecast but it was expected to blow over quickly.

In many ways it was fortunate that the plane had been found in winter. Of course, the weather was changeable in the extreme and the conditions for travel might prove difficult, but their activities were protected by the darkness and the lack of traffic in the area at this time of year.

As Ratoff watched, the men on the far side of the plane wreck abandoned their digging and gathered to peer at something in the ice. After a moment, one of them yelled to him. He set off towards them, ducked under the nose of the plane and joined the soldiers, to be met by the sight of a leg protruding from the ice next to the fuselage. The leg was encased in a black army boot that reached almost up to the knee and greyish trousers. Ratoff ordered the men to uncover the body and soon the entire corpse, or what was left of it, became visible.

It looked to Ratoff as if it had been deliberately laid there beside the plane. Some of the passengers had evidently survived the crash and been capable of moving around and tending to those who had died on impact. The man was dressed in the uniform of a high-ranking German officer, though Ratoff did not recognise the insignia. He wore an Iron Cross at his neck, his hands were crossed over his breast and his face was covered with a cap. His other leg was missing: apparently it had been ripped off at the hip. The gaping wound, revealing the white bone, was clearly visible but the leg itself was nowhere to be seen. Ratoff bent over the body with the intention of examining its face but found the cap frozen to it.

Straightening up again, he ordered his men to free the body from the ice and take it into one of the tents. He wondered how long the passengers had survived after the crash-landing. The accident had happened at this time of year. Ratoff and his men were clad in special Arctic-survival gear but even so the cold pierced them to the bone. They also had the gas lamps and had been specially trained to endure the cold. The passengers of the plane, on the other hand, would have been utterly defenceless. Those who survived the crash must have slowly frozen to death. It could not have taken many days.

Thirty-five miles away, eight members of the Reykjavík Rescue Team stood staring down into the blue depths of a jagged fissure in the ice, from which they could hear the faint ringing of a mobile phone. They had set out shortly before daybreak and soon found the tracks of the snowmobiles; the trail had changed direction about two hours from the team's base camp, heading due west towards a large belt of crevasses. Back at camp they succeeded in pinpointing the mobile phone signal and the rest had been easy. The snowmobiles appeared to have careered into the chasm at full speed, as if Elías and Jóhann had not seen it coming until it was too late.

One of the rescue team lowered himself into the crevasse on a rope; his two comrades lay at a depth of about eight metres. As he came alongside them, he could see that their injuries were horrific, as if they had crashed repeatedly into the walls of the fissure as they fell and the snowmobiles had then landed on top of them, rendering them almost unrecognisable. Their faces were reduced to raw, featureless pulp; eyes obscured by a mass of swelling, ears bloody clumps, bodies twisted into unnatural shapes as if every bone in them were broken. He had never seen anything like it before and, turning his head away, he vomited.

The team set to work, first hauling up the snowmobiles, then lowering stretchers on to which they strapped Elías and Jóhann. These they raised in turn with slow care to avoid bumping the battered bodies against the ice walls, and set the stretchers in the back of the team's snow-cat. A bitterly cold north-easterly had started to blow, whirling up loose snow which cut into any exposed skin like razorblades and soon hid all sign of their tracks around the crevasse.

Júlíus stood watching the operation, his head bowed, oblivious to the cold. He had been leading expeditions for fifteen years; there had been accidents and injuries before but nobody in his charge had ever died. Now he had lost two young men for whom he was responsible, two boys whom he had given permission to leave camp to test-drive the new snowmobiles. He might have known they would get carried away, forget the time and end up in trouble, but this was far beyond his worst imaginings. He heard someone calling him from the vehicle. One of the volunteers, a medical student called Heimir, was resting two fingers over Elías's neck. Júlíus waited, holding his breath.

'It's weak but there's still a pulse,' Heimir announced.

'He's alive?'

'Just about. But I doubt he's got long.'

'Can we tend to him here or should we take him back to camp and summon a helicopter?'

'Like I say, he could go at any minute. It's probably safest not to try and move him. We should do the best we can and call the helicopter. How quickly can it get here?'

'It shouldn't take long,' the leader said, switching on his radio. 'But I still think we should get him out before the storm hits. There's severe weather expected any minute and we'd be better off back at camp than in the open. Let's move.'

Suddenly Elías gave a faint moan. His blue lips moved slightly.

'Is he trying to say something?' Júlíus asked.

Heimir bent down to Elías's bloodstained face and laid his ear to the boy's mouth. After a minute he straightened up and looked at Júlíus.

'He's drifting in and out of consciousness.'

'Did he say anything?'

'It was very unclear. I think he may have said "Kristín".'

'Yes, he would,' Júlíus said. He remembered how he had assured her that Elías was safe and a pang of self-recrimination went through him.

But when he called the Coast Guard helicopter it transpired that the only available aircraft was currently fetching a wounded fisherman from a trawler halfway between Iceland and Greenland. In cases when the Coast Guard could not get to the scene, it was customary to call the Defense Force at Keflavík Airport and ask them for

160

help. Júlíus was assured that the Coast Guard would contact the Americans and ask them to send a helicopter to pick up the two men.

Why had Elías's sister thought he was dead? Júlíus wondered, as he walked back to the edge of the crevasse and looked down into the chasm. How could she have found out before us?

He dreaded having to tell her that she was right. Elías was not dead yet but he was unlikely to pull through. His injuries were severe, he had been lying in the ice for hours, and he would certainly be hypothermic. Júlíus scanned the horizon, willing the helicopter to arrive before the storm struck. It was Elías's only hope.

15

She woke up at the third ring. Monica
Garcia worked as the director of the Fulbright Commission in Iceland, an educa-
tional exchange programme based at the
US embassy in Reykjavík, where she had an
apartment. She disliked being called in the
middle of the night and stirred sleepily; she
had been hoping for a peaceful night after
the extraordinary last twenty-four hours at
the embassy. But the strident ringing persisted until at last she propped herself up
on her elbow and snatched up the receiver.

'Monica?' said a voice.

'It's one in the morning,' she protested,
registering the luminous numbers on her
radio alarm. 'Who is this?'

'It's Steve. I'm sorry, but it's an
emergency.'

'Steve? Why are you calling me in the

162

middle of the night?'

'I think some men from the embassy are trying to kill me.'

'Why would anyone want to kill you, Steve? What have you been smoking?'

Groping for the lamp on the bedside table, she switched it on, just managing to avoid knocking over a glass of water and dislodging a small pile of books on which an open copy of *War and Peace* lay uppermost.

'Two men, both around six foot, blond, neatly dressed in civilian clothes. They're after my friend as well. I told you about Kristín. She knows something about military activities on Vatnajökull and whatever it is, it's important enough for them to send paid assassins round to her house. She came to the base to find me, and the men turned up at my place shortly afterwards but we managed to escape.'

'She fled *to* the base? Steve, I don't understand a word of this.'

She sat up in bed and shivered: the room was freezing as the radiator had broken again.

'I know, it's complicated. I'll explain later but you have to trust me.'

'Where are you now?'

'I'm still on the base. What's going on at the embassy? What's happening on the glacier? Do you know?'

'Everything's been turned upside down. That's all I can tell you. I've no idea why.'

'How do you mean upside down?'

'Military intelligence has assumed control by direct order of the defense secretary. Some sort of special operations personnel showed up, took over everything and sent the ambassador on leave. Three special forces companies landed at Keflavík just over twenty-four hours ago and may well have gone to Vatnajökull, for all I know. Beyond that I really don't know what's going on. It's as if there's been a military coup. They installed a whole load of computer equipment — I don't have a clue what it's for — and set up a command and control centre. The embassy staff aren't being told anything. We've been ordered to stay out of the way and keep our mouths shut. They say they'll only be here for a few days.'

'Have you come across a man by the name of Ratoff?'

'No, never heard of him. Who is he?'

'It's a name Kristín overheard. He may be in charge. Look, I have to hang up. Is there anything you can do to help me, anything at all, Monica?'

'I'll try to dig something up for you. If special forces have taken over the embassy, they're probably in control of the base too, so I'd be very careful about looking for help there. Do you remember the Irish pub in Reykjavík? The one downtown?'

'Yes.'

'Call there at 4 o'clock today or come down yourself. I'll see what I can find out for you in the meantime.'

'Thanks, Monica.'

'And Steve, for Christ's sake, be careful.'

He put the phone down and turned to Kristín. They were in his office in one of the army administration blocks. Kristín was keeping watch by the window, the profile of her face silhouetted against the glass, black against black. She had phoned air traffic control in Keflavík, posing as a journalist from Reykjavík, and asked if there had been a plane crash recently on Vatnajökull. She was informed that no plane had crashed on the glacier for decades, not since the famous Loftleidir incident. When they asked what paper she was calling from, she had hung up.

Kristín vaguely remembered the accident. 'A Loftleidir plane — that's the old Icelandic airline — was forced to make an emergency landing on the glacier,' she told Steve. 'Everyone survived.'

'Is that the plane Elías saw then?' Steve asked.

'I haven't a clue. I don't know what happened to the wreckage. And anyway, what would the army want with an old Loftleidir plane? It must have been forty years ago. It's absurd.'

They had been in the office around ten minutes and Kristín was growing jumpy. Although they had parked Steve's car a few hundred yards away among other vehicles outside a large apartment block, it would not remain undiscovered for long if the men put out a search. The office had been Steve's first thought as he accelerated away from his block, leaving Ripley and Bateman behind in the parking lot. But he had not come here to hide as his workplace would be an obvious location for them to check; rather, the building housed part of the Defense Force archives, to which he had access.

He and Kristín ran down the long ground floor corridor and descended into the basement where the archives were kept. Punching in a code to deactivate the alarm, Steve turned a key in the heavy steel door and pushed it open. Inside stood another door, covered in wire netting, which opened into one of the archives. The storeroom was divided into several compartments by coarse wire netting which formed a series of cages, each of which was filled with long rows of filing cabinets, and beyond them shelves of files and boxes.

'Welcome to America's memory,' Steve whispered.

'How are we supposed to find anything in this warren?' Kristín asked, gazing in dismay at the rows of units stretching off into the distance. 'What are you looking for anyway?'

'There may be something here about operations on Vatnajökull,' Steve said. He was familiar with the archives, having temped there one summer, and knew where to lay his hands on records of surveillance flights over Iceland in the last fifty years. If there was a plane on the glacier, he reasoned, it might well belong to the US Air Force or Navy.

He was so happy that Kristín had turned to him in her hour of need that it did not even occur to him to refuse her request. No longer in any doubt about the danger she was in, he was determined to stand by her, to help her in any way he could; besides, his journalistic instincts had been roused and he was becoming increasingly curious about the case on his own account.

They walked rapidly along the shelves,

checking the labels on cupboards and files. Some way towards the back, Steve stopped and pulled out a box. He looked inside, then replaced it and continued searching. He did the same thing several times; took out a box containing a number of files, leafed through them, then put it back. It was hopeless — he had no idea where to start in this sea of information — and before long they returned to his office, empty-handed.

For some minutes he stood by the window, peering out, chewing his lip in frustration. 'A friend of mine has access to more files than me,' he announced finally. 'We should see what he says.'

'I'm sorry to have landed you in all this. I didn't know where else to turn,' Kristín said as they left the building.

'Forget it,' Steve answered, his eyes flickering round nervously. 'I'm as interested as you in finding out what's up there.'

They decided to leave the car behind and walk. Steve knew the base very well and kept to the back alleyways, stealing through communal gardens, darting hurriedly across brightly lit streets where necessary, taking care to stay under cover. Kristín had no idea where they were going. As for most Icelanders, the base was a foreign country to her. The only time she had been to Midnesheidi was with her parents to the international airport in the days before the new terminal had been built. She recognised the Andrews movie theatre, and glimpsed in the distance the old terminal building and officers' mess. She remembered two of her old classmates from school who had gone on to work for Icelandic contractors on the base and used to come home to Reykjavík every weekend laden with cigarettes and vodka that they bought cheap from the American servicemen, to the great envy of their friends.

'I never expected to see you again,' Steve ventured as they picked their way through the snow behind one of the apartment blocks.

'I know,' Kristín said.

'I always meant to try to talk to you about it but somehow . . .'

'I've thought the same. It was my fault.'

'No, it wasn't. No way. It was nobody's fault. Why does everything always have to be somebody's fault?'

When Kristín did not answer, Steve let the subject drop. There was little traffic in the area although they twice spotted military police patrols. Steve stopped by a building not dissimilar to his own but in an entirely different part of the base. They all looked identical to Kristín. He told her to wait, he would not be long, so she lurked round the side of the block trying to make herself inconspicuous, stamping her feet, blowing on her hands and pulling her hood tight against the chill air. It was about fifteen minutes before he returned, accompanied by a man whom he introduced to her as Arnold. He was plump, about Steve's age, with sweaty palms, shifty eyes and a lisp. They climbed into his car and drove off.

'Arnold's a librarian,' Steve said smiling. 'He knows his way round the archives and he owes me a favour.'

Kristín had no idea what this implied and Arnold did not enlighten her, just glowered at Steve.

He pulled up at a two-storey administration block not far from the old terminal. After letting them in through the back entrance, he led them straight down to a basement archive, considerably larger than the one they had visited earlier, occupying three levels.

'What years are we talking about?' Arnold asked flatly.

'Flights over Vatnajökull since the beginning of the war, I suppose,' Steve replied. 'I don't know what for. Routine surveillance flights, maybe, or reconnaissance. Aerial photography. Nothing major, as I said.

Nothing risky. Nothing that presents a threat to US national security.'

'Surveillance? Aerial photography?' Arnold scoffed, not even trying to disguise his irritation. 'You've no idea what you're on about.'

'Forced landings as well. Crashes on the glacier. A plane. Anything like that. Pilots who might know about flights over the glacier. Anything at all like that.'

Shaking his head, Arnold walked down to the next level. They followed, their footsteps echoing hollowly against the walls. Kristín found the noise they were making unbearable. Arnold passed a row of shelves, slowed and stopped. Turning back, he descended to the level below, clattering down the metal staircase, and walked along one of the rows. There he took down a box file and opened it, then closed it again. Eventually they came to a large filing cabinet and Arnold pulled out one of the drawers.

'Here's something,' he said to Steve. 'Records of photographic surveillance flights in 1965. By the old U-2 spy planes, just before they switched to satellites.' Arnold stepped aside as if to avoid getting any closer to this irregularity than he already was, then announced that he would wait for them by the entrance upstairs and vanished.

Steve squatted down.

'Let's see . . . what have we here? . . . Nothing. Only some crap about routine surveillance flights off the north coast. Nothing about Vatnajökull. Nothing about aerial photography.' He examined more of the files.

'Maintenance reports!' he sighed. 'Technical jargon. Wait a minute, here are some names of pilots.' There were several. Steve took out a pen and paper and started to scribble them down.

'Arnold's a laugh a minute,' Kristín observed.

'He smuggles more dope into the base than anyone else I know,' Steve said matter-of-factly.

'I thought he was a librarian?'

'A wolf in sheep's clothing.'

'So what did you say to him?'

'Some lie about you being — what do you call it? — a GI baby? That you're trying to trace your father.'

'Who was a pilot?'

'You got it.'

'And he didn't think we kept rather unorthodox hours?'

'All these guys must be dead,' Steve muttered, without answering. He was still busy noting the pilots' names.

'What do the reports say?'

'Nothing of any interest. Just descriptions of routine surveillance flights. Very limited information. Naturally they don't keep anything important down here.'

'Nothing about Vatnajökull? Or photographs?'

'Not that I can see.'

'Might Arnold know?'

'No harm in asking. I'm going to check if we've got anything on these pilots.' He finished copying down the names.

Arnold was hovering by the door when they came back upstairs. Telling Kristín to wait a minute, Steve went over and had a word with him in private. Arnold looked extremely nervous. They argued for a while, then Steve came back.

'He says he doesn't know anything about Vatnajökull and I believe him. He'll give us five minutes to look up the names of these pilots on his computer.'

Arnold led them down a long corridor, cursing all the while, opened the door to his office, groped his way to the computer and turned it on. He reached out to switch on his desk lamp but Steve stopped him; the blue glow from the computer screen provided the only illumination in the room. Before long they had opened the army

173

employment records and were looking up each name in turn. Kristín stationed herself by the window, terrified that the glow from the computer would attract attention. What was it that Elías had seen?

'They're either dead and buried or repatriated to the States long ago,' Steve sighed and typed in one last name. Arnold had disappeared.

'Hang on, there's something here. Michael Thompson. Retired. Still resident on the base. Pilot. Born 1921. He's been here at Midnesheidi since the sixties. He lives nearby. Come on,' Steve said, jumping out of his chair. 'We'll have to wake the poor bastard up. Maybe he'll have some answers.'

They left by the way they had come in. Arnold was nowhere to be seen and Steve told Kristín he had probably slipped off home. The snow was still falling incessantly as they made their way through the darkness to the oldest part of the military zone. Compared to others the US army had established around the world, the base was tiny. The NATO Defense Force had numbered only four to five thousand personnel at its height but its population had been dramatically reduced since the end of the Cold War. Many of the accommodation blocks now stood empty and derelict, especially in the oldest quarter, relics of a forgotten war. It did not take them long to get there, despite wading through knee-deep snow on little-used paths. They did not speak on the way except once when Steve expressed surprise that Michael Thompson should still be living on the base. Most of the servicemen sent to Iceland could not wait to move on to their next posting after completing their maximum three-year tour of duty, usually praying fervently for somewhere tropical.

16

Thompson's name was on the entry-phone. Steve rang the bell. The retired pilot lived in an apartment block like Steve's but more rundown. No maintenance had been carried out for years; the paint had flaked off here and there exposing the concrete, the light above the front door was broken and only a handful of the apartments looked occupied.

Steve pressed the doorbell again and they waited, glancing around anxiously. He rang the bell a third time, holding the button down for so long that Kristín tapped his hand. Shortly afterwards there was a crackle from the entry-phone and a reedy voice uttered a hesitant: 'Hello?'

'Is that Michael Thompson?' Steve asked.

'Yes,' replied the voice.

'I'm sorry to wake you like this but I need

to talk to you urgently. Could you let me in?' Steve said, trying to speak as quietly as possible.

'What?'

'Could you let me in?'

'What's going on?'

'May I come in?'

'What is it you want exactly? I don't understand.'

'It's about Vatnajökull.'

'What?'

'Vatnajökull,' Steve said. 'I want to ask you about flights over Vatnajökull. I know it's very unexpected and an extra . . .'

'Flights?'

'Lives are at stake, man. For Christ's sake, please open the door.'

After a short pause and more crackling on the entry-phone, the lock buzzed and Steve ushered Kristín inside in front of him. They did not turn on the light in the hall but groped their way up the stairs, holding on to the banister. Thompson lived on the first floor. They tapped on his door and he appeared in the rectangle of light, peering out at them. He had put on slippers and a robe, beneath which his legs protruded, chalk-white and bony. He was very thin, with a stoop and a Clark Gable moustache, long since turned white, barely visible against his pale skin.

'It must be serious to make you barge in on me in the middle of the night like this,' Thompson commented, showing them into the living room. They sat down on a small, black leather sofa and he took a seat facing them, looking at them sceptically in turn.

'My brother called me earlier this evening,' Kristín began, feeling that it might just as well have been a month ago. 'He was on a training exercise on Vatnajökull when he spotted a plane and some soldiers. Then his mobile phone was cut off and I haven't heard from him since. Shortly afterwards two Americans turned up at my apartment in Reykjavík and tried to kill me. I escaped and came to Steve for help because if there are soldiers on the glacier, I assumed they must have come from here.'

'You say they tried to kill you?'

'That's right.'

'What are you talking about? What do you mean by barging into my home and spinning me a story like this? And anyway, what's it got to do with me?'

'You're a pilot. You've been here a long time. Do you know anything about a plane on Vatnajökull?'

'I haven't the faintest idea what you're talking about,' the old man answered angrily. 'Now please leave before I call the police.'

'Wait. I know we must seem crazy,' Steve said, 'but we're desperate. This is not a hoax, we're not nuts and we don't mean to be disrespectful. If you can't help us, we'll go. But if you can tell us anything that might help, we'd be incredibly grateful.'

'My brother witnessed something he wasn't supposed to see,' Kristín said. 'And soldiers who presumably must come from this base. They believe he told me more about what he saw than he did and now they're after us too. Steve had the idea that if there was a plane on the glacier then a pilot like you would know about it.'

'But who is this *they* you keep going on about?' Thompson asked.

'We don't know,' Steve said. 'There are two men. We don't know who sent them.'

'But we've heard,' Kristín added 'that special forces troops landed here in Keflavík a short time ago, on their way to Vatnajökull.'

Thompson was silent.

'They were going to kill you?' he asked again.

They stared back at him without speaking.

'There used to be so many rumours,' he

179

said at last in a resigned tone. 'We never knew for certain what they were looking for. We thought it might be a plane and that it must have had some extremely dangerous cargo; they organised regular monitoring flights over the country and the sea to the north of it. Once a month we flew over the glacier, over the south-eastern section, photographing the surface of the ice. Our commanding officer, Leo Stiller, organised the flights. I never spotted anything myself, but every now and then they would believe they had seen something that gave them strong enough grounds to take a closer look.'

'Leo Stiller?' Steve repeated.

'A good guy. Killed in a helicopter accident here on the base. His wife moved to Reykjavík after he died. Her name's Sarah Steinkamp.'

'Who analysed the photographs you took?' Steve asked.

'I believe they were sent to military intelligence headquarters in Washington. I don't know much about that end of things. Only that all sorts of rumours used to do the rounds; they still crop up from time to time. Leo was into all kinds of conspiracy theories. He never did know when to shut up. I'm sorry to hear about your brother. Judging from the way they've behaved in the past I imagine he'd be in danger up there.'

'So what is this plane?'

'I don't know.'

'Why's it important?'

'I don't know that either.'

'But what do you believe is in the plane?' Kristín asked. 'What did you pilots think when you talked amongst yourselves?'

Instead of answering her, Thompson rose slowly to his feet and suggested he make some coffee; they looked chilled to the bone and he could never really get going in the morning until he had had a coffee, he explained. 'Not that it's morning yet,' he corrected himself, 'but it's near enough; not much point going back to bed after a night like this.'

As he clattered around in the little kitchen that opened off the living room, Kristín gesticulated frantically at Steve.

'We can't sit around drinking fucking coffee whilst he takes a trip down memory lane,' she whispered urgently. 'Elías is out there . . .'

He signalled to her to slow down, relax, let the old man decide the pace.

'I was wondering,' Steve called into the kitchen, 'if it's not rude to ask, why you're still here. I'd have expected you to have gone home to the States long ago. Everyone else leaves here the first chance they get. Isn't there some sort of rule about it?'

Thompson reappeared carrying three mugs.

'Do you take milk or sugar?' he asked.

Kristín rolled her eyes in despair. Steve shook his head.

'Coffee's no good unless it's strong and black.' Thompson looked at Steve. 'It's hardly surprising you should ask,' he said. 'I came to this strange little island in 1955. I flew helicopters in Korea and was posted here when the war was over — if it is over. Before that I was stationed in Germany and the Philippines. It was quite a shock to the system, I can tell you, coming here to the far north where the climate's miserable, it's cold and dark for half the year, there's nothing to do on the base and the locals despise us. Yet here I am.'

'Why?' Kristín asked. 'And I'm not sure all the people despise Americans,' she added.

'You Icelanders have a very ambivalent attitude. You discourage all contact and behave as if the army has nothing to do with you, but then you say you can't manage without it. I don't understand you. You make a huge profit out of us; we pump bil-

182

lions into your economy, have done for decades, yet you behave as if we didn't exist. Sure, you're a small nation and I can understand that you want to protect your independence. You've always protested, standing outside the gates here with placards and chanting slogans, but now the Cold War's over and the military operations are being scaled down, suddenly those voices are silenced and instead everybody wants to keep the base. Just so long as you don't have to have anything to do with it. We're the ones who are effectively living on an island out here on Midnesheidi.'

'If that's the case, why are you still here?' Kristín asked.

'Because of a woman,' Thompson said, switching without warning to Icelandic. Kristín was so startled that she spilt the scalding coffee she was sipping.

The white Ford Explorer pulled up in front of the administration block where Steve worked. The doors opened and Ripley and Bateman climbed out. They had found Steve's car and followed the trail to this building, accompanied by military police and a number of soldiers in jeeps. With the cooperation of the admiral, Ripley and Bateman had organised a manhunt; search parties were moving through the base, stopping traffic, setting up roadblocks and searching the buildings, aircraft hangars and residential blocks. Information was also being gathered about any friends and colleagues Steve might conceivably turn to on the base.

Ripley and Bateman walked up to the entrance of the office block and tried the door. It was locked. They walked round the building to the back door.

'And here they are,' Ripley announced, eyeing twin sets of tracks that led away through the fresh snow in the direction of the oldest residential quarter.

'Who did he call?' Bateman asked, as they set off to follow the trail on foot.

'Her name's Monica Garcia. Works for the Fulbright Commission.'

The snow crunched underfoot.

'We need dogs,' Ripley said.

Kristín put down her coffee mug on the table, staring at the old pilot in surprise. Steve understood nothing of their conversation after they switched to Icelandic. Like most Americans stationed in Iceland, he knew no Icelanders apart from Kristín and rarely left the base except on official business. The base was a world to itself, with all the services necessary to support a small society. In that it was no different from any other American military base around the world. A number of Icelanders worked there but they lived in the surrounding towns and villages and went home at the end of the working day. The base had always been cut off, not merely geographically but also politically and culturally, from the rest of Iceland.

'You mean an Icelandic woman?' Kristín asked.

'She had one of those unpronounceable names you lot go in for: Thorgerdur Kristmundsdóttir, but I knew her as Tobba which was much easier to say. She passed away several years ago now. Lived in a village not far from here. Taught me Icelandic. But she was married and wouldn't dream of leaving her husband. She worked at the store on the base — that's how I got to know her, how we were able to meet. She awakened my interest in this country and little by little I became as captivated by Iceland as I was by Tobba. Then the whispering started: that she was involved with a Yank up at the base. I suppose that's the kiss of death for an Icelandic woman.'

Kristín glanced at Steve who was watching them uncomprehendingly.

'I kept applying to stay on — you have to

do that every three years, and after she died I didn't know where else to go. They gave me a special dispensation and now they've stopped bothering me. I travel around the country a lot in summer; I've even worked as a guide taking small groups of servicemen to the historical sites as well as the usual tourist spots: Gullfoss, Geysir and Thingvellir.'

Thompson fell silent.

'I sometimes visit her at the cemetery,' he added.

'I'm sorry, Mr Thompson,' Kristín said. 'But we're in a desperate hurry . . .'

'Yes, of course. The biggest commotion over that plane was in 1967,' Thompson said, gathering himself. He seemed to have returned to the present and had reverted to speaking English. 'I believe four soldiers lost their lives on the glacier that time. Are you old enough to remember the astronauts?'

'The astronauts?'

'Armstrong and co.?'

'Neil Armstrong? The first man on the moon?'

'The very same. Well, did you know that he and a number of other American astronauts came to Iceland for a training exercise two years before he landed on the moon?'

'Sure, everyone knows that.'

'Well, for a time in '67, Leo was in command of surveillance flights. It was a routine job, all the pilots had to do it. But on one flight Leo thought he saw something below him on the ice and flew back and forth taking photographs. I wasn't involved; Leo told me this afterwards. They tried and failed to land a helicopter but it was in the middle of winter, like now. So they sent a small expeditionary force up there with a metal detector and after that preparations began for a major operation, conducted in the utmost secrecy. But everyone heard about it; it's a very small community here.'

'Who are *they?*'

'Military intelligence, mainly. They knew the Icelanders were sensitive about troop movements, especially in those days, so someone had the brainstorm of sending Armstrong and the astronauts to Iceland for training exercises in the lava fields to the north of the glacier. The Icelanders welcomed the astronauts with open arms, of course, and were very understanding about all the military manoeuvres connected with the mission. You were told that the landscape in the interior resembled conditions on the moon. Preposterous! But you guys swallowed it. In actual fact, it was designed to deflect attention from the biggest movements of troops and equipment undertaken by the Americans in Iceland since the war. Whatever that plane contains, those are the lengths some people are prepared to go to in order to find it.'

'But why not go to Hawaii if they needed to practise in a lava field?' Steve asked.

'I have a notion where the idea came from,' Thompson continued, seemingly invigorated by recounting these long-ago events. 'There was a pilot here with the Defense Force from around 1960 who flew Scorpion fighter jets: Parker, Captain Parker was the name. When a group of astronauts made a refuelling stop here at Keflavík, incognito, in the summer of '65, the press office decided to cash in on the fact and the story really caught the public imagination. This guy Parker was in charge of the group. So when they needed to send an expedition to Vatnajökull in '67 without attracting any attention, Parker had the bright idea of inviting Armstrong over, figuring that it would cause even more of a sensation, because by then Armstrong had commanded a spaceflight, the Gemini 8 mission.'

'And nobody knew about this?' Steve asked.

'So many people were involved that something must have leaked out, though none of it could ever be confirmed. They failed to find the plane — if indeed it exists. The whole thing was a complete fiasco. It was rumoured that the secret service had taken control of the embassy in Reykjavík during the operation, as well as the base here in Keflavík. The leader of the expedition was called Carr, General Vytautas Carr. Old-school. Hard as nails.'

'But they didn't find the plane?'

'I don't know what happened. It was April but winter was far from over. There was one of those Easter blizzards, as you call them — a storm that blew up out of nowhere and lasted for days. They simply weren't pre-pared for Arctic conditions in April, became blinded by wind and snow, and had to get off the glacier, losing four men in the process. Two of them fell into a crevasse, the other two got separated and died of exposure. They were driven off the glacier, exhausted and defeated, and by the time the weather improved, the plane had van-ished, if it was ever there. Like I said, Leo and the others often used to discuss it but I don't know how much is true, though the astronauts did come here, that's for sure.'

'If the plane has emerged from the ice and the soldiers saw my brother . . .' Kristín left

189

the sentence unfinished.

'I don't know,' Thompson replied. 'I don't know what to say, dear. You must hope for the best but there's something about that plane. According to one guy, it crashed shortly after the end of the war and the plan had been to dismantle it and remove it from the glacier. He claimed it had come from Berlin. For a long time there was talk of gold, the Third Reich's last gold reserve. The story went that American soldiers stole it from the Germans and meant to fly it across the Atlantic. But it was also rumoured to be carrying a cargo of those art treasures the Germans plundered from all over Europe.'

Nobody spoke.

'And what do *you* think the plane contains, Mr Thompson?' Kristín asked eventually.

'You heard what I said. There are so many possibilities.'

'What do you regard as most likely then?'

'Someone said it was carrying a bomb built by the Nazis that we intercepted before the Russians could lay hands on it and that we were trying to get it back to the States.'

'A bomb?' Steve asked. 'What kind of bomb?'

'I don't know but it might explain why

190

they're so obsessed with finding the damn thing.'

'Do you know who Ratoff is?' Kristín asked.

'Never heard the name,' Thompson said. His mind was clearer now; he had a good memory and had no difficulty recalling the distant past once he had got going.

'Where did they approach the glacier from? Do you know?'

'From the south. I can't remember what the place was called. A couple of brothers lived nearby and acted as their guides. Farmers. That's all I know, I swear to God. And that's nothing but gossip and half-truths. I don't believe anyone knows the whole truth.'

Arnold's head snapped back as Bateman struck him a violent blow to the face and a new cut opened above his eyebrow. He would have screamed but they had bound him to the chair and gagged him with duct tape. He breathed frantically through his nose, his eyes goggling at the two men in white ski-suits. Blood seeped into his eye.

They had burst into his apartment, demanding to know if he owned the old Toyota in the parking lot in front of the building. Their tracker dogs had stopped by the car, refusing to budge, and the bonnet felt warm to the touch. It had taken a single phone call to trace the owner, and Arnold's name was on the doorbell. This was the second time Arnold had been woken that night and he was in such a foul temper when the men tried to question him over the entry-phone that he refused to let them into the building. Before he knew what was happening, the door to his apartment had been kicked in.

He told them what he knew: he had taken the couple to the archives and left them there. But the men wanted to know far more — what Steve and Kristín were looking for, where they were now and how they intended to leave the area. Arnold inwardly cursed that son of a bitch Steve.

His face was covered in blood; these men did not waste time. It was not the first occasion Arnold had been in trouble with the military police but he had never seen these two before, nor had he experienced their methods of interrogation. They tied him to a chair and quite simply beat him to a pulp. He did not have a clue where Steve and the Icelander were or what they were looking for. He held out as long as he could, determined not to tell his interrogators the one thing that might come in useful, but his stamina was limited.

Bateman took out a thick roll of silver tape and bit off a ten-centimetre strip. Like Ripley, he was wearing white rubber gloves. Holding the tape in both hands, he stuck it firmly over Arnold's nose and mouth, then stood in front of him, observing his vain attempts to gasp for oxygen with scientific detachment. When it looked as if Arnold was losing consciousness, Bateman grabbed one corner and tore it away from his nose, leaving a red welt where it had taken a small piece of skin with it.

Arnold's nostrils flared frantically as he sucked in air. The tape still covered his mouth but he inhaled with all his might. Bateman picked up the roll of tape again, bit off another strip and wordlessly fixed the tape over his nose.

'I'm not going to resuscitate you if you keep this up much longer, Arnold,' Ripley said to him.

He writhed in the chair, his blood-drenched face becoming as suffused and swollen as a balloon. Bateman tore the tape off his nose again, this time removing it from his mouth as well.

'I own a Zodiac,' Arnold shouted breathlessly, when he could finally speak between desperate gulps of air. 'Steve knows where it is. He'll use it to get off the base. Don't do it again; I beg you, for Christ's sake, let me breathe.'

'A Zodiac?' Bateman asked.

'I use it for smuggling. I smuggle drugs in and out of the base. I've been doing it for two years. Mostly cocaine but also speed and dope and . . . I sell it in Reykjavík. I have two contacts there called . . .'

'Arnold,' Ripley said in a level voice. 'I'm not interested in your little schemes. Tell me where the boat is.'

'I keep it in a bay to the west of the base. There's a gap in the perimeter fence where the road from the big tool store takes a right turn into the lava field. The boat is hidden about five hundred yards away, pretty much directly below the gap in the fence.'

'Excellent. And where are they headed, Arnold?'

'To a beach just outside Hafnir. You'll find it on the map.'

17

'There have been some funny goings on here,' observed the scruffily dressed detective in his early fifties, surveying Kristín's flat.

Just before midnight the police had received a phone call from a man in the neighbourhood reporting a young woman in a distressed state who had burst into his family home, demanding to use their phone and speaking incoherently of murder — presumably at her house — before borrowing some clothes and vanishing. He had not intended to report the incident and it was more than three hours before he made up his mind to do so, largely at his wife's urging. Although he did not say as much, he was rather ashamed of himself for having let such a thing happen to his family.

The police took a statement and checked

195

the phone's display to identify the number called by the mysterious woman. No one was home at the corresponding address but on investigation they discovered that the house-owner had a daughter. Her age seemed consistent with the description of the woman who had forced her way into the family's home; she also lived in the same neighbourhood and this was deemed sufficient grounds to dispatch two officers. No one answered when they knocked on the door of the flat, located in a two-storey maisonette. The occupants of the upstairs flat said they had been out all evening.

Noticing a small hole in Kristín's door, conceivably made by a bullet, the police called a locksmith. When they entered the flat the first thing they saw was a body lying slumped on the desk.

The detective stood over the man's body, inspecting the contents of his wallet. According to his business card his name was Runólfur Zóphaníasson and he was involved in 'Import–Export'. Apart from that his wallet contained a driving licence, some money, a sheaf of restaurant receipts, and debit and credit cards. The detective glanced around the flat: the furniture appeared to be in place, all the pictures hung straight on the walls, nothing on any of the surfaces seemed to have been disturbed, and there was no sign of any weapon. The body might just as well have fallen from the sky. Cautiously straightening the man up, he examined the bullet wound in his forehead and the gun in his hand.

'Strange angle, don't you think?' he asked his colleague, who was younger and a good deal better dressed. 'If you were going to shoot yourself in the head, would you aim straight at your forehead?'

'I've never given it any thought,' his colleague replied.

'And if he did hold the gun up to his forehead, shouldn't there be signs of scorching or powder marks? Or blowback on his forearm?'

'So you don't think it was suicide, despite the note on the computer?'

'According to his driver's licence, the man lives on the other side of town, in Breidholt. If you were going to kill yourself, would you go to someone else's house to do it?'

'Why do you keep asking me how I would do it if I was going to commit suicide?' the younger detective asked, running a hand down the handsome tie that complemented his suit exactly. 'Is it secret wishful thinking?'

'Not secret enough, obviously,' replied the older man, who in contrast was wearing a torn jumper and battered hat. 'This Kristín who lives here, what does she do?'

'Lawyer with the foreign ministry.'

'And Runólfur here was in the Import–Export business, whatever that means. There's no sign of a struggle, and the upstairs neighbours say they weren't at home. Still, it's a small gun. It wouldn't have made much noise.'

'You're the firearms expert.'

'Indulge me, if you will, in my attempted reconstruction,' the elder officer said, ignoring his colleague's jibe. 'If you were going to kill yourself, would you shoot a bullet through the front door first?'

'Let's see, the door was open. He must have meant to shoot himself in the head but missed and the bullet entered the door. After that he aimed straight at his forehead to be sure of hitting it. Something like that?'

'So he shot himself with the door of the flat open?'

'Looks like it.'

'This is one of the most cack-handed suicides I've ever seen. Why shoot himself here? Was he involved in a relationship with this Kristín?'

'I imagine Kristín would be in a better position to answer that than I am.'

'I suppose we'd better put out a wanted

notice. But don't say anything about her being a suspect in a murder inquiry, only that we need to speak to her.'

'Is it really conceivable that a government lawyer could have killed this man?'

'If I were going to murder someone, I'd go for a salesman every time,' the older detective replied, carefully scrutinising the hole in the man's forehead.

18

Arnold's directions proved accurate. Before he left them at the administration block, he had told Steve how to get out of the base without using a gate or climbing over the wire. Kristín could not begin to imagine what sort of favour he owed Steve, but it must have been considerable. She preferred not to think about it.

After leaving Thompson, they headed west, away from the airport and Leifur Eiríksson terminal. The military traffic in the area had intensified; police roadblocks had been set up at intervals around the base and soldiers now patrolled the perimeter fence on the Keflavík side. To the south and west the base was bracketed by sea. Avoiding the more frequented ways, they darted from building to building, shielded by the darkness, until the built-up area petered out, giving way to lava and snowfields which ran down to the shore.

The sky was cloudless and full of stars, and with the moon lighting their way they covered the distance quickly. Arnold's detailed description of the landmarks soon led them to the Zodiac. All they needed now was to follow the shore south past Hvalsnes and into Kirkjuvogur bay, to the hamlet of Hafnir, where they could abandon the boat and hitch a lift into Reykjavík. The Zodiac had a quiet outboard motor, a twenty-horsepower engine that chugged into life at the first attempt. As Steve steered away from shore, Kristín had the impression that this was not the first time he had navigated along this stretch of coast. An icy wind buffeted her face and although the boat did not achieve much of a speed, it smacked into the waves at regular intervals, forcing her to cling with all her strength to the rope fastened at the bows. Her anorak was soon drenched by the spray.

A quarter of an hour later they abandoned the boat at Hafnir. They had not spoken at all during the journey.

'Is this how they smuggle the drugs?' Kristín asked at last, once Steve had made the rubber dinghy fast.

'I wouldn't know,' he said. They left it at that.

As they made their way north from Hafnir towards the Reykjanes dual carriageway, they saw the distant reddish-brown glow illuminating the sky above Keflavík and Njardvík. After about forty-five minutes' walk in complete silence they noticed headlights approaching out of the darkness behind them. The car slowed down as it drew near, finally stopping a little way ahead of them. It was a baker on his way to Keflavík; he offered them a lift up to the main road. From there it should not take them long to hitch a lift to Reykjavík.

Michael Thompson had given them the Reykjavík address of Leo Stiller's widow, Sarah Steinkamp, in case she could shed any more light on Stiller's theories. Apart from that, he claimed to know little about her situation and was unwilling to discuss her; he looked in on her every few years for the sake of his old commanding officer, he said, but she was a difficult person — angry, bitter and depressive — so he never stayed long.

She lived in the old Thingholt district, on the ground floor of a small, dilapidated two-storey wooden house. The corrugated-iron cladding had rusted away where it met the ground and the small windows were only single-glazed. Long ago, the front door had been painted green but most of the paint had now flaked off. A large fir tree stood in the middle of the small garden that had once been enclosed by a wooden fence, the palings of which were now rotten and had largely collapsed.

Kristín and Steve approached the house with caution; they had seen no sign of their pursuers but still peered nervously into the darkness that surrounded them. Despite being confident that they had escaped unseen from the base, they were taking no chances. They stepped into the circle of weak light shed by the tiny lamp above Sarah Steinkamp's door, an icy wind chapping their faces. It was about seven in the morning.

Steve pressed the doorbell. There was a small copper plate on the door with a name engraved on it in faint lettering. It was almost illegible but Kristín thought she could make out 'Sarah Steinkamp'. There were no other names; the upstairs apartment must be un occupied. Its dark windows stared down at them like empty eye-sockets. Steve pushed the bell again. Even when he put his ear to the door he could hear no sign of life inside.

He rang the bell yet again, more forcefully

this time but still nothing happened. They took a few steps backwards from the doorstep and out into the glow of the streetlamps, straining their eyes towards the windows on the raised ground floor but could not see any lights inside. Steve rang the bell a fourth time to be sure and they heard it jangling deep inside the house. They had just turned away, on the point of abandoning hope, when a ground floor window opened. The unexpected noise in the still morning made them both jump. A tremulous woman's voice asked what was going on.

'Are you Sarah Steinkamp?' Steve asked. There was no answer. 'I'm sorry to call so early in the morning but it's urgent.'

'What do you want with her? Who are you?'

'It's about . . .' Steve began. 'Could you let us in, please? My name's Steve; this is my friend Kristín. She's Icelandic.'

'Icelandic?' said the quavering voice. They could not make out her face in the darkness, just a faint, disembodied silhouette at the window.

'And you? You don't sound Icelandic.'

'I'm American. We need your help. Could you let us in? You're Leo Stiller's widow, aren't you?'

'Leo? What do you want with Leo? Leo's dead.'

'We know that. We want to talk to you about Leo,' Steve said, doing his best to sound agreeable.

They stood motionless for a long time in front of the house, unable to see even whether the figure in the gloom was still at the window. Just as they had given up all hope, the door opened a crack, revealing a woman of tiny, almost dwarflike, stature. The security chain rattled.

'What do you want with my Leo?' she asked, her eyes fixed on Kristín. She spoke English with a thick European accent that Kristín could not place exactly but suspected might be Eastern European.

'It's because he was a pilot,' Steve said. 'We need some information about him.'

'What kind of information? What are you talking about?'

'Could we come in and talk to you?' Steve asked.

'No,' the woman said irritably. 'You can't.'

'It's terribly urgent that we talk to you,' Kristín said, taking two steps towards the door. 'You are Sarah, aren't you? Sarah Steinkamp?'

'Who are you?' the woman asked. 'How do you know my name?'

'My name's Kristín. My brother's in danger. A retired pilot, Michael Thompson, suggested we talk to you. You know him, don't you? He lives on the base.'

'I know Thompson,' the woman said. 'He was a friend of Leo's. Why's your brother in danger?'

'Because of a plane,' Kristín said. 'Your husband was a pilot at the base, wasn't he?'

'Yes, Leo was a pilot.'

'That's why we want to talk to you,' said Kristín, who had inched her way forwards to a spot beside the front door. She had a better view of the woman now: long grey hair, a wrinkled face, her body painfully thin and a little hunched, clad in a worn, brown dressing gown. Admittedly, they had disturbed her at the crack of dawn but Kristín sensed that their sudden appearance had also disturbed her on some more profound level. She hesitated. It was an uneasy stand-off, the woman half-hidden by the door as if she felt a physical threat.

'What plane?' the woman repeated.

'A plane on the Vatnajökull glacier,' Kristín replied.

'On Vatnajökull?' the little woman said in surprise.

'Yes, my brother saw a plane on the glacier and then I lost contact with him. He saw soldiers too.'

The old woman pulled her dressing gown more tightly around her.

'Come in,' she said in a low voice, undoing the chain and opening the door wider. Kristín hesitated, then stepped inside the house, Steve at her heels, entering a hall that served both flats. A staircase led up to the floor above but directly opposite them the door to the old woman's flat stood open. Inside it was dark and stiflingly hot; she must have left the radiators on full blast all night. Kristín lost sight of the little woman as she vanished into the gloom. She stood stock still, not daring to move forward, screwing her eyes up towards where she thought she saw a movement. Then a match hissed and she saw the woman's face briefly illuminated in the flame. She was lighting candles; the house appeared to be full of them and the old woman walked around lighting one after another until Kristín lost count. They cast a soft, flickering glow over the sitting room. Kristín noticed a piano and a violin, family photographs crowding the walls and tables, a threadbare sofa and armchairs, and thick rugs on the floors. The woman invited them to sit down but she herself remained standing by the piano.

'I feel like Gretel,' Kristín whispered to Steve.

'Then I'm Hansel,' Steve breathed back. 'As long as she doesn't put us in her oven.'

'Please excuse the intrusion, Mrs Steinkamp,' Kristín said, once her eyes had adjusted to the candlelight. 'We had no alternative. We won't keep you long.'

'I don't understand how Leo could have anything to do with you,' the woman said.

'It's a long, complicated story,' Steve replied.

'But it's more than thirty years since he died,' the woman pointed out.

'Yes, how did he die?'

'He was killed in a helicopter crash. An error, they said, but I never received any explanation. They never conducted an inquiry but I have my suspicions. I moved away from the base and came to Reykjavík. They send me his pension every month.'

'What happened?' Kristín asked.

'Leo was an outstanding pilot,' the woman said, the dim glow of the candles playing over her features. She had clearly once been an elegant, even beautiful, young woman but Kristín suspected that life had not been kind to her; age had set its stamp on her hard and there was a glittering determination in her eyes that hinted at past troubles.

208

She must have been in her late seventies. Kristín examined the family pictures on the walls and piano; they were old, taken in the first half of the century, all photos of adults or elderly people, encased in thick, black frames. She could not see any children in the pictures, nor any recent photos or colour pictures. Only old, black-and-white images of men and women, posing for the photographer in their best clothes. The woman caught her looking at them.

'All long dead,' she said. 'Every single one of them. That's why there aren't any new pictures. Those are mourning frames. Is that enough of an answer for you?'

'I'm sorry,' Kristín said. 'I didn't mean to pry.'

'Leo told me to keep my maiden name, Steinkamp. That was Leo all over. He was a Jew like me. We met in Hungary after the war and he took me in. My family were all dead. All I had left were photographs. Everything else had gone. Our neighbour in Budapest had saved them. Leo tracked him down and I've kept the pictures with me ever since.'

'They're beautiful photographs,' Kristín said.

'Are you investigating Leo?'

'Investigating?' Steve said. 'No, of course

not. We just need information.'

'They never investigated anything. They said it was an accident. Said he'd made a mistake. My Leo didn't make mistakes. He was a perfectionist, you know? Always checking. He saved my life. I don't know what would have happened to me if he hadn't found me . . .' She was silent for a moment, then asked: 'What sort of information?'

'About the plane on Vatnajökull. Did Leo ever tell you anything about it?'

'Leo knew all about the plane on the glacier. He said it belonged to the Nazis.'

They stared at the woman in astonishment.

'And then he died,' she added.

'The Nazis?' Kristín repeated. 'What do you mean? What did he mean?'

'There was a Nazi plane on the glacier. That's what Leo said. Then he died. In a helicopter crash. But Leo was a very good pilot. How peculiar that you should come knocking on my door after all these years, asking questions. No one has mentioned the plane since those days.'

'But it crashed after the war was over,' Kristín said, confused.

'No, it did not,' Sarah corrected, her small eyes meeting Kristín's steadily. 'It crashed before the end of the war. The Nazis were trying to escape, scattering in all directions to save their wretched skins.'

'Thompson said it was carrying American soldiers who had stolen some gold,' Kristín said.

'Of course he did.'

'Did Leo tell you the same story?'

'No, he knew what was really happening and he did not keep secrets from his wife.'

'What exactly did he tell you?' Steve asked.

The woman still appeared suspicious and uncertain, as if in two minds about whether to answer them, but then she seemed to come to a decision.

'Leo made a fuss about it at the base. About the plane. They wanted to cover it up but my Leo wanted to know what was going on. He wouldn't shut up. He couldn't stand all the secrecy.'

'And what happened then? Did he get any answers?' Steve asked.

'No, nothing,' Sarah Steinkamp replied. 'The plane appeared out of the ice, then vanished again.'

'What do you mean?' Kristín asked.

'Leo said that the glacier was like that. He said the plane had been buried in the glacier but then reappeared. End of story.'

'Was this in 1967?'

211

'Yes, 1967, exactly.'

'So why did Leo believe it was a Nazi plane? What did he mean by Nazi?'

'Surely even you know who the Nazis were, young man!' the old woman snapped, her expression hardening. 'Or has everyone forgotten them, as if they never existed?'

Kristín had stood up. She shuddered as the full implication of this woman's history dawned on her: the photographs, Budapest, Steinkamp.

'Murderers!' the old woman exclaimed, and Kristín heard the frozen agony in her voice. 'Bloody murderers! Never forget what they did,' she cried, her eyes blazing as she stood there surrounded by the family pictures in their thick black frames. 'They murdered my entire family. Burnt them in the ovens. Murdered our children. That's what the Nazis were like, and never you forget it.'

Kristín looked at Steve rather than meet Sarah Steinkamp's gaze. She felt guilty and ashamed for rousing this pensioner from her warm bed and stirring up a lifetime's horrors. To her amazement, Steve ploughed on, lost in the complexities of the riddle they were struggling to solve.

'But why did Leo believe the plane belonged to the Nazis? What made him think that?' he persisted.

'Who are you?' the old woman asked, suddenly sounding brusque, as if she had regained her senses. 'Who are you? I don't know you at all. I am tired and you are upsetting me. Please leave now. Please go away and leave me alone.'

Kristín signalled to Steve that enough was enough. They took their leave of her without more ado. She stood by the piano, watching as they turned and walked back out to the front door. They closed it carefully behind them and felt a mingled sense of relief and sadness on emerging once more into the icy winter air.

19

Vytautas Carr strode briskly into the control room. The reinforced doors closed slowly behind him with a heavy sucking sound. The room was filled with the same chilly gloom, the only light coming from the screens, most of which were flickering. A number of employees sat at the computer consoles and other controls which operated the organisation's satellites, some talking on the phone, others silently intent on the screens which were reflected in their eyes. Phil, Carr's assistant, came over and invited him to follow him. They walked through the control room and into a much smaller room, closing the door behind them.

'We'll start receiving them live any minute, sir,' said Phil, a thin, tense man with a cigarette permanently jammed between his lips. He was one of the satellite operators.

He had rolled-up shirt-sleeves and horn-rimmed glasses balanced on his nose which were invariably smeary with fingerprints, though he never seemed to notice. Carr reflected that for a man charged with seeing things with superb clarity, it was odd that he never seemed to clean his spectacles.

'How long will we have them?' Carr asked.

'The satellite takes approximately thirty-seven minutes to pass over the area, sir. It's cloudless at the moment but a storm's gathering.'

'Does Ratoff know we're watching?'

'I imagine he does, sir.'

Iceland's recognisable outline appeared on the screen in front of Carr alongside part of Greenland's east coast. The image vanished, to be replaced by another showing the south-eastern corner of the island. Phil pressed a button and yet another frame appeared, this time of the southern half of Vatnajökull. He zoomed in until the snowy surface of the glacier became visible, criss-crossed with crevasses, and finally a group of tiny dots could be seen moving over the ice. Carr felt as if he were looking through a microscope at minute organisms swimming around on a slide, like a scientist observing a complex experiment. During his long army service the world had changed almost beyond recognition and the extent of the US army's capabilities these days never ceased to amaze him. The image was magnified yet again until he could make out what was happening on the glacier. Removing his own glasses, he gave them a wipe, before replacing them on his nose and focusing intently.

When he spotted the plane, half-protruding from the ice, his heart skipped a beat. He saw the men digging on either side of it, their tents and vehicles forming a semicircle around the wreck, and the glow of the blow-torches as they began the task of cutting the fuselage in half.

'Are we recording this?' Carr asked.

'Sure,' Phil said. 'I guess we should be getting a glimpse of the cargo soon, sir?' he added with a grin.

'Yes, the cargo. Quite.'

Carr watched the men on the glacier for many minutes in silence. The image was grainy, the men no more than dots swarming over the surface of the ice, the plane indistinct. But the job appeared to be progressing well; Ratoff was on schedule, and the work was being carried out in an orderly fashion. The plane would soon be free of the ice.

Without warning, the rhythm of the movements on the screen changed and there was a commotion on the glacier: from thousands of miles away, Carr watched as men rushed over to the plane. Even from that great distance, it looked to Carr as if it had broken in half. The plane was open.

Ratoff hurried out of the communications tent when he heard the calls and ran down to the wreck. As he was forcing his way through the crowd that had gathered, distracted from their jobs, the front of the plane bent and the fuselage broke in half, collapsing under its own weight on to the ice with a deafening screech and crash, leaving the tail-end still half-submerged. Ratoff peered through the gaping hole into the cabin, then turning to the soldiers, ordered them to prepare the severed section for removal from the glacier. At the same time he issued orders that no one was to enter the plane without his express permission.

The men with the blow-torches moved aside with their equipment to give Ratoff room to climb inside the plane. Bending slightly, he stepped into the cabin, the first passenger aboard in over half a century, and as he did so the sounds outside were instantly muted; he was met by a heavy silence that had not been disturbed in all these years. The experience was like stepping back in time and it filled him with a sense of mingled excitement and anticipation. Four Delta Force officers stood guard outside; they knew their orders. Meanwhile the soldiers scattered again, returning to their tasks, and soon it was as if nothing had happened.

In the weak daylight that penetrated this section of the fuselage, he found two bodies, both middle-aged men, one dressed in the uniform of a German army officer, the other, to his astonishment, in the uniform of a two-star US general. An American! He bore insignia that Ratoff did not recognise and looked to be in his late fifties. A strong-looking aluminium briefcase with heavy locks was handcuffed to his left wrist.

That's three bodies so far, Ratoff noted. They lay close together on the floor, side by side, as if carefully arranged. Where it was visible, their skin was bluish-white and he could see no sign of decay, the ice having preserved them as well as any morgue. Ratoff assumed these men had not survived the crash; those who did must have laid them here. One had a gaping wound to his head and must have died during the landing. The other appeared largely unscathed; his fatal injuries must have been internal.

He looked better prepared for the cold, wrapped up in two overcoats and a fur hat, not that they had done him much good.

Ratoff turned and retraced his steps, re-emerging into the daylight. The tail section was still largely trapped in the ice and Ratoff needed a leg-up from one of the Delta officers to climb in through the opening. Inside it was dark, so he took out a torch, shining it towards the rear of the cabin where he made out three other bodies huddled together as if the men had been trying to share body heat during the final miserable hours of their lives. So the plane contained six corpses, counting the one found outside: according to Ratoff's briefing, there should have been seven.

Once again, any exposed skin was a translucent bluish-white, taut and firm to the touch, and as before Ratoff found no signs of decomposition. He noted crudely made splints on the legs of a couple of the bodies and again was baffled to discover that one of them was dressed in an American uniform. He must be the pilot; the leather bomber jacket he wore was standard World War II issue for US fighter pilots. There was a small American flag sewn on to the sleeve and the man's name was embroidered on a strip of black linen on his left breast. The name was American too; there was no mistaking it. He could not have been much more than twenty-five years old.

It was inexplicable. What was an American fighter pilot doing flying German officers and an American general across the Atlantic in a Nazi plane painted in US camouflage colours?

To reach the innermost part of the Junkers' tail, Ratoff had to bend double. With the help of his torch it did not take him long to find two wooden boxes the size of beer crates, one of which he dragged towards the front of the plane where the light was better. The lid was nailed down but he found a severed piece of iron stanchion on the floor and, using it as a lever, was able to force the lid, the nails screeching as they were slowly torn from the wood. Soon the box opened fully to reveal rows of small white bags, each tied at one end. There must have been about twenty of them. Ratoff picked one up, discovering that it was made of soft velvet and felt heavy in his hand. Releasing the drawstring, he slid out an ice-cold gold bar with a swastika, the emblem of the Third Reich, stamped in the centre of it. Ratoff stared at the bar, weighing it in his hand with a smile, then cast his eyes around.

But only two crates, he thought. A tiny

haul. So where was the rest? Ratoff had been anticipating far more than these two boxes; he had expected the plane to be packed with gold bars bearing the Nazi seal. He slid the bar back into its bag and replaced it in the crate, closing the lid and hammering the nails back in again.

Could they have moved it out of the plane? Moved the entire cargo and buried it in the ice somewhere nearby? Or somewhere further afield even? When Ratoff considered it, however, it dawned on him that the plane was hardly big enough to have carried all the gold he had been assured it contained: he had been expecting at least several tons. So if Jewish gold was not behind the organisation's interest in monitoring this god-forsaken, frozen desert for half a century, he reasoned, what on earth was? Two crates of gold would hardly trigger the Third World War. Two pathetic boxes. What other secrets did the plane harbour? What was this icy tomb carrying that caused his superiors to have a heart attack every time they thought it was re-emerging from the ice?

Ratoff's eyes had by now adjusted to the gloom inside the wreckage, but although he searched high and low, he could find no more boxes. The only personal item he discovered belonging to any of the passengers was the briefcase. Carr had given him special orders to remove all documents from the plane, of whatever type. Frustrated by the absence of the treasure trove he had pictured in his mind's eye, he attacked the briefcase with the scrap of metal that he had used on the crate, and with some difficulty succeeded in forcing the lock. Nothing but worthless files and papers. He would take a better look at them later. A search of the bodies also yielded an unremarkable cache of wallets and passports. The men in German uniform ranged in age from forty to sixty. One bore a rank that Ratoff thought might be that of a general. He wore several unfamiliar medals on his chest, and like the man who had been laid beside the plane, had an Iron Cross fixed at his throat between the points of his collar, the German army's highest honour in the war.

On re-emerging despondently into the light, Ratoff noted that his men were already preparing to transport the front section of the plane down to the base. He gave orders for the corpses to be removed from the wreckage and taken to the tents to be placed in body-bags, then returned to the front section of the Junkers, heading straight for the cockpit, intent on piecing together a fuller picture. There were seats for a co-pilot and navigator but from the bodies of the other personnel on board, it appeared that the American had flown the plane single-handedly. Spotting the flight chart the pilot had made, he shoved it in his pocket, along with the log book and was just turning to leave the cabin when he caught sight of a small red exercise book protruding from under the co-pilot's seat. He scooped it up and put that in his pocket as well.

Carr was on the phone as he crawled out of the aircraft again.

'Are you spying on me, sir?' Ratoff rasped when he had taken the receiver.

'Why waste billions on all this equipment if we don't use it?' Carr retorted. 'Well, what have you found?'

Ratoff gestured to the communications officer to leave the tent. All communication from the glacier was conducted on the Delta Force closed channel. Ratoff waited until he was alone, then spoke again.

'What's going on, sir?'

'What do you mean?'

'I've found only two crates of gold. You said the plane was full of it. Two boxes! That's the lot.'

'Maybe they buried it in the ice. Maybe it'll never be found.'

'Maybe the gold's not what it's about,'

Ratoff suggested.

The line filled with static.

'You never told me there was an American pilot on board,' Ratoff continued. 'And a two-star general from our side.'

'Be careful, Ratoff. I'm under no obligation to tell you anything.'

'It looks to me as if some of them survived the landing,' Ratoff said. 'Our pilot and two of the Germans. Judging by the numbers you gave me, one of the Germans is missing. In any case, they can't have survived long up here in the depths of winter — they had inadequate clothing and no provisions. And somehow I doubt they kept themselves warm by lugging gold around. Anyway, the plane's too small to have been carrying a heavy cargo. So if you're not looking for gold, what are you looking for? Maybe you'd like to tell me what I'm doing in this shithole.'

'You say there are only six bodies?'

'Correct.'

'There should be seven on board.'

'Is that something to worry about?'

'Well, the seventh man has never come to light. Perhaps they buried him further away. Perhaps he tried to get to civilisation.'

'If the plane wasn't carrying gold,' Ratoff repeated, 'what is it that you're after, sir?'

'Ratoff,' Carr said warily. 'If I wanted someone to ask questions I wouldn't have come to you. You know that.'

'Is it the briefcase?'

'Ratoff.' Carr's voice had fallen to a low growl. 'Don't fuck with me. Just do as you're told. You were chosen to lead this operation for a reason.'

Ratoff decided not to push it any further for the time being.

'The only thing I found was the general's briefcase, which I haven't opened. Then there's the pilot's log book and another book. I don't know what it contains. I haven't looked at any of it.'

'Fine. I repeat: bring out all documents, briefcases, books, passports, names, anything in writing that you find on board. Take it into your safekeeping, Ratoff; do not allow anyone else access to it and deliver it to me and only me. Observe the procedure. Bring me the lot. Every last scrap.'

'Of course, sir.'

'Take my advice: you'd be doing yourself a favour to remain ignorant of those documents. We've been over this already. Follow the plan.'

'You've always been able to rely on me, sir.'

Carr ignored the edge he believed he

225

could detect in Ratoff's voice. 'When will you be in Keflavík?'

'We'll be airborne in two days' time, assuming the storm doesn't delay us.'

'Excellent.'

They ended the conversation. Ratoff considered the briefcase, chart and books he had piled on a chair. Over the years, he had heard innumerable stories about the plane's contents but when he had to accept that it was nothing but documents, it was as if all suspense, all anticipation and all his hunger for the mission had died within him. No gold. No bomb. No biological weapon. None of the more recognisable of the missing Nazi war criminals, as far as he could see. No art treasures. No diamonds. Only documents. Worthless documents. Scraps of yellowed paper.

Still angered and disorientated by disappointment, he took the documents to his own tent. Inside stood a camp bed, a chair and a collapsible desk at which he sat down. First he examined the log book, noting where and when the plane had taken off and the intended flightpath. Then he turned to the red exercise book; leafing through it, he was surprised to see that the pilot had kept a diary during his last days on the glacier. Putting it aside for the moment, he opened the briefcase and took out three files, bound with thin, white straps. He opened the first and flicked quickly through the pages which turned out to be in German; the yellowed paper felt stiff and brittle to the touch. The second contained similar documents. He knew a little German, having been stationed for two years in his youth at the US base in Ramstein, but not enough to grasp the precise meaning of the pages.

The third file contained several more documents, all marked confidential, whose entire text was in English. Among the papers was a single unsigned memorandum. Ratoff immersed himself in reading. He perused the material quickly and gradually began to piece together what the documents contained, rising involuntarily to his feet and pacing the narrow confines of the tent. 'Is it possible?' he whispered to himself.

After he had finished reading, he stood, dumbfounded, staring blankly at the papers, briefcase, passports, diary. It took him quite a while to grasp the implications and put them in the context of what he already knew. He scanned the names that were mentioned, scrutinised the signatures again. They were powerfully familiar.

Little by little his scattered thoughts fell into place. He understood the lies. He understood all the misinformation that had been disseminated. At once, he understood the plane's significance. He knew now why they had been searching for it for decades.

Ratoff grimaced as the truth finally dawned on him. If they had indeed executed this plan, and then gone on to organise this massive military operation to protect the secret, then surely he was in danger? He would be eliminated at the first opportunity; they would have killed him regardless of whether he had read the documents. Carr had known at the outset that if it was successful the mission would be his death warrant. He smiled grimly at the irony. He would have done the same in their shoes. He looked at the documents again and shook his head.

The wind snatched and tore at the canvas, sending it billowing to and fro, wrenching Ratoff back to reality. When he went outside, the snow was gusting so hard he could not see his hand in front of his face.

Carr watched as the glacier edged sideways and finally disappeared from the screen. Few knew Ratoff better and Carr understood instinctively what the director of the operation was doing at that moment. He left the room, prowling ponderously through the control room, out into the corridor and back to his own office where he closed the door firmly and sat down at the desk. He picked up the telephone receiver. It was time for the next step.

He asked for a Buenos Aires number. Then for a flight to Iceland.

20

Kristín had cared for Elías since he first entered the world. She was ten years old when he was born and immediately took a great interest in the baby, far greater than her parents in fact. She remembered wishing that her mother would have a little boy. Not that it mattered in the end — what she wanted above all was a sibling as she was bored of being an only child and envied her friends their brothers and sisters. But her parents could not bear noise and the house was a haven of peace and quiet. Both spent long hours at the office and would bring their work home with them in the evenings, which left them no time to pay Kristín any attention. She learnt to move about the house noiselessly and to look after herself; learnt not to disturb them.

Looking back later she could not understand why they had had Elías. As grown-ups, she and Elías would sometimes discuss the fact. He must have come as a complete shock to them. When her brother was being rowdy Kristín often sensed just how deeply he irritated their parents, as if they resented any time spent on their children, as if they found their offspring a nuisance and regarded them with disapproval. Feeling this neglect brought Kristín even closer to her brother. Yet their parents were never cruel, never smacked them or doled out harsh punishments; the worst of it was that if either child misbehaved, their indifference would become even more marked, the silence in the house even deeper, the calm and peace and quiet more consuming.

While Kristín had quickly learnt to adapt by creeping around, trying not to disturb them unnecessarily and taking care of herself, these were lessons Elías never grasped. He was noisy and demanding, 'hyperactive', their parents said. Their aggravation was obvious. He cried for the first three months after he was brought home from the hospital and at times Kristín would cry with him. As Elías grew up he was forever spilling his milk, knocking over his soup bowl, or breaking ornaments. Kristín quickly developed a stifling sense of responsibility and would chase him around with a cloth, trying to limit his damage. By the time she was fourteen she was his sole carer: on her way to school she would drop him off at day nursery, and after school would fetch him, feed him, play with him, see him to bed at the right time and read to him. Sometimes she felt he was her own child. Above all she made every effort to keep the peace, to make sure that her parents were not disturbed. That was her responsibility.

It took many years for her to discover the reason for their indifference and neglect. She had occasionally noticed the signs but did not recognise them for what they were until she was older. Bottles she could not account for would surface in peculiar places, either empty or half-full of clear or coloured liquid: in the wardrobe, in the bathroom cupboards, under their bed. She left them there, never removing them from their hiding places and they would vanish as if of their own accord.

There were other, more distressing signs. Her father would often leave on long business trips, or lie ill in bed for days. Her mother was frequently incapacitated, or saw things that no one else could see, though this happened rarely and at long intervals, so Kristín learnt to live with it, as Elías would in his turn.

'I do wish we could spend more time with you,' their mother once said to Kristín, and she noticed that oddly sweet smell on her breath. 'God knows, we do our best.' She was drunk when her car hit a lamppost at 90 kilometres an hour.

All these memories passed through Kristín's head as she stood in her office, hearing news of her brother's condition from a complete stranger. She and Steve had gone directly to the ministry from Sarah Steinkamp's flat in Thingholt, a walk of no more than ten minutes. She lowered the telephone receiver slowly and her eyes filled with tears. She had not slept for more than twenty-four hours and still had lumps of dried blood on her ear and cheek. A familiar sense of guilt overwhelmed her.

'They don't think he'll make it,' she said quietly.

Steve took the telephone and introduced himself to Júlíus, the leader of the rescue team. It was still very early and no one had turned up to work yet but the security guard, recognising Kristín, had let them in. They did not intend to stay long.

Steve now heard the full story. They had found Jóhann's badly battered body in a crevasse. Elías had fallen into the same crevasse but still showed signs of life, though Július was forced to admit that they saw little chance he would pull through. His condition was very poor. Július and his team were on their way back to camp and were expecting a Defense Force helicopter before long, but they did not know if they would make it back to camp before the storm struck.

'Has Elías managed to say anything about the accident?' Steve asked.

'He's said his sister's name, nothing else,' Július replied.

Kristín had recovered sufficiently to take back the phone.

'Elías didn't have an accident,' she said steadily. 'Somewhere on the glacier there are American soldiers and a plane that is somehow connected to them. Elías and Jóhann were unlucky enough to run into them and were taken captive and thrown into the crevasse.'

'Do you know where?' Július asked, and Kristín heard the screaming of the wind over the phone. He was on a snowmobile and had to shout to make himself heard.

'We believe it's in the south-eastern section of the glacier. We spoke to an old pilot who used to carry out surveillance flights in the area. I'm going to get myself up there, though I don't know what assistance we can hope for. US special forces have taken over the base on Midnesheidi and the embassy here in Reykjavík. We've no idea if the Icelandic government is involved and the police want to interview me about a murder, so I can't turn to them.'

'A murder?'

'It's a long story,' Kristín said. She had heard the police announcement on the radio that she was wanted for questioning in connection with the body of a man found in an apartment in the west of Reykjavík and immediately suspected that they would try to implicate her in some way.

'The main thing is,' she continued, 'can I look to you for help if we make it? If we find the soldiers and plane, will your team be in the area?'

'You can take that as read. But Kristín . . .'

'What?'

'It's a bloody big glacier.'

'I know. How many are in your team?'

'There are seventy of us. We have to get Jóhann and Elías airlifted to town, then we can set about looking for those soldiers. But first we've got to wait for the Defense Force helicopter . . .'

'Why not use the Icelandic Coast Guard chopper?'

'It's busy.'

'Júlíus, I'm not sure you'll get any help from the base at the moment. There's a different crowd in charge there now and from what we've seen I doubt they'll provide any assistance.'

'They're sorting it out back at camp. I've no idea what's going on at the base. But I've already lost one man and the other — I have to be honest, Kristín — Elías is in a very bad way. There's a massive storm brewing here. You're telling me that I won't get the help I need because of some special forces coup? I'm wondering — and I have to ask you straight — have you lost your marbles? I've never had a more bizarre phone conversation in my life than the last two with you.'

'I know,' Kristín said, 'I've wondered the same myself. But there's a reason why my brother's dying in your hands and it's far, far more complicated than either you or I know. I'm just saying that I'm not sure you'll get the Defense Force chopper. Call the Coast Guard and don't give up until they send theirs, whatever they say about using the one from the base. Insist on the Coast Guard chopper.'

'Got it!' Júlíus shouted.

'Then wait to hear from me again.'

Kristín turned to Steve.

'When are we going to meet this friend of yours, Steve? Monica, wasn't it?'

'Later,' Steve answered. 'We ought to try to rest until then.'

'Rest?'

'Elías is alive,' Steve said carefully. 'He's still alive. There's hope.'

'They didn't succeed in killing him,' Kristín said. 'They won't get away with it. We'll meet Monica, then head up to the glacier.'

'Then we'll need equipment. A guide. A four-wheel drive. Where are we going to find all that?' Steve asked apprehensively.

'We have to find those brothers Thompson mentioned. Surely they'll help us if they're still alive? Failing them, the people who live there now. And I think I know where I can get hold of a four-wheel drive.'

'Kristín, we need to think seriously about what we can achieve against a bunch of soldiers.'

'I haven't a clue,' Kristín answered, 'but I have to see what's going on with my own eyes. I have to find out what they're up to.'

Desperate as she felt about Elías, it was no longer simply about her brother. She was driven by an inner compulsion and by other forces impelling her forward that she could not put a name to. Her normal reserves of energy exhausted, she had reached a place that was beyond fatigue. She wanted to know what the plane contained and she intended to find out. And when she found out she was going to tell people, expose the bastards who had tried to kill her brother and succeeded in killing his friend.

'But first I have to check out what was going on in 1967.'

The reading room of the National Library was deserted and the only noise was made by Kristín turning a heavy wheel to scroll through microfilms of newspapers from the 1960s. She sat in front of the clumsy microfiche reader watching the pages roll past, one after the other. The number of editions on each microfilm depended on the physical size of the newspaper; with some titles, two years' worth could fit on the same film. Kristín watched the headlines fly by, history being replayed on fast-forward: the Vietnam War, the assassinations of Martin Luther King and Bobby Kennedy, the student uprising in Paris in '68, Nixon's presidential candidacy.

She savoured this brief interval of solitude, the silence that reigned in the reading room. Of course she was grateful to Steve for coming to her assistance and appreciated his help and his calm reactions, but at last she had time to catch her breath, to think about what had happened over the last few hours and to plan what to do next.

In the meantime, Steve had gone to a small hostel on a backstreet nearby. He said he only needed the room for part of the day and had some dollars on him, so the warden was quick to pocket the money and did not bother to enter him into the guest book. He and Kristín were planning to travel east to the glacier later that day but before that he intended to gather more information about the operation on the glacier; ring some people, find out whatever they could tell him. He had hardly had time to think since Kristín rang his doorbell yesterday evening and now he took the chance to go over the events of the night, trying to form a picture of what he had experienced. Clearly, Kristín was in real danger and he was glad to be able to help her; even though he could not work out exactly what was going on, as long as she needed him, he was content.

Kristín found the astronauts' visit in 1967. There were twenty-five of them and the press had followed their every move. One of the pilots with them was called Ian Parker, the name Thompson had mentioned, the man who used to fly Scorpions. He had also been a member of the earlier group; the newspapers reminded their readers that eight astronauts had come to Iceland on a training mission in 1965. On that occasion the group had been taken into the un in habited interior, to the volcanic desert around Herdubreidarlindir and Askja, a trip that was repeated when Neil Armstrong and his fellow astronauts visited the country. He was the only member of the team to have been awarded his astronaut wings, the only one who had actually been in space, having piloted the Gemini 8 in 1966 during the first successful manned docking of two spacecraft in orbit.

Unsurprisingly, Armstrong attracted the most column inches. The article described him as a very reserved man with a short back and sides haircut; quiet, serious, interested in the technological challenges of space flight, and quoted as saying that the only drawback with the US space pro-gramme was the huge amount of attention he attracted wherever he went.

'The huge amount of attention he at-tracted wherever he went,' Kristín repeated to herself.

Her ex-boyfriend, Ómar the lawyer, had no

intention of lending her the car at first. In fact, he was more inclined to call the police when Kristín appeared without warning at his office in the centre of town. He had heard the radio announcements. Later, surely, pictures of her would be broadcast on the TV news that evening and in tomorrow's papers.

'Jesus, Kristín! What's going on?' he burst out when he saw her standing at the door of his office.

'What have you heard?' she asked.

'All I know is that you're wanted by the police because of a dead man in your apartment,' he said, rising from his desk. 'What on earth have you done?'

'I haven't done anything,' she assured him.

'That's not how it sounded. Why are you on the run from the police? Surely it's some misunderstanding?'

'Calm down,' Kristín said, closing the door. 'I need to ask you a favour.'

'A favour?'

'Yes, I'd like to borrow your jeep.'

'My jeep?'

'Yes. Look, I'll fill you in on the whole story as soon as I have time but I'm in a terrible hurry and there's no one else I can turn to. You have to help me.'

He stood staring at her as if she was a

complete stranger; a tall, good-looking man with attractive brown eyes who had caught her off her guard at a Law Society party and been part of her life for the next three years.

'I'm desperate,' she said. 'You'd be doing me an incredible favour.'

'Are you in some kind of danger?' he asked in a gentler tone, and she remembered that for all his faults he could be considerate at times.

'No,' she lied. 'And I am going to get in touch with the police just as soon as I can but there's something I have to do first and you can help me.'

'What are you planning to do with the jeep?'

'I have to take a short trip into the countryside — I won't be long, trust me.'

Ómar wavered. He could see that Kristín was desperate and had no good reason to refuse her request.

'Just for today?' he asked.

She nodded.

'And you'll leave it in front of the office by the end of the day?'

'Yes. Thank you so much, Ómar. I knew I could rely on you.'

'If you don't return it, I'll be on to the police straight away.'

'No problem,' Kristín said, kissing him on the cheek. 'Don't worry about a thing.'

'Did you really kill that man?'

'Of course not. Don't be silly. I'll tell you all about it when I get back. I promise.'

Now she and Steve were sitting in a handsome, brand-new blue Pajero. The jeep was equipped with a car-phone and tinted windows; apart from her brief respite in the library, it was the first time Kristín had not felt hunted in the last eighteen hours. She fought down the instinct not to leave the jeep's warm, leathery interior.

She had found a parking space in front of a florist near the restaurant, from where they could monitor the comings and goings around the pub. It was getting on for four o'clock, dusk was falling. A group of men clad in thick jumpers, leather jackets and jeans — trawlermen, Kristín guessed — stopped outside the pub and, after a loud altercation, went inside. A young couple followed them. A fat man in a thick windcheater came out. Everything seemed calm.

It was ten past four when Steve nudged Kristín.

'There's Monica,' he said, pointing to a tall, slim woman in her early forties, with dark hair, wearing a thick, beige overcoat and a belt around her waist. She hurried inside. They waited to see if anyone was following her, then stepped out of the car. Looking through the window Steve saw that Monica had taken a seat at the back, in a corner. The fishermen were now lining the bar and making a racket, roaring with laughter and shouting to one another. Four men sat by one of the large windows facing the street, trying to ignore the fishermen. Otherwise, only the odd table was occupied. The interior was wood-panelled and furnished with rustic wooden tables and heavy chairs in a forlorn attempt to evoke an Irish pub ambience, and a small staircase led to an upstairs room where they sometimes had live music. Kristín and Steve made their way over to the corner and sat down beside Monica.

'What's happening, Steve? What the hell's going on?' Monica asked the moment she saw them. The words came tumbling out; she was agitated and tiny pearls of sweat beaded her upper lip.

'I don't know,' Steve said. 'I swear I don't know.'

They described the events of the previous evening and night for her and she listened, tense and restless, rubbing her hands together as if she was finding it hard to concentrate. Steve noticed her continually looking over his shoulder as he was speaking. While they were waiting outside in the jeep, Steve had explained to Kristín that he and Monica used to work together when she lived on the base, before she got her job with the Fulbright Commission.

'Did you find anything out?' Steve asked, when he had finished his story.

'No one will say a word,' Monica answered, running her hand through her hair. 'The embassy is in a state of siege. I've never seen guns in there before but now everyone is armed. They're special forces, I think. It's like living in a time-bomb that could go off any minute. Most of the embassy staff have been forced to take leave. When I asked what was going on, I was sent to see some officer who said that the situation would be sorted out in a few days and that everything would then go back to normal. He asked me to be patient. He was very polite but I got the impression he wouldn't hesitate to shoot me given half a chance.'

'In a few days?' Kristín repeated. 'They'll have left the glacier by then and presumably the country too.'

'What about this Ratoff?' Steve asked. 'Did you find anything on him?'

'Nothing. Not that I've had much chance to look. Obviously, if he works for the secret services, it won't be easy to track him down. I don't even know if it's a Christian name or a family name, or even his real name at all.'

'Nor do we,' Kristín interjected impatiently. 'It's just something I overheard. So what do you know about troop movements on the glacier?'

'I spoke to a friend on the base, Eastman. He's one of the guys in charge of the hangars and he told me the situation there is very mysterious. The word is that special forces troops arrived on a C-17 transport plane that's now waiting on standby on one of the runways. It's almost unheard of: no one's allowed near the plane — they have their own guards. The troops who arrived on it must be the men your brother saw on the glacier. Eastman didn't know where they were heading. The whole thing's shrouded in the utmost secrecy.'

'What about the two men who tried to kill Kristín?' Steve asked.

'The embassy's crawling with dubious characters. For all I know, any one of them could be a paid assassin.'

'Are they tapping the phones?'

'Yes, Steve. They're tapping the phones.'

'So they know who makes calls, both to and from the embassy?'

'That's what I'm trying to tell you.'

'What do you mean, trying to tell us? Jesus Christ, so they know about you and me, about us! Have you sold us down the river, Monica?' Steve said slowly in disbelief. 'Is this a trap?' He was on his feet now, tugging at Kristín, who had not yet absorbed the implications of what Monica was telling them. Following the line of Monica's gaze Steve glanced around to see Ripley entering the pub, dressed in a padded, white ski-suit. He strolled unhurriedly over to their corner. Steve looked back at Monica.

'They threatened my boys,' Monica said desperately; she too was on her feet.

Kristín could not believe what she was seeing when she looked over at the door and spotted Ripley making his way towards them, and out of the corner of her eye glimpsed Bateman coming down the stairs. He was dressed like Ripley; they no longer looked like religious salesmen; now they might have been tourists. She could see no way out of the trap — she and Steve were in a back corner of the pub, in the place chosen by Monica. There was no escape route.

'Third time lucky,' Ripley said, pushing

247

Kristín down into her seat again. She stared at him, her knees buckled and she fell rather than sat. Ripley took a seat beside Monica, and Bateman pulled up a chair and joined them, indicating to Steve to return to his chair.

'Well, isn't this cosy?' Ripley said, beaming. 'Is the beer good here? Before you try anything silly, I should point out that we're both armed and won't hesitate to shoot, so perhaps we can do this in a civilised way.'

'We have a car outside and we're going to invite you — not you, Monica — to come for a drive,' Bateman added.

'And if we refuse to go with you?' Steve said, still searching Monica's face.

'Ah, you're the knight in shining armour that she found on the base, aren't you?' Ripley said, smiling to reveal a row of improbably even white teeth.

'What a charming couple,' Bateman continued, looking at Kristín. 'Do you make a habit of screwing Americans from the base or is Steve here the exception?' He reached out a hand as if to caress her cheek.

Kristín jerked her head back. Steve sat stock still. Monica lowered her eyes in shame.

'Well, it's been delightful but regrettably we'd better get moving,' Bateman said.

'Monica, here, who's ready to betray her friends at the drop of a hat, will leave first and make herself scarce. I'll go next and escort our political scientist. We're going to stand up very slowly and walk out of here very calmly. Ripley and Kristín will follow, and that'll be that. It couldn't be simpler.'

'Where are you taking us?' Steve asked.

'We'll find some nice quiet spot,' Bateman said. 'Don't you worry about that.'

'What's in the plane on the glacier?' Kristín asked.

'Now that's the kind of curiosity that we find so stimulating,' Bateman said. 'But don't you think it would be better if you let us get on with what we have to do?'

Bateman stood up to let Monica pass. She bustled away from the table, keeping her eyes on the ground as she passed them and hurried across the pub to the exit, looking neither left nor right. Opening the door, she vanished into the winter dusk.

'Right, Stevie, on your feet,' Bateman said, standing up himself and taking hold of Steve's shoulder and tugging at him. Steve stood up, looking helplessly at Kristín as Bateman turned him round and pushed him along in front of him. He did nothing roughly as he did not want to attract any attention.

'Now you,' Ripley said. Neither the fishermen at the bar nor any of the other custom-
ers seemed to notice. Kristín rose slowly
and they set off. She felt sick, her legs weak
as if they did not belong to her; the whole
situation seemed unreal, as if it was happening to someone else, as if time had
slowed down. When they reached the bar,
one of the trawlermen inadvertently blocked
her way, forcing her to stop in her tracks.
Ripley tried to move him aside but he would
not budge or give Ripley so much as a
glance. Kristín saw Steve climbing into the
white Ford Explorer outside the pub. So
this is how it would end: abducted from a
busy pub, without so much as putting up a
fight, for a lonely, unpleasant finale.

'He called you a faggot,' Kristín said in
Icelandic, before the fisherman could say a
word. She had noticed him staring at her
while she sat with Steve and Monica but
had tried not to catch his eye. She knew all
about men who stared from a distance: they
were trouble.

'Oh, yeah? Who said that?' the fisherman
demanded, instantly squaring up.

'Faggot. He called you a fucking faggot,'
Kristín said, pointing at Ripley.

'Don't say a word more,' Ripley ordered,
pulling at Kristín. 'Your boyfriend will get

shot if anything goes wrong in here.'

'He said you were all fucking fairies,' Kristín yelled at the bar, tearing herself away from Ripley. They now had the fishermen's undivided attention. If Ripley meant to pull the gun out of his ski-suit, he did not manage it. She saw the barrel of a revolver glint in his hand, then watched as the fisherman who had showed an interest in her punched him hard in the face.

'I'll show you who's the faggot,' he said.

Ripley collapsed on the floor and as the trawlermen surrounded him, Kristín edged slowly out of the crowd. She glanced outside at the Explorer. Steve was in the back, Bateman behind the wheel, inevitably beginning to wonder what had delayed his partner. He craned his neck to peer into the pub but Kristín was not sure what he could see.

Noticing a door behind the bar, she vaulted over the counter and fled into what transpired to be the kitchen. Out of the corner of her eye she saw Ripley trying to fend off two fishermen before he was overpowered; the Icelanders were raining down blows on his body and head. Kristín sprinted through the kitchen and out of a door that opened into a small backyard which was connected to the street via a narrow alley. Running along it then pressing her back against the wall to peer into the street, she saw that the white Explorer had not moved. Inside she could just make out Bateman and Steve.

She began to creep towards the car, then saw Bateman gesticulating at Steve and yelling something at him. Next minute he jumped out of the Explorer, slamming the door behind him, and ran into the pub. Without a moment's hesitation she raced to the rear door on the street side and tried to open it but discovered it was locked. Noticing her, Steve banged on the window. He could not open the door on his side either; he was locked in the car.

'For fuck's sake,' Kristín panted. Looking round frantically she saw a small warning sign that had been erected in front of some nearby roadworks. Dragging it towards the car, she heaved it as hard as she could against Steve's window. The glass shattered, small splinters showering the interior and the road. Immediately the car alarm went off and inside the pub she saw Ripley's head jerk round. Bateman was supporting him. The fishermen were standing in a huddle by the bar. Bateman shouted something as Steve squeezed out of the window, ripping his jacket on the jagged edges of the glass.

'Our car!' Kristín screamed as she tore

ahead of Steve past the restaurant. She did not dare to look back. Steve was following hard on her heels; she could hear him breathing heavily just behind her.

Bateman emerged from the pub supporting Ripley and laid him on the steps. He had his gun in his hand and, scanning his surroundings, caught sight of Kristín and Steve jumping into the jeep parked in front of the florist.

'It's the Special Squad!' exclaimed a teenage boy clutching a skateboard and pointing at Bateman. Bateman ignored him. He did not notice that people all round him had stopped and were watching him sprint along the street, gun in hand. He ran hunched over, like a hunter after his prey, his arms held straight down by his sides so the gun almost brushed the tarmac.

Kristín got behind the wheel of the Pajero and turned the key in the ignition and stamped on the accelerator simultaneously. The engine screamed into life. Shoving the automatic into reverse, she backed out of the parking space and down the street with wheels spinning, the tyres smoking on the wet tarmac. With a quiet popping sound, a small hole appeared in the windscreen just to the right of her head and another directly below it: Bateman was shooting as he ran.

Kristín backed across the road, clipping a car approaching from the opposite direction, which made the Pajero spin forty-five degrees. She slammed the automatic into drive and screeched off down the road. They heard a low hiss as shots penetrated the chassis and Kristín ducked in the hope that this would protect her. Steve lay in the footwell on the passenger side, eyes wide with anguish.

Behind them, Bateman tore around the corner into the street in pursuit but he soon gave up the chase and shrank ever smaller in the rearview mirror before disappearing from sight.

21

South Iceland,
Saturday 30 January, 1800 GMT
They stopped twice to fill up with petrol on their journey east. Kristín drove the whole way. According to the weather forecast, there was a severe storm affecting the east and north-east of the country but down on the southern lowlands through which they were now driving conditions were fine apart from some drifting snow. It was very dark; there was little traffic on the Sudurland highway and the further east they drove, the fewer vehicles they encountered. Soon only the occasional pair of headlights lit up the Pajero before disappearing just as suddenly, plunging Kristín and Steve into darkness again.

They were each wrapped up in their own thoughts and spoke little, except when the radio news reported the shooting incident in the city centre and Kristín interpreted for Steve. A man believed to be associated with the gunman had been admitted to hospital with injuries. Eight fishermen had been arrested but could not be interviewed at present because they were still under the influence of alcohol. The police were investigating possible links between the shooting and the murder of Runólfur Zóphaníasson, and were calling for witnesses to both incidents to come forward. It also emerged that a lawyer employed by the foreign ministry, who was wanted for questioning in connection with Runólfur's murder, had still not been traced. Sources confirmed that she was a suspect in the murder of Runólfur, who had been involved in unspecified business with the ministry, and that she may also have been present at the shooting in the city centre. No details were given about the gunman. The incident was almost unheard of in Reykjavík where gun crimes were extremely rare.

Steve rang Michael Thompson from the car-phone. In the interim Thompson had dug out the details of the farmer who lived at the foot of the glacier and was able to tell them the name of his farm. Having obtained the phone number from directory enquiries, Kristín called Jón to make sure he was home. He said they were welcome to visit, though he did not know how he could help them.

They sat for a while without saying a word.

'Have you thought about me at all since?' Steve asked eventually, squinting in the glare of a pair of headlights that shot past, leaving them in darkness again. He had been sitting mostly in silence, eyes fixed on the monotony of the white road ahead, ever since they left Reykjavík.

'From time to time,' Kristín said. 'I did try to explain.'

'Sure. You didn't want to be a GI whore.'

'It's not that simple.'

'I don't suppose it is.'

'I'm so sorry to drag you into this stupid mess.'

'What, that little game of cowboys and Indians?' There was no humour in his voice, only weariness.

Kristín was lost in thought for several minutes.

'It's partly political. I oppose the presence of the American army on Midnesheidi. I could understand its strategic significance during the Cold War, but that didn't mean I agreed with its presence. I've always regarded it as a blot on the landscape. It's as simple as that. The Icelanders shouldn't have an army and they certainly shouldn't get into bed with one. Far too many people have prostituted themselves to the Defense Force already — businessmen, particularly. I should never have allowed things to go so far between us but . . .'

She groped for the right words.

'You're against the army. So what?' Steve said.

'It's not that simple,' Kristín repeated. 'I'm opposed to the NATO base. Not as a member of an organisation or anything like that, but in my heart; I just can't stand the thought of an army on Icelandic soil, whether it's American, British, French, Russian or Chinese. Never, over my dead body, will I accept its presence here. And the more the debate has come to revolve around money, unemployment, redundancies and the economy, the stronger I've felt about it. It should never have come to this. It's unthinkable that we should be financially dependent on an army. What does that make us? What have we become?'

'But . . .'

'War profiteers. No better than war profiteers. The whole damn Icelandic nation.'

'Aren't you just a Commie bastard?' Steve asked, with a wry smile.

'I should be of course but I'm not. I'm . . .'

'A nationalist?'

'An opponent of the army.'

'But the base's activities have been massively scaled down. They may close it any day now.'

'I think you're here to stay. For a thousand years. Don't you see? For eternity. And you can't imagine how horrific I find that prospect.'

They raced along the road, a beam of light piercing the darkness at a hundred and twenty kilometres an hour.

'I'm not the American army on Midnesheidi,' Steve pointed out at last.

'No, I know. Perhaps we took things too fast. Perhaps we should have got to know each other better.'

'Let me tell you who I am, so there's no doubt about it,' Steve said. 'I'm a New Yorker. No, that's not quite right, I'm from Albany, New York, and you'd know what I'm talking about if you'd read any William Kennedy.'

'*Ironweed,*' Kristín chipped in.

'Did you see the movie?'

'I did.'

'The book's better but I don't really see how else they could have filmed it. Anyway, Albany's full of Irish like me. Plenty of Quinns. The salt of the earth. My great-grandparents emigrated at the turn of the century to escape the poverty. They settled with their family in Albany and led a hand-to-mouth existence but left their children better off. Granddad went into the whole-sale business, importing goods from Ireland, and made a decent living from it, and Dad took over from him. You couldn't call it a business empire but he does okay. The Albany Irish fought and died in the wars the US fought in Europe, Japan, Korea and Vietnam. They were no soldiers but they joined the army because they believed their country needed them. As for me, I chose to study political science because I wanted to understand what led the US to establish bases in places like this, to understand what turned us into the world's police force. I know all about people's hostility here but what about them getting their snouts in the trough? The truth is I've hardly gotten to know this place at all. Still, someone once told me you're all descended from the Irish, so perhaps you're safe sharing a car with me after all.'

'There were a few Irish hermits living here over a thousand years ago.'

'There you go.'

'But I don't think . . .'

They started when the car-phone began to ring. They stared at it, but when Steve moved to answer it, Kristín said:

'Oh, leave it. It'll just be my ex, pissing himself about his fancy jeep.'

By the time they drove into Jón's yard, the blizzard that had blown up on the way there had developed into a complete whiteout. The old farmer was standing in the door-way, visible through the thick curtain of snow, lit up by the porch light, a stooping figure in jeans and felt slippers. There was no sign of the soldiers; they had moved all their equipment up to the glacier, and the wind, which was gusting strongly here at the foot of the ice cap, had filled their tracks and tyre-marks with drifting snow. Kristín and Steve ran from the jeep to the farm-house and Jón closed the door behind them, showing them into his living room where Kristín took in old family photos, book-shelves and thick curtains in the dim lamp-light. The heating was turned up high and a powerful odour of the stables hung in the room's stuffy air. Jón went into the kitchen to put on some coffee while they made themselves comfortable.

'I heard about the shooting in Reykjavík,' he said quietly, his eyes on Kristín as he invited them to take a seat. His voice was hoarse and quavered a little. He had thick hands, callused with hard work, slightly bow legs and strong features long since mellowed by age.

'And I suppose you're the Kristín they keep asking about on the radio,' he added.

'My brother is dying on the glacier,' Kristín said slowly and clearly. 'He fell into the hands of some American soldiers up there; they took him and threw him down a crevasse. He was found by his rescue team but they think he's unlikely to live. The friend who was with him is dead. We hear that you've helped these soldiers over the years, guided them on the glacier, done whatever needed doing.'

The accusatory note in her voice did not escape Jón and he looked surprised. What an extraordinary young woman she was. He had always kept the promise he and his brother had given Miller long ago and never told a soul what he knew, had kept quiet all these years. Even after Karl died. And now here sat this woman, accusing him of colluding somehow in her brother's death. What would Karl have done in his shoes? he asked himself.

'The expedition leader goes by the name of Ratoff,' he volunteered.

'Ratoff!' Kristín exclaimed triumphantly. 'That's him. That's the man they mentioned.'

'He's not like Miller.'

'Who's Miller?' Steve asked, catching the name, although they were speaking Icelandic.

'A colonel in the American army who was in charge of the first expedition. In 1945.'

'So the plane on the glacier's American, not German?' Kristín asked, once she had translated Jón's reply.

'No, on the contrary, I think it's much more likely to be German,' Jón said slowly. 'It crashed at the end of the Second World War; flew over our house and vanished into the darkness. We knew it had gone down. It was flying too low. Miller told my brother and me that the plane was carrying dangerous biological weapons — some kind of virus that the Germans had developed. That was why they had to find it urgently. It didn't occur to us not to help them.'

'So it crashed before the end of the war?'

'Shortly before peace was declared.'

'That fits in with what Sarah Steinkamp told us,' Kristín said, looking at Steve. 'She said there were Germans on board. Hang on, a virus?' she said to Jón. 'What kind of virus?'

'Miller was very vague about it. I got the impression he'd given away more than he should have done. We were on good terms; Karl and I would never have dreamt of betraying his trust.'

Jón looked from Kristín to Steve and back again.

'Miller said the pilot was his brother,' he added.

'His brother?' Kristín said. 'In a German plane?'

'I don't know,' Jón replied. 'He didn't mean to tell us; he was under a great deal of pressure and it just slipped out.'

'Did Miller tell you the plane was German?'

'Yes.'

'So why was an American pilot flying it?' Kristín asked, perplexed.

'When my brother and I saw the plane fly over the farmhouse in the dark all those years ago, we reckoned it was big enough to be a Junkers Ju 52. Of course no one would know it nowadays. It was the same model as Himmler's private plane. We didn't know then that it was German.'

She looked at him blankly.

'The war was something of a hobby for my brother and me,' Jón explained. 'Especially the aircraft. Karl knew all about the aircraft they used and said straight away that it looked like a Junkers.'

She continued to stare at him, still not quite sure what he was talking about.

'Miller was tireless in his hunt for that plane. We didn't understand why until he told us about his brother. Karl took a photo of Miller that I still have somewhere.'

Jón rose from his chair and walked over to a large dresser. The top half was a cabinet containing glasses and plates, the lower half heavy, carved drawers. Bending down, Jón pulled out the bottom drawer and rooted around until he found what he was looking for. He handed them an old photograph.

'He used to turn up here from time to time, saying he was on his summer vacation, and would go up to the glacier. We let him stay with us. He'd be here for up to a week or two. Came every three to five years to search for that plane, though it must be more than thirty years since his last visit. We were told he'd died. He wrote to us for years,' Jón added, handing them some yellowed letters. 'These are thank-you letters to me and my brother that he used to write after he'd been to stay. An exceptionally nice chap, Miller.'

The letters were addressed to Jón in an elegant hand and the sender had taken care to spell his patronymic and the name of the farm correctly. They were postmarked

Washington; the stamps featured Abraham Lincoln.

'What was his Christian name?' Kristín asked, examining the photo.

'Robert,' Jón replied. 'Robert Miller. He told us to call him Bob. Isn't that what most Americans are called?'

'Did he ever find anything?'

'Not a thing, poor man.'

'He wanted to find his brother?'

'That goes without saying.'

'Did he tell you anything about his brother?'

'Not another word. And we didn't ask any questions. He asked us not to take any more pictures of him. This is the only one we have.'

The photograph had been taken outside the brothers' stables one summer's day. Miller stood holding the bridle of a black horse, face turned to the camera; a thin figure in checked shirt and jeans. He had raised a gloved hand to shield his eyes from the sun but his features were clearly visible: a prominent nose and mouth above a receding chin, a high brow and thinning hair.

'That horse was only half broken and it came close to killing Miller,' Jón said, pointing to the animal. 'Bolted across the yard with him the moment he got in the saddle, heading straight for the electric cable that used to run between the buildings. Fortunately Miller noticed the wire in time and managed to throw himself off.'

Jón was silent for a while, as if considering whether to say more or stop there. They raised their eyes to him enquiringly. He shifted from one foot to the other in his woollen socks, before eventually inviting them to follow him.

'What does it matter?' he said. 'Come with me. I can show you something that proves that plane was German.'

They waited while he pulled on a thick down jacket, boots, a woollen hat and gloves. Their own coats were in the car and he told them to fetch them while he waited at the door, then led them out into the blinding whiteness. Soon the house was invisible and they could see no more than a yard ahead in the snow-filled night. Kristín walked behind Jón, carefully placing her feet in his tracks. She could only just make out his shape in front of her and when he stopped abruptly, she stumbled into him and felt Steve collide with her from behind. Jón had reached a door which he heaved open, sending it slamming back into the wall. He fumbled in the darkness and turned on a light, revealing that they were inside a cowshed that was now used as a stable. It took all Steve's strength to close the door behind them against the force of the wind.

There were six horses in the stable, giving off a heat that made it warm inside. They stood in their wooden stalls, watching the unexpected visitors with quizzical expressions, steam rising from their nostrils, their winter coats almost comically thick and woolly. Kristín, who had always loved horses although she had never ridden, paused to pat a chestnut mare. Jón led them along the passage that ran behind the animals, parallel to the dung channel. Kristín was surprised by the old man's vigour and nimble movements. The three innermost stalls were empty and in one stood a large chest with a key in the lock, which Jón now turned, before lifting the lid.

'It must have been about twenty years ago,' he said with a grunt. The lid was surprisingly heavy. 'He may not have been the only one to survive the crash. He veered just too far to the east, or he would have stumbled on the farm.'

'Who would?' Kristín asked.

'The German,' Jón said, lifting a tattered German uniform jacket out of the chest and holding it up for them to see.

22

Vatnajökull Glacier,
Saturday 30 January, Evening
Count von Mantauffel has gone in search of
help. He took two bars of chocolate and we
tried to wrap him up as warmly as we could.
He's the toughest member of our party and is
desperate to get off the ice. We thought if he
headed south-east he might be able to find
his way down, but there's not much hope; he
knows it and we know it. The cold will be the
death of him.
  The cold will be the death of us all.

Ratoff was sitting in his tent, reading the
diary he had found under the co-pilot's seat
by the dim light of the gas heater. The gale
ripped and tore at the tent, its screaming so
loud that conversation was impossible. Two
of the soldiers' tents had already been carried away and were probably halfway across
the Atlantic by now. Blinded by wind and
snow, there was nothing more they could

do until the storm had exhausted itself.

The pilot had been carrying papers that identified him as one William Miller. Instantly, Ratoff knew where he had seen that face before: Colonel Miller was the former chief of the organisation; the pilot must have been his brother. Ratoff had already been struck by the strangeness of seeing the bodies emerge from the ice well preserved and undecayed after so many years. The pilot looked as if he had merely been asleep for half a century. Now he could picture Colonel Miller precisely as a young man. The thought intrigued him.

The diary was written in pencil, its entries sporadic. They were not separated by date or time, as if the author had lost all sense of the passing days, and some were very short, hardly more than a sentence jotted down, a disjointed thought or a message from the pilot to those who eventually found the plane. Ratoff could not tell how much time the diary spanned but by his calculations it would not have taken the men long to freeze to death. He flicked through the pages, dipping into them here and there, trying to work out the sequence of events. From time to time the pilot addressed a particular reader — presumably his brother — as if he had intended him to find the diary.

It's dark round the clock here. Cold and dark. We put Dietrich outside on the ice. He died in agony, I'm afraid. We won't be putting any more outside for the moment. The plane almost filled with snow. Such an incredible wind. But nothing could stop von Mantauffel. He said he had no intention of dying here; I'm afraid he's right that no one will be coming to rescue us. But I'm glad he's gone. He was a disturbing presence, playing the victor in spite of having lost the war. The others are more polite. We're all dying — that makes men polite. I can't see how we can be saved. I just can't see it.

Ratoff turned the pages.

. . . to gain altitude but it was hopeless. The wings were heavily iced up and there was serious turbulence, alternating updrafts and downdrafts. It was nightmarish flying weather: gale-force winds, snowfall and pitch darkness. Out of nowhere, we felt the plane hit the ice. Completely out of the blue; I still can't grasp how it happened. The left wing probably struck first, but after that it was just noisy chaos. We bounced and the propellers caught in the ice, the wings sheared off in a shower of sparks and the fuselage ploughed on but it didn't break up . . .

Ratoff read on. His tent flapped violently,

271

the gaslight dancing over the pages of the diary.

I saw Berlin for the first time in my life the day before yesterday. I think it was the day before yesterday. Strange to be visiting the German capital in the middle of a war. See what you've done by persuading me to fly over the Atlantic? What are you mixed up in? Are they going to do a deal with the Nazis? Are they trying to shorten the war? Planning to attack Russia? You hear so many rumors. The Germans don't want to talk about it. I know they're part of some kind of negotiating team, but what are they negotiating?

Our general died on impact. He got up from his seat shortly before we crashed; one of the Germans as well. I don't know what they were thinking of. They yelled at me to do something but there was nothing I could do.

My God, it's cold. I can hardly hold the pencil.

The door flap was wrenched open from outside, causing the tent to belly out, the canvas stretching so taut that the seams creaked as if they were going to split. Bateman was on the line again in the communications tent. Ratoff stood up, zipped the tent flap firmly behind him and followed the man. They could barely keep their footing in the relentless blizzard even over the

272

few short yards between the tents.

'Tell me you have dealt with the inconvenience,' Ratoff shouted, trying to make himself heard above the wind.

'Negative, sir,' Bateman said. 'Ripley's unconscious in hospital. The woman escaped with her friend. He's one of us . . .'

'What do you mean?'

'An American. I think they're on their way to you. There's a retired pilot on the base who's been asking questions about the brothers who farm near the glacier. It didn't take him long to admit why he wanted the information. He said they'd come to him for help. Said they were heading for the glacier.'

'Then good luck to them. It's hell on earth up here,' Ratoff yelled. 'Has our mission been compromised?'

'They don't seem to have talked to anyone except the pilot. And as yet the embassy hasn't received any official reaction from the government or any other institution in Reykjavík. The girl's so busy evading us that she hasn't had much chance to warn anyone about what's going on. Anyway, I think we've managed to frame her for murder, which is a bonus.'

Ratoff set the receiver back in its cradle and heaved a contemptuous sigh. They were

273

pathetic; outmanoeuvred and now hospital-
ised by a woman. By a civil servant, for
Christ's sake, and an Icelandic one at that.

23

Central Reykjavík,
Saturday 30 January, 1800 GMT

The two detectives who had inspected Kristín's flat only the previous evening were now standing at the bar of the Irish pub. The area around the building was cordoned off with police tape; a crowd of curious bystanders had gathered in the darkness on the other side of the street, floodlights had been set up both inside and out, reporters and photographers were circling, desperate for a quote, and the premises were surrounded by police cars with flashing lights. Ripley and one of the fishermen had been admitted to hospital. Delicate, intricate flakes of snow were falling lazily, only to melt as they landed on the floodlights. The older detective removed his hat and scratched his head.

'Like a spaghetti western,' he remarked.

'You were right about Kristín. She was

here,' the younger detective replied. 'The witness statements match the picture we have of her.'

'I'm not sure I've quite grasped this yet. There are at least four people with Kristín at the scene, three men and one woman. One of them, who the fishermen claim was American, is lying on the steps outside after being beaten to a pulp by our jolly jack tars. The other woman makes herself scarce. Another man, after trying to come to the aid of his companion, runs down Tryggvagata taking pot shots at Kristín and a third man. The gunman is American too, if the fishermen are to be believed. Kristín and her companion get into a jeep and drive away. The American on the steps has no ID. His car is parked outside and has plates registered to the Defense Force in Keflavík. What's going on? You studied in America. You know the people. I've only seen the films.'

'I can't make head or tail of it, any more than you. Perhaps we'll get some answers from the embassy.'

'Inspired. The embassy will solve it. We'll just talk to the embassy and they'll clarify everything and then we can go home to bed.'

'Is your indigestion troubling you again?'

The older police officer turned to look at

his partner. His expression was oddly sad, despite the glint of mockery in his eyes under their red brows. His hair was red too; his face intelligent, stubborn, determined.

'What? Am I not jolly enough for you?' he asked sarcastically.

'When were you ever?'

On arrival at the US embassy on Laufásvegur, they were informed that neither the ambassador nor the attaché was in the country. The chief press officer was indisposed but they could speak to a General Wesson from the Keflavík base. He was the highest-ranking officer at the embassy in the ambassador's absence. The detectives shrugged. The general kept them waiting for an hour and fifteen minutes in a small anteroom outside the ambassador's office. Finally the door opened and they were greeted by an overweight man of about fifty, with thinning hair, a broad face and strong, rather protuberant teeth. He led them into the office and invited them to take a seat. The younger detective took care of the questions since his partner had a poor command of English.

'What can I do for you, gentlemen?' the general asked. With him was a thin young man who introduced himself as Smith and took up position at a carefully calculated

277

distance behind the general.

The detective cleared his throat. 'I don't know if you've heard but there was a shooting incident in the city centre earlier today involving a vehicle registered to the Defense Force. An American citizen was injured and is now in hospital.'

'I've been made aware of events, Inspector, and I find it shocking that those men should have set on him like that. Have you discovered any motive for this outrage? I hear it was a brawl between fishermen and our man got caught in the middle. Naturally we will be demanding a thorough investigation.'

'Well, General, the fishermen claim that he not only started the brawl but that his companion, who also sounded like an American, entered the pub waving a gun and subsequently started firing in the street.'

'That's preposterous. Are you trying to pin this on our man?'

'I am merely reporting how witnesses described the incident.'

'But it's ludicrous. I hear the fishermen were blind drunk. Do you mean to blame an American citizen for their barbaric behaviour?'

'We're keeping an open mind, sir. But reports indicate that the man's companion pursued an Icelandic woman, firing shots at her. His vehicle is registered to the Defense Force. Can you enlighten us as to what might have been happening?'

'No, I'm afraid I cannot. I haven't had any contact with the Defense Force about the matter yet. If it transpires that the man came to the aid of his companion in the pub by pulling out a gun, it would of course be reprehensible, but perhaps understandable in the circumstances.'

'Ask him if he knows the identity of the man in hospital,' the elder detective interrupted in Icelandic. He had until now been sitting quietly, surveying the room with an air of supreme indifference.

The general listened to the question but did not reply.

'What do you mean when you say "our man"?'

'Pardon me?'

'You said "our man", as if he came from the embassy.'

'That's not what I meant.'

'Ask him if it's normal practice for a three-star general to take over the embassy when the ambassador is on leave.'

The younger officer put the question. The general smiled broadly, his strong teeth gleaming, and leant forwards.

279

'I don't think the way we run our embassy has any bearing on the matter.'

'Ask him if he knows who Kristín is.'

'No, I don't know anything about her,' the general answered.

'Ask Jaws here if it's possible that the gunman and his companion were at the pub on military business.'

The younger detective hesitated, then repeated the question in English. Smith bent down to the general who smiled even more broadly.

'I'm afraid you've been watching too many Hollywood movies. We don't shoot at Icelanders. We protect them and consider them friends of the United States. We also direct unprecedented sums of money their way by means of generous contracts. I'm afraid I can't help you gentlemen any further. If you came here to offend a friendly nation, you did a good job of it. Good day.'

He rose. Smith came round to the front of the desk and waited for the policemen to stand, which they did, belatedly. The elder detective with the hat looked Smith up and down, then turned to Wesson.

'Smith and Wesson? Is that some kind of joke?' he asked.

Smith smiled thinly. 'You're the joke, buddy,' he replied in fluent Icelandic.

The two men's eyes met.

'Who are you really? What are you hiding?'

'Gentlemen, you will have to excuse me. Smith will show you out. I have no further comment.'

As the two detectives drove away from the embassy, the car-phone started ringing. The call came direct from the switchboard of the National Commissioner of Police. The man on the line introduced himself as a lawyer before launching into a tirade about his jeep being stolen.

'I lent my jeep to my ex-girlfriend, the woman you're looking for, and she hasn't returned it,' he announced.

'Are you talking about Kristín, the woman wanted for questioning?' the elder police-man asked.

'Yes, her,' the lawyer replied irritably. 'Thank God one of you lot is a bit quicker on the uptake. I've been passed from one fool to another by your switchboard.'

'What did she want with the jeep?'

'I don't see how that matters,' the lawyer said indignantly. 'I'm asking you to please just find my vehicle.'

'Did she say where she was going?'

'Well if I knew where she was going or where she was now, I wouldn't be wasting my time reporting this.'

'Is there a phone in the jeep, a car-phone perhaps?' The detective's patience was wearing thin.

'Of course.'

'Have you tried calling it, sir?'

'Of course I've called the phone, *officer*. She's either not picking up or has it switched off.'

The lawyer gave them the number.

'So are you going to find her then?' he demanded.

'Sir, the Reykjavík police force will not rest until your precious car is recovered,' the detective said wearily and hung up. It was not long before the phone rang again. This time it was the chief inspector.

'Have you been offending our friends at the American embassy?' he asked angrily.

'Not as far as I know,' the policeman answered. He sounded genuinely astonished. News travels fast, he thought.

'I've just had the justice minister on the line. He's had a call from some chap who said you'd made fun of the appearance of the most senior official at the embassy. And mocked their names to boot. Is that right?'

'We're investigating a crime and they could have been more accommodating. We've got a body and a shooting on our hands. Do you really think this is the moment to worry about a man who could chew carrots through a barbed wire fence?'

'Don't give me that, Detective Inspector. I'm told you were rude and arrogant.'

'He wasn't even the ambassador, just some general who looks like a cod and is about as cooperative.'

Knowing his officer of old and realising that it would be futile to pursue this, the chief inspector tried a new line of attack.

'This Kristín you're advertising as wanted for questioning, have you any idea where she is?'

'Not a clue,' the detective admitted, scratching his head.

24

South-East Iceland,
Saturday 30 January, Evening

Kristín lifted the tattered German uniform jacket and ran her hands over the cloth, feeling buttons, pockets, lapels. The fabric was surprisingly soft to the touch; it was a peculiar thought that it had belonged to a German officer who had died in it up by the glacier. There were three medals pinned to the left breast. She handed the jacket to Steve who also examined it carefully.

'I found him in a small gully not more than five kilometres above the farm to the east,' Jón said slowly, his eyes shifting from one of them to the other. 'I buried him on the spot, the little that was left of him. Put up a small cross. The way I saw it, he was one of *them.* You're the only people I've told. There was nothing left of the poor sod but bones.'

'How long ago did you say this was?'

Kristín asked.

'About twenty years.'

'Hang on, are you saying he'd been lying practically on your doorstep for more than thirty years?'

'Hardly on my doorstep. No, he was quite some way from here, well hidden among the rocks.'

'Why didn't you report your discovery?'

'It was nobody else's business. This was ten years after the major recovery expedition and there's hardly been any sign of the military round here since. It's not for the likes of me to go contacting senior officers in the army. I wouldn't know where to start.'

'So why did you take the jacket? Why didn't you bury it as well?'

'I don't really know. Maybe I wanted a souvenir. As I said, I'm very interested in the war and anything to do with it. It was Karl's hobby too, before he died. I remember when the plane flew over; Karl and I used to speculate about it endlessly. It's easy to climb on to the glacier from here; hardly more than a gentle slope for those who know it well, though you have to watch out for crevasses. We scoured the glacier time and again in search of the plane but we never found it. The glacier's like that. It's quick to swallow up anything that sinks into it.'

'Then spits it out again a hundred years later,' Kristín added.

'Yes. Or longer. Or never.'

While Kristín found it impossible to imagine what a German plane would have been doing this far north, Jón assured her that it was not unusual to see enemy aircraft flying over the south-eastern corner of the country during the war. They came from the airport at Stavanger in Norway, he explained, having been specially adapted to carry extra fuel; the return flight across the North Atlantic lasted more than eleven hours, during which time the temperature in the cockpit could drop to $-30°C$ or lower. The planes were mostly Junkers Ju 88s. Generally these were reconnaissance missions but occasionally the Germans carried out air raids. He remembered a Heinkel He 111 fighter, for example, carrying out a machine gun attack on the British camp at the village of Selfoss in 1941, during which one man was killed. German aircraft were also spotted on rare occasions flying over Hornafjördur; they hugged the mountain range before disappearing from view behind Mount Eystrahorn. And a Focke-Wulf 200 once bombed the British tracking station just outside the village of Höfn. So Jón was not particularly surprised that a German plane should have crashed on the glacier. What did puzzle him was that it should have happened in the closing stages of the war when it could not have taken off from Norway, which was no longer occupied by then. It could only have come from Germany.

Jón also told Kristín about an American military aircraft that crashed on the Eyjafjallajökull glacier during the war. There had been little information about the accident at the time due to the news blackout, but everyone had survived and made it safely back to civilisation.

'When Miller first turned up here, Karl and I remembered the Eyjafjallajökull accident and were eager to do anything we could to help him. I suppose our sense of loyalty may have been a bit exaggerated but we gave him our word and we kept it. We kept our promise. That's all there is to it.'

Steve ran his hand over the German jacket again, examining the three medals on the breast. He did not recognise them or know what they would have been awarded for but they indicated that whoever owned the jacket must have been fairly senior in the German army. He wondered what the German officer had been doing up there on the glacier all those years ago.

'There was a box half-buried in the ground beside the German,' Jón said at last, as if as an afterthought. 'I took that as well. It looked as if it had been handcuffed to him. He still had the cuff round his wrist. Must have lugged it down off the glacier.'

'A box!' Kristín exclaimed.

'Yes, or something of the sort. It should be here as well.'

Jón rummaged around in the chest again. Kristín and Steve looked round at the horses which were watching them with ears pricked.

'I don't really know whether to call it a box or a case,' Jón said. 'It's made of metal. Here it is.' He lifted up a scratched and dented metal box, the size of a small brief-case, with a handle and a lock that had clearly been tampered with. The metal had rusted clean through in places. Jón opened the box.

'I found some papers inside. All ruined. Nothing else. I haven't taken anything out.' He passed the box to Kristín. She inspected it for any outer markings, then looked inside and saw the papers. They had been badly damaged by the weather, years of relent-lessly alternating heat and cold, and fell apart when any attempt was made to separate out the sheets, but the odd word could still be made out on the most intact piece. The documents had been typewritten but the individual letters were now mostly blurred or illegible, though she could tell they were in German. In one place it was still possible to make out the words 'Operation Napoleon'.

'Have you any idea what this means?' she asked Jón.

'I don't understand a word of German,' he said. 'But it must have been important if he was prepared to lug that case on his wrist all the way over the glacier in the middle of a storm.'

'Thompson said something about a bomb on board the plane,' Steve reminded Kristín.

'What was that?' Jón asked. He had been a farmer all his life and had never seen any reason to learn English or German or any other language, for that matter, apart from his native Icelandic.

'We heard there was a Nazi bomb on board that the Americans were transporting to the States.'

'A bomb?'

'Yes. A hydrogen bomb that the Germans had been planning to drop on London at the end of the war. Or on Russia. Who knows?'

'Wait a minute, didn't you say you'd put a cross on the German's grave?' Kristín asked. 'Is it still there?'

'No, it isn't, I'm afraid. I didn't do a very good job. I don't really know why I did it at all. It was just two pieces of wood nailed together. I haven't been there for a long time but the cross fell down years ago. I . . .'

Jón broke off.

'What?' Kristín prompted.

'I don't like to say. I'm rather ashamed of myself.'

'Why?'

'I marked the cross.'

'Marked it?'

'I carved a name on it.'

'A name? You mean you knew the German's name?'

'Goodness me, no. It wasn't a man's name.'

'Not a man's name? What do you mean?'

'I had an old dog that I was forced to put down at around that time, so I buried him with the German. I don't know what came over me. Bloody disrespectful, I know. I rather regret it now, but I comfort myself with the thought that he probably didn't deserve any better. Few of them did.'

'So you marked the cross with the name of the dog?'

'Yes, Ogre.'

'Ogre?'

Jón looked at his feet and smiled ruefully as he recalled his ill-tempered and mangy old companion. 'He was a tiresome dog.'

Kristín glanced at Steve who shrugged.

'Could I use your phone?' she asked Jón.

He mumbled his assent. They went back out into the blizzard, Kristín carrying the metal box, Steve the uniform jacket, and followed Jón into the house, oblivious to the incessant ringing of the car-phone in the jeep.

25

Vatnajökull Glacier,
Saturday 30 January, Evening
We're trapped inside the plane. I can't hear the wind any longer and it's not as cold as before. We have two kerosene lamps; I don't know how long they'll last. Don't know how long we've been here. Don't even know where 'here' is. Probably the Vatnajökull glacier. At times the fuselage groans as if it's being wrenched apart. Our only hope is Count von Mantauffel, but it's not much of a hope. We'll probably never be found. He took the metal box with him, handcuffed to his wrist, as if he didn't even have a key to it himself. And if he doesn't, who does? Or maybe it contains something so important that he daren't leave it behind. I'm sitting in the cockpit, keeping away from the Germans. There are two of them still alive, talking their gibberish, scowling at me occasionally. Blaming me for everything.

If we could force the door off its hinges we might be able to dig our way out. The windows are too small to squeeze through. We didn't realise we'd be trapped. Crazy weather the whole time. We haven't started thinking rationally yet. It's horrible having the corpses in here, all battered from the landing. I didn't see the glacier until we crashed into it. God! I couldn't see a thing. I thought I was off the south coast. One minute we were in the air, the next I was skimming the ice. The two men who were standing over me in the cockpit were hurled back into the cabin. Killed instantly. I'd asked them repeatedly to sit down.

We're trying to keep ourselves warm. We don't talk much. Sometimes I hear them mention von Mantauffel. I haven't told them but there's a chance we were spotted. I was flying so low that I saw buildings below me through the blizzard. That's when I knew we were done for. I tried to gain height but we were too near the glacier. There were two men standing by the house gazing up at the plane — they must have seen us. They're bound to report it. They have to report it.

Berlin was bombed flat like London. The airport had been destroyed, so we took off from outside the city. The delegation I'd arrived with stayed behind. Who was the Swede? An exceptionally courteous man.

Seems they're all counts there. I'm going to try to write down what happened in case you ever find us. It passes the time, too.

After we parted in Copenhagen I went to meet the two intelligence officers you mentioned. They never told me their names. They were waiting for me in the park just like you said. They drove me out of the city in a military jeep, heading south to a town called Flensborg where two Germans met us, a lieutenant and a major, and the Swedish count, a member of the royal family apparently. From there we drove toward the front line. The roads were full of refugees and bomb craters — the battle of the Ardennes had been going on for several days at this point. We drove through Schleswig-Holstein where I was given a German uniform to change into. Next we passed through Hamburg where there was gasoline waiting, then on, following the course of the River Elbe, to Berlin, reaching it that evening. If anyone stopped us, all the Swedish count had to do was wave his papers and we'd be ushered through.

They gave me back my jacket, then held a long meeting at the aerodrome. I didn't recognise anyone — they were all Nazi big shots, but the Swede was obviously an old acquaintance of theirs. There were German generals with him, two of them. And one from our side, as you said — I don't know where he came from. I wasn't allowed to attend the meeting — I'm just the driver. Some soldiers loaded two crates of gold bars on to the plane, and provisions of some kind. That was all. The plane is painted in our camouflage colors. A wonderful machine, the Junkers — powerful engines, tremendous weight-bearing capacity and range.

The meeting overran — it took forever. That's why we're in this goddamn mess. Otherwise we'd have missed the storm and ice, I'm convinced of that. At one point our man marched out of the meeting but the Swede persuaded him to go back in. A long time later the two of them came back out and held a conversation by the plane, going on about the Russians and the Ardennes, and Argentina and God knows what else. Anyway, the meeting dragged on and on. I tried to talk to the German soldiers but they couldn't understand a word of English. I gave them some cigarettes. They were only boys, not even twenty. They smiled at me.

In the city there was a total blackout, like everywhere else, and it was strangely silent. They know it's over. I don't understand what they can be negotiating about. The end of the war? Are they going to end the war with a treaty? We know there's not long left. Can *they shorten it? It would save thousands of lives. The Russians will beat us to Berlin. Is that the problem? Why these secret talks?*

I'm almost sure I saw Guderian at the meeting — I recognized him from the newsreels.

One of the lamps has gone out. I know you chose me because you trusted me to keep a secret and needed one of us to fly the plane across the Atlantic. I don't blame you so don't regret it. Never regret it.

I think we're disappearing into the ice. We're being buried alive.

Ratoff closed the book. The wind was dying down; the noise was not as shrill as before. Standing up, he opened the tent flap and peered outside. The night was pitch black but it was gusting and snowing less heavily now. The only illumination came from the floodlight on top of the communications tent. He realised it would take time to get things in motion since it would probably be necessary to dig the plane out again, but the longer the troops were on the glacier, the greater the risk they would attract attention. The sooner the wreckage and the Delta operators were back at base, the better. He considered calling out the Defense Force helicopters. This had been part of the back-up plan, but the drawback was that their activities tended to attract intense interest, not only from Icelandic air traffic control, who would ask endless questions, but also from the media, who scrutinised their every move. He had to make a decision: the storm had delayed the operation by at least a day and their presence on the glacier had now been discovered. There was an Icelandic rescue team in the area that had lost two members and was probably moving closer towards them every second.

Ratoff went into the communications tent and asked to be put through to the admiral in Keflavík.

26

'Is he dead?'

She could hear nothing but static.

'Is Elías dead?' Kristín shouted into the phone. 'Is he still with you?'

The connection was very bad and only the odd word was audible; Júlíus — the leader of the rescue team — kept breaking up. She was standing out in Jón's entrance hall, holding a heavy, old, black telephone receiver and pressing her forehead against her arm and the wall above the phone. She closed her eyes tightly, concentrating on trying to hear what Júlíus was saying. Jón and Steve were in the kitchen. Steve was on his feet.

'Júlíus!' Kristín shouted.

'Heli . . . n't . . . yet,' she heard him say. '. . . s . . . dropping . . . doctor on the team. Elías . . . alive.'

'Is he alive? Is Elías still alive?'

'. . . hanging in . . . Coast Guard helicopter's on its way. The storm . . . pretty much . . . down.'

'Are you going to look for the soldiers?'

'. . . es . . . find people . . .'

'I can hardly hear you so I'm going to tell you this, then hang up. The American soldiers are probably no more than about ten to fifteen kilometres from the edge of the glacier, directly above the farm of Brennigerdi. They're armed, so be careful. They're digging a German plane out of the ice. It's up to you what you do but these men may be extremely dangerous. We're at the foot of the glacier now and we're going to climb up from this side. Hopefully we'll meet you up there.'

Again, the line filled with the hiss and crackle of empty space, so she put down the receiver and rejoined Jón and Steve in the kitchen.

'I think he's still alive,' she said, heaving a sigh.

The news had given her a renewed spark of hope, a new burst of strength to carry on. The relief was indescribable; she knew she could not have borne it had he died. Admittedly, the connection had been very poor but she would allow herself no doubts;

she was convinced that Júlíus had managed to save her brother's life.

'I think they're planning to pay the soldiers a visit. We'll try to rendezvous with them up there.'

'Good,' Jón said. 'I can give you detailed directions. It's not hard from here.'

'Kristín, can I have a word?' Steve said, and asked Jón to excuse them. They went into the sitting room. 'Are you absolutely sure you want to do this?' Steve said. 'The rescue team will sort things out. They'll inform Reykjavík what's going on. Won't you wait and see what happens? Going up there ourselves could mean taking an unnecessary risk. There's nothing more we can do.'

'I want to see them with my own eyes, Steve. I want to see what kind of people they are. And I want to make sure they don't get away with what they've done. I have to be on the spot to be certain of that.'

Steve was about to object when she went on.

'You lot can't be allowed to play your war games wherever you feel like it.'

'What do you mean "you lot"?'

'You saw those men at the pub. You know what they've done on the glacier. What kind of people would sanction that sort of brutality?'

'You came to me, Kristín, don't you forget that.'

'I came to you for information.'

'And help. That's the point. You just can't stand the fact.'

'That's bullshit!'

'No. I know that attitude. We're the invaders. We're the military power. We fight in wars. We're the bad guys. But as soon as anything goes wrong, we're expected to save the day. We're welcome to pump billions into your banana republic, yet you regard us as no better than thugs, fit only to be kept behind a wire fence. We're welcome to intervene in world wars started by Europe and keep an eye on the Russians and hold down the Arabs but the shit hits the fan the moment . . .'

'Fuck you, Steve. Don't be so sanctimonious. You're the guys who are forever seeing Reds under the bed, who drove Chaplin and all the rest out of the country.'

Steve looked at her in her borrowed clothes, the black shadows of strain and exhaustion beneath her eyes, her implacable expression. He knew he would not be able to dissuade her from going up to the glacier whatever he said. She had come too far to stop now.

'I am going up to the glacier.'

'You'll be taking on armed soldiers, Kristín.'

'The rescue team will help. They can hardly massacre all of us. Anyway, Júlíus has alerted Reykjavík. They won't be able to hide what they're up to for much longer.'

'Is everything all right?' asked Jón, appearing at the sitting room door. The old man had largely kept to himself since they returned from the stable and Kristín had wondered if he was suffering from a conflict of loyalty towards Miller. Maybe he felt guilty for having assisted the Americans and kept quiet about the fact.

'Everything's fine,' Kristín reassured him. 'What about you? Is everything all right with you?'

'What does that matter?' Jón asked. 'I don't have much time left.' He said this without any sense of regret, as if it were just another fact of life he had resigned himself to.

'But are . . .'

Jón interrupted; he did not want to talk about himself.

'If you mean to go up to the glacier you should rest for an hour or two,' he said. 'You're welcome to lie down in Karl's room.'

Kristín nodded reluctantly. She did not

feel tired, despite not being able to remember when she last slept, but it made sense to rest a little now. Jón escorted them upstairs to a room off the landing with a large mattress and a desk; there was yellow linoleum on the floor and the walls were lined with books. It felt cool compared to the overpowering heat downstairs.

Kristín lay down on the bed. Realising that Steve intended to lie on the floor, she shifted to make room for him. He stretched out beside her. She could not relax. When she closed her eyes she could feel the fatigue creeping up her legs like an anaesthetic and spreading through her body.

'Thanks for your help, Steve,' she murmured.

'It's nothing,' he replied.

She opened her eyes and turned to him.

'It is. You didn't have to help me. You could have sent me packing, forgotten the whole thing. I don't deserve any favours from you.'

'What, a damsel in distress?'

She laughed quietly. 'Yes, and that makes you the knight in shining armour.'

'I'm no knight. I'm just a Yank from the base.'

'Yeah, you're just a Yank from the base.'

Something in her voice had changed. He

looked at her, their faces almost touching. In spite of everything that had happened to her, the chase and the danger, her anxiety for Elías, her fears for her own life, her anger; in spite of it all she had never felt so alive, so confident, so perfectly in control. It was as if her ordeal had given her a new lease of life, stripping away the veils of mist and forcing her to get a grip on herself, take control of her life, acknowledge her feelings — and find an outlet for them.

'You remember when I ran out on you?' she said.

'The peace protester turned Yankee whore? How could I forget it? I understand a little better now but still . . .'

He trailed off. He could not help admiring her for the unfailing courage and loyalty she had shown her brother, for the way she refused to be cowed by the superior forces ranged against her but managed to elude her would-be assassins and was now undertaking a difficult, dangerous journey, the outcome of which remained uncertain. She seemed to have discovered some hidden well of strength that had just been waiting to be plumbed. He had had an intimation of this potential, this suppressed life-force, the first time they met, and when he looked at her now, knowing her courage and what she was capable of, he felt himself falling even further under her spell.

'Why did you let things go as far as they did?' he asked.

'I didn't have any doubts about you until that evening on the base. Maybe it was the time and place. I must have needed more time to get used to the idea. Suddenly it was all too much and I couldn't go through with it. It wasn't your fault. Anything but your fault. It was all that crap to do with the military. Isn't that idiotic? I can't believe how stupid I was.'

Neither spoke.

'Well, I don't suppose the last twenty-four hours will have done anything to improve your opinion of Americans.'

Kristín sighed.

'I don't hate Americans. It's just that there's an army on Icelandic soil and I'm opposed to its presence. That's all there is to it.' She was anxious not to put him off. Steve had come to her aid voluntarily and she owed him. She had seen all that was good about him over the past twenty-four hours: his stoicism, his courage, his unlimited capacity for understanding.

'Let's change the subject. We should try to get some rest,' he said now.

'I'm glad I came to you,' Kristín said. 'I

305

don't know how I would have coped without you. Thank you, Steve.'

'It was a good thing you did. I always hoped we could somehow . . . I'd have approached things very differently if I'd known . . .'

He broke off.

'When this is over,' Kristín said, 'when all this is over, let's try again and see what happens. Would you be up for that?'

Steve nodded slowly. She kissed him.

'What was that all about?' he asked.

'No idea. The friendship between our two great nations, perhaps,' she murmured, kissing him again, this time on the mouth as she started tugging at the zips of his winter clothes. Women in wartime, her conscience reminded her, but she was past listening.

27

Lake Thingvallavatn,
Saturday 30 January, 2100 GMT

The second meeting between the Icelandic government and the American military authorities was also conducted in secrecy. This time it was held at the prime minister's holiday retreat on Lake Thingvallavatn, a four-bedroom house equipped with all mod cons, including a sauna and hot tub, and commanding a panoramic view of the lake. The minister for justice had joined the Icelandic contingent, and facing them across the table once again were the admiral, representing the American Defense Force at Keflavík, and at his side Immanuel Wesson, provisional head of the US embassy in Reykjavík.

The clock on the wall showed 9 p.m. exactly. At suppertime the prime minister had been notified by the police and air traffic authorities that a rescue team, currently on Vatnajökull, had passed on the message that armed US soldiers had been sighted on the glacier. Two members of the team who had apparently come into contact with them had subsequently been found — one dead, the other badly injured and not expected to live.

'The survivor's name is Elías,' an aide had told the prime minister, handing him a dossier. 'He's believed to be the brother of the woman Kristín who vanished from her home, leaving behind the body of a man called Runólfur Zóphaníasson.'

'Are the two cases connected?' the prime minister asked.

'It appears they are,' the aide confirmed. 'A wanted notice has been put out for her in the national media. This Kristín is also believed to be connected to a shooting incident in the city centre earlier today.'

'Do we have anything on that?'

'Not much as yet. It's believed that two or more Americans were involved in the incident. One of them is lying badly injured in hospital, the other fled on foot and we don't know where he is. Kristín's whereabouts are also unknown.'

Shortly afterwards, a report had reached the prime minister that two of the Defense Force helicopters were airborne and heading east. No flightpath or destination had been submitted, nor had air traffic control received any request for permission to fly through Icelandic airspace, as protocol demanded. Furthermore, the prime minister had been informed that an Icelandic Coast Guard helicopter was on its way to airlift the two rescue team members who had been found on the glacier, after the Defense Force's unprecedented failure to respond to an earlier mayday from the team. The violent storm that had been raging on the glacier was now dying down and members of the rescue team were heading towards the area where the troops had been reported. News of the events on Vatnajökull was spreading fast: the evening radio bulletin had carried a short but accurate summary and promised listeners that updates would be broadcast soon.

The prime minister's immediate reaction on learning of these developments was to summon the admiral from Keflavík to a meeting, but the admiral beat him to it. He phoned the prime minister, requesting an urgent meeting to be held in secret outside Reykjavík, adding that the US defense secretary was prepared to address them by telephone if necessary. The prime minister was audibly taken aback. He understood from the previous encounter that the operation on the glacier was a sensitive issue for the Americans, but surely there was no chance of suppressing it now?

He introduced the minister for justice, explaining that he had been briefed, before relaying the information that he had received about the latest events on the glacier and in Reykjavík. The Americans listened in silence.

There had been few pleasantries when the Americans arrived. The admiral seemed on edge, the general impassive. Unlike the admiral, he was in uniform, while the Icelanders in contrast were casually dressed in jumpers and jeans.

'Is it true that there are armed American troops on Vatnajökull?' the prime minister asked, once he had outlined the situation.

'You know why we have troops on the glacier,' the admiral answered, 'and I thought we had come to an agreement at our last meeting. It's what's known in military parlance as a simulation exercise, involving visiting NATO forces from the Netherlands and Belgium and revolving around a staged plane crash. There are approximately one hundred and fifty personnel involved. The troops are carrying blank rounds which are not under any circumstances lethal.'

'Why weren't we informed about the weapons?' the prime minister asked. 'At our previous meeting you only mentioned transporting that damn plane off the glacier and across the Atlantic. It was supposed to happen without anyone being any the wiser. Now a man has died. We were led to believe that it was a scientific expedition, not a war game. How do you explain this behaviour? This gross violation of our treaty? This insult? Your disgraceful conduct has put a severe strain on relations between our countries. A severe strain.'

'We are in no way responsible for what happened to the member of the rescue team,' the admiral responded. 'Furthermore, the exercise will be completed before noon tomorrow and our personnel will be gone from the glacier, leaving no trace of their presence. It's really not a major issue. I would like to think that we can stick to the explanation we agreed on: a two-day exercise, nothing more.'

'The rescue team has reported that your men are armed. The leader moreover suspects that the two Icelanders they found in the crevasse had in some way disturbed your activities. Is that possible?' asked the minister for justice, a bearded man in his early forties, with small, perpetually anxious eyes.

'We have no information to suggest that that is the case,' the admiral replied. The general had not contributed a word. He was occupied in looking around the room, at the Icelandic paintings on the walls, and outside at the veranda with its hot tub and the impenetrable darkness beyond, unrelieved by any lights.

'We are working under extremely difficult conditions in the field,' the admiral continued, 'but I can assure you that no one has given orders to open fire on Icelanders or indeed anyone else.'

'The shooting incident in the city centre earlier today — is that in any way connected to this matter?' the prime minister asked. 'Are your men shooting at Icelandic citizens now? All the evidence suggests that Icelanders have become some sort of target in your war games.'

'We are aware of the shooting but I can give you a categorical assurance that it has absolutely nothing to do with the operation on Vatnajökull,' the admiral replied. 'They are two completely unrelated matters.'

'And the two helicopters that have been dispatched from the base?'

'Three of our men were involved in an accident. Nothing too serious. The choppers are on their way to fetch them.'

'We have also been informed that you failed to respond to a mayday from the glacier requesting the assistance of the Defense Force helicopters,' the foreign minister intervened. 'Is there any truth in this?'

'I am not aware of that,' the admiral said, dropping his gaze to the table and shuffling his notes. 'I don't believe that such a thing occurred, though naturally I will have the allegation investigated.'

'There is one thing we need to ask you, gentlemen,' the general said, opening his mouth at last. All eyes turned to him. He cleared his throat. 'This rescue team — we want it out of there.'

He spoke brusquely, as if he had other better things to do than waste his time on diplomatic talks or making roundabout excuses like the admiral.

'What do you mean?' the prime minister asked, disconcerted. The admiral slowly closed his eyes.

'Out of there, I said. We want the team out of there. They'll ruin our exercise if they start interfering. We don't want them there. We want rid of them. Do you have a problem with that?'

The Icelanders looked at one another in

313

silent astonishment.

'Do you have a problem with that?' Wesson repeated.

'We have no authority over the rescue team,' the prime minister replied. 'We can't simply order them to stop. In any case, I gather they were already on the glacier before our last meeting. If you had given us sufficient warning about your intentions we could have closed the area to all traffic. But as you didn't see fit to . . .'

'Then we can't be held accountable for their welfare,' the general interrupted. 'I'm sure they'd think twice if they received a call from the prime minister.'

'I suggest you take care who you threaten, General,' the prime minister said in an even tone. 'One man has died on the glacier, another is critically injured, so please don't insult me by saying that it has nothing to do with you.'

'May I remind you, Prime Minister, that a sizeable percentage of this country's gross national income derives either directly or indirectly from us.' The general spoke in the same flat, emotionless tone, his face impassive.

'I don't think this meeting is going anywhere,' the prime minister said, rising to his feet. 'We'll be issuing a formal protest about this matter and demanding a thorough public investigation, both here and in America, into the accident involving the two rescue team members. We will close all roads between the glacier and the base until we have full and accurate disclosure about what is going on out there. We'll apprise the media of the situation and you can imagine how they will apportion the blame. I will address the nation personally. You can talk all you like about percentages. Good day.' Gathering up his papers from the table, he replaced them in his briefcase and closed it with a snap. The justice minister followed his example.

'There's a bomb on the glacier,' the general said, unmoved, his gaze still fixed directly ahead. 'You should call the team home, if only for their own sake.'

'A bomb? What do you mean, a bomb? What kind of bomb?'

'The kind that explodes. It's German and it's old and we're trying to remove it but it's a delicate operation. We have experts on site, our best men, but the rescue team is in danger. You have the power to stop them, thereby preventing a potential catastrophe.'

'There's a bomb on board the plane? What do you mean by German?'

'The German scientists brought it with

them. We believe we are dealing with a primitive hydrogen bomb.'

The prime minister was struck dumb; he could hardly believe he was hearing this.

'It's our first broken arrow,' the admiral added. 'We call them broken arrows, the nuclear weapons lost in air crashes or through other accidents. There are a small number scattered here and there around the globe and you will understand that we go to considerable lengths to control information about them. But the first, Prime Minister, is on Vatnajökull.'

'And it's still live and extremely dangerous,' Wesson added.

28

They were well equipped with powerful torches, good climbing boots and warm winter overalls provided by Jón but the temperature had risen after the earlier storm, turning the snow soft underfoot and making every step a struggle. The moon dipped in and out of the clouds, shedding a pale light on the rim of the glacier. The temperature was falling again.

In the end they had not managed any sleep but the rest had done them good. Before setting off, Kristín had tried once more, unsuccessfully, to reach her father, then had finally gathered enough courage to call the police. She was put through immediately to the detective investigating the city centre shooting. He listened attentively to her detailed account of the improbable events that had occurred and her explanation of why she had not contacted the police sooner. She concluded by telling him that she was now at the foot of Vatnajökull.

'So the man we found in your flat — Runólfur — had no connection with any of this,' the detective commented when Kristín had finished speaking. Far from disputing her account, he went out of his way to give the impression of taking what she said seriously. He did not want to risk making her hang up by arguing with her. It was late and the entire force was working round the clock on the shooting and murder.

'No connection at all,' Kristín confirmed; she had tried to give as clear and impartial an account as possible. 'In fact, I think he saved my life.'

'They told me at the ministry that you might have killed him and gone into hiding as a result. They thought it was plausible. But that, if so, you would have been acting in self-defence. They said this Runólfur bloke had been threatening you.' His voice, friendly, steady and sensible, had a calming effect on Kristín. She sensed she could trust this man and tried to put a face to the voice but somehow could not imagine what he would look like.

'That's why I didn't know where to turn. And because the men who attacked me referred to a conspiracy. They murdered a man in my flat. Don't you see, I was desperate?'

He absorbed this information. Kristín's account, crazy as it was, nevertheless tied in with what he had found out so far, and he could see no reason to disbelieve her. Her willingness to work with the police was obvious but he sensed the extreme difficulty of her situation.

'We detained the man from the Irish pub briefly,' the detective continued, 'but the embassy insisted he be moved to the US military hospital on the base. The Icelandic government conceded to their wishes, on condition that he doesn't leave the country.'

'That's insane. He'll be halfway across the Atlantic by now,' Kristín said.

'I agree. First Class.'

'And what about the other one?'

'We know nothing about the other man. We went to the embassy which is, as you say, crawling with soldiers, and talked to a general, some kind of stand-in ambassador, but couldn't prise anything out of him. We know they have something to hide; we need your help to find out what it is.'

Her manner was so convincing that he had decided to take a gamble and trust her, at least more than he trusted the Americans.

'I know what it is,' Kristín said. 'It's to do with the wreck of a plane on Vatnajökull and I'm on my way there now. I've only got a single name, Ratoff. That's all. Maybe he's in charge of the operation.'

'We've heard nothing about any plane wreck,' the detective commented.

'My brother saw it.'

There was a pause while the man on the phone thought.

'Why don't you come and see us in town and we'll try to sort it out from here.'

'It'll be too late. It would be better if you sent some of your people here. And why don't you get in touch with the rescue team on the glacier? The man in charge is called Júlíus. He can confirm what I've told you about Elías and Jóhann.'

'You know that a travel ban has just been announced for the Vatnajökull area due to a volcanic eruption alert? There have been newsflashes on all channels. They've declared a state of emergency.'

'Eruption alert? What bullshit! What do you think American soldiers are doing there if there's a risk of an eruption? What you mean is that the spineless, arse-licking government has kowtowed to the Yanks yet again.'

The detective suppressed a laugh. He was

beginning to like her. 'I believe the term is "fostering positive relations".'

'I'm on my way,' Kristín said again.

'You really ought to come in to the station and tell me more. What's this plane you keep talking about?'

'I haven't got time to go into it but there's something inside the wreckage that they're determined to hide. I don't know what. It could be anything.'

'And that's the big secret?'

'Exactly. It's up to you what you do, but I'm going to the glacier,' Kristín repeated, and ended the conversation. Part of her wanted to trust the detective, who seemed a decent man, but she knew the only way for her to uncover the whole truth was to go and find it out for herself.

Steve was four metres behind her and the gap between them was growing. The weather was still but cold. Their overalls creaked, the snow creaked and she felt as if her lungs were creaking too. Jón had given them very precise directions as to the best way to access the glacier, yet she was surprised to find how easy the route was, in spite of everything. The only thing holding them back was their lack of fitness. She could hear Steve puffing and blowing behind her, swearing profusely every now and then. She was out of breath herself, every footstep she took in the snow an effort.

Kristín did not know what to expect when she reached the glacier. Hopefully she would find Júlíus there and possibly even members of the Coast Guard. Besides notifying the police, she had called an acquaintance on the national TV news desk to ensure that the media would quickly start following up the rumours of American troops on Vatnajökull and the possible presence of a German World War II plane on the glacier. The Yanks would not be able to cover it up much longer and she had every intention of being on the spot when the story broke.

She had barely slept a wink since she woke up at the crack of dawn two days ago, dreading a confrontation with Runólfur at the office, and exhaustion was beginning to take its toll as she laboured up the steep slope to the ice cap.

'Do you know what I saw in you?' Steve had asked as they lay in bed at Jón's farm.

'Saw in me?'

'The first time I met you.'

'At that reception?'

'You seemed a bit lonely, as if you didn't

know many people.'

'Receptions are not my favourite . . .'

'I've never had such a powerful response to anyone.'

'What do you mean?

'I'm not sure what it was. It's hard to explain.'

'What response?'

'I saw . . . I knew at once that I . . . I wanted to get to know you, to find out who you were, hear you speak, see you laugh and smile, be with you, just you and me.'

Kristín smiled. 'You're not very good at this, are you?'

'No, I guess not,' he replied, smiling. 'I'm just trying to tell you how I felt the first time I saw you.'

From Steve, Kristín's thoughts moved on to Elías. He would have made light work of a climb like this and teased her for being such a wimp. Well, he had finally succeeded in forcing her out into the wilderness. She saw the rim of the glacier drawing nearer in the moonlight. A little way to the east the land was scored by deep gullies and ravines, in one of which Jón had found the German.

She pictured her brother in the hands of the soldiers, and lying, critically injured, at the bottom of the crevasse. It was not the first time she had suffered this choking sensation on Elías's account.

She had been eighteen, Elías eight, and she had sent him to the shop for a bottle of Coke. When he came out of the shop, she heard later, he had run straight into the road without looking and was hit by a car. He landed on the bonnet, bounced on to the windscreen, shattering it, then was flung over the roof, fetching up on the road. He was knocked unconscious and a large pool of blood had accumulated under his head. They did not live far from the shop, so Kristín had heard the shrill sirens accompanying the arrival of police and ambulance, and knew instinctively that they were for Elías. She set off at a run and saw men lifting his small frame off the road and into the ambulance. Kristín could see no sign of life in her brother. The driver who had hit him was sitting on the kerb, clutching his head in despair and a group of bystanders had gathered. She walked over to the ambulance in a daze and was permitted to ride with Elías to the hospital.

Elías was in surgery for eight hours. He had cracked his skull and suffered a brain haemorrhage; he had also broken a leg and two ribs, one of which had pierced his right lung, and fractured his right arm in two places. Kristín sat in the waiting room, consumed with guilt, rocking to and fro, staring into space, now and then emitting anguished whimpers from deep within. She had sent her brother out for a bottle of Coke and now he was dying.

Her parents cut short their holiday in the Canaries and flew home, but only after she had managed to convince them that Elías was seriously injured. They blamed Kristín not only for what had happened to him but also for spoiling their holiday; she had found it hard to tell which upset them more. She was supposed to look after her brother. It had always been that way. They had placed the responsibility on her shoulders and she had failed.

She would never be free of the guilt. Even though Elías later made a full recovery, the guilt remained deep inside her like a malignant tumour that could not be excised. Stranger still, she could never shake off the conviction, however absurd, that if anything happened to Elías later in life, it would be because of the accident, because of his head injury. That because of her, he might be more vulnerable to falls or car accidents. That was why she could not bear his lust for adventure — the skydiving, scuba diving, glacier trips — and did her best to curtail such activities. She often felt that he went out of his way to provoke her, yet she had never told him of her fear, of the guilt that gnawed away inside her. Did not dare put it into words. Perhaps she had bottled it up inside her until she needed it, like now.

'Wait for me,' Steve shouted and she realised that she had forged far ahead.

Work on the glacier was proceeding at full speed again. The snow had been cleared from one side of the Junkers but the other was still surrounded by deep drifts. Nevertheless, men were busy fixing slings around the front half of the plane. Ratoff was expecting two helicopters. As soon as the slings had been fixed around the fuselage, the bodies would be put back inside the cabin and the opening would be sealed off, enabling the helicopters to remove all the detritus in one go. Inevitably the use of the choppers would compromise the secrecy of the mission, but the men would spread tarpaulins over the wreckage in an attempt to disguise it. Not that Ratoff was worried about rumours: the more the better.

The head of communications gestured to the radar screen. A cluster of small green dots was crawling down the glass, their

movement so slow as to be almost impercep-
tible.

'The rescue team is on the move, sir.'

'Get me the embassy,' Ratoff ordered.

Ratoff watched the two dots approaching
from the south, crawling slowly up the green
radar screen in the communications tent.
He saw the rescue team converging from
the north, creeping down the screen. He
was prepared and had sent soldiers to
intercept them in an attempt to stop or at
least delay them, but the two dots in the
south were a mystery to him. He wondered
if it could be that pain-in-the-ass of a girl
from Reykjavík, the young man's sister. His
mouth twisted in a smile: she had certainly
made fools of Bateman and Ripley, even put
one of them in hospital.

A reception committee was on its way to
meet them at the edge of the glacier. Incidentally, he noted from the screen that the
troops he had sent in the opposite direction
to meet the rescue team had come to a halt.

29

Vatnajökull Glacier,
Saturday 30 January, 2315 GMT

Júlíus watched the soldiers approaching, the powerful headlamps of their snowmobiles lighting up the darkness. There were about twenty of them, clad in helmets and goggles which completely obscured their faces, with rifles slung over their backs. Within a minute they had halted in unison and stood waiting for the rescue team, as if they had drawn an invisible line that they had every intention of defending. Júlíus's team consisted of some seventy men and women, travelling on skis, snowmobiles and two tracked vehicles. As they neared the soldiers, Júlíus signalled to them to slow down, and they eventually came to a standstill about ten metres from the waiting troops. It was an improbable meeting in the dark, snowy wasteland: the troops armed with automatics and revolvers, clad in Arctic camouflage, the winter uniform of soldiers who wished to pass unseen, and facing them, the un-armed Icelandic rescue team whose luminous orange jackets recalled, in contrast, the necessity of visibility in their work.

Júlíus, who was travelling in one of the tracked vehicles, told his team to stay put while he talked to the soldiers. He stepped out of his vehicle and walked towards the waiting men, noticing as he did that one of them dismounted from his snowmobile and came forward to meet him. The other soldiers rapidly followed suit. They met halfway, standing not quite toe-to-toe. The officer pulled the scarf down to uncover his mouth but even so Júlíus found it hard to make out his face behind the goggles. He looked young, though, much younger than Júlíus himself.

'You have entered a US military prohibited zone,' the officer announced in American-accented English. 'I have orders to prevent you from proceeding any further.'

'What do you mean a US military prohibited zone?' Júlíus responded. 'We've heard nothing about any prohibited zone.'

'I am not at liberty to reveal any further details. The zone won't be in force for long but whilst it is we insist that it is respected. It would be simplest for everyone if you co-operated with these instructions.'

Anger welled up inside Júlíus. He had seen the broken bodies of his team members lying at the bottom of a crevasse, one dead, the other unlikely to live, and was convinced that the men in white camouflage were behind the apparent accident. And now, to cap it all, these foreign soldiers were trying to deny him free movement in his own country.

'Cooperate! You're a fine one to talk about being cooperative. What are you up to here? Why did you have to kill one of my men? What's this about a plane on the glacier? What's all this fucking secrecy?'

'I need to ask you to hand over all your communications equipment, mobile phones, walkie-talkies, and any emergency flares,' the officer ordered, ignoring Júlíus's question.

'Our communications equipment? Are you insane? We're responding to a distress signal from your so-called prohibited zone. There are Icelanders in danger . . .'

'You are mistaken. There are no Icelanders in this area apart from yourselves,' the officer interrupted. He remained calm and impassive, though his tone betrayed a hint of impatient arrogance. Júlíus took exception to his conceited manner; under any other circumstances, this was a man he would be only too happy to punch. He was not afraid of the other soldiers and their guns; the entire situation seemed farcical and unreal more than dangerous.

'And what if we refuse? Will the American army shoot us?'

'We have orders.'

'Well you can shove your orders up your arse. You have no right to stop us. There is no prohibited zone on the glacier. All we've heard about is a volcanic eruption alert but I bet that's a fabrication as well. You have no right to throw your weight about in Icelandic sovereign territory. And you certainly aren't having any of our equipment.'

They stood eye to eye. A biting northerly wind was blowing over the glacier, sending loose ice crystals rippling across the surface like smoke. The rescue volunteers stood in a silent pack behind Júlíus, showing no sign of fear in the face of armed soldiers. Like their leader, they had no intention of being pushed around by a foreign military power.

'We're carrying on,' Júlíus announced.

He turned and walked back towards his team, so failed to notice the officer signalling to the man nearest him. The soldier removed his rifle from his back and knelt to assume a firing position. Júlíus had almost reached the first tracked vehicle when a volley of shots rang out. Instantly, the grille and bonnet of the vehicle in front of him were riddled with holes, the silence split by a deafening series of cracks as the bullets punctured the steel. Júlíus flung himself down on the ice. Fire blazed up from the engine and a small detonation blew the bonnet sky-high, to land with a crash on the roof of the vehicle. The members of the rescue team who were sitting inside it kicked open the doors, hurled themselves out on to the ice and crawled to safety. Soon the entire vehicle went up in flames, illuminating the winter darkness.

The shooting stopped as quickly as it had started. His breathing coming in gasps, heart hammering in his chest, Júlíus rose up from the ice, stunned at what had just happened. Calmly, the young officer walked right up to him again. The soldiers had all unslung their weapons and now had the rescue team comprehensively covered.

'Your mobile phones, radios and emergency flares,' the officer repeated in the same flat, toneless voice. Júlíus stared at the flaming wreckage. He had never experienced anything like this before, never encountered military force, or seen weapons used in combat, and for a moment his anger gave way to trepidation about what might await him and his team. He tried to penetrate the soldier's goggles, taking in the grey forest of weaponry behind him. None of the men's faces were visible. His gaze turned to his own people, some of whom had fled the burning vehicle while the others were standing at a loss by their snowmobiles. It was fifteen degrees below zero on the glacier and he could feel the warmth from the blaze.

Kristín spotted them first. She and Steve had approached the glacier at a point where the edge was not particularly high or steep, so they barely noticed the change in terrain from snow-covered rocks to ice and were already some way on to the surface of the ice cap when she saw lights ahead in the darkness. Four snowmobiles. She had stopped to wait for Steve who had been lagging behind again. By the time he caught up the snowmobiles had reached her.

Both had the same thought as their eyes met. They had assumed that the glacier would be kept under close surveillance, so it came as no surprise that a reception committee had been sent to meet them, but the speed at which they had been intercepted was shocking. There was no hope of outrunning the snowmobiles, but then they had no intention of trying. As the familiar sensation of fear bloomed again in Kristín, she reminded herself that those who needed to know had been informed of what was happening. That was her life insurance. Whether it would work or not was another matter. She and Steve stood still and waited. Strangely, given the circumstances, it was her feet that preoccupied her at that moment. From painfully cold they were beginning to turn numb, despite the extra pair of woollen socks that Jón had lent her.

The four men surrounded them on their snowmobiles. One, whom Kristín took to be the officer in charge, switched off his engine and dismounted. He was clad in goggles and Arctic survival gear like the other three, with thick gloves on his hands. He drew the scarf down from his mouth.

'I must ask you to turn around and leave the glacier,' he said. 'You have entered a US military prohibited zone.'

'Prohibited zone?' Kristín repeated contemptuously. She knew instinctively that these were the soldiers her brother had seen, perhaps precisely those who had intercepted him on the glacier. Perhaps the very men who had thrown him into the crevasse.

'Correct. A US military prohibited zone,' the soldier repeated. 'We have permission to carry out exercises here. The area is closed to all unauthorised personnel. Please turn back.'

Krístín stared at him and had difficulty hiding her feelings. Rage boiled up inside her. After all the trials she had gone through since the two men burst into her flat, at last she was standing face to face with the truth. These soldiers were proof that the US army was involved in activities on the glacier that would not tolerate the light of day. They were proof that her brother had not had an accident but had seen something he was not supposed to see. And now this man was standing in front of her, giving her orders; an American soldier throwing his weight around in her country as if he ruled the place.

'Turn back yourself,' she snarled, snatching at his goggles and looking him in the eye. He jerked his head away and the goggles snapped back on to his nose. The cold intensified the pain and, momentarily losing control of himself, he struck Krístín in the face with the butt of his rifle, knocking her on to the ice. Steve tried to jump him, seizing him around the shoulders, but the soldier drove the butt into his stomach with all his strength and Steve bent double and fell to his knees, winded. As she tried to pull herself up, Kristín was bleeding from mouth and nose but the officer shoved her down with his foot, knocking her flat on her back again.

'Turn back,' he ordered.

'Tell Ratoff I want to meet him,' Kristín choked.

'What do you know about Ratoff?' the officer asked, unable to conceal his surprise and realising belatedly that he had said too much.

Kristín smiled despite the cut on her lip.

'I know that he's a murderer,' she replied.

The soldier stared at her impassively and then at Steve, as if wondering what action to take. After weighing up the options, he fished a mobile phone from his breast pocket, punched in a number that was answered instantly, and stepped aside, making it hard for Kristín to hear what he was saying.

'A male and a female, affirmative, sir,' he said in a low voice. 'She knows your name. Just a minute, sir.' Turning, he walked back to where Kristín lay, propped up on her elbows in the snow.

'Are you Kristín?' he asked.

She met his gaze without answering.

'Do you have a brother who was up here on the glacier yesterday?' the officer asked.

'I don't know. You tell me,' Kristín hissed from between clenched teeth.

'That's right, sir,' the officer said into the phone. 'Understood,' he added, then ending the call, turned to his men.

'We're taking them with us,' he announced.

30

Vatnajökull Glacier,
Sunday 31 January, 0000 GMT
He lost control — Kreutz, that is. He looks like
he must be the youngest, in spite of his rank.
At first he was talking calmly to his companion,
but he grew more and more agitated until he
was screaming at him. I couldn't understand a
word they were saying. I don't know what it
was but something made him go completely
crazy. He jumped to his feet and began pac-
ing back and forth, hammering the cabin door,
shouting and thumping on the fuselage. In his
madness he knocked over one of the kero-
sene lamps and we haven't been able to
relight it since. The other German tackled him
and eventually overcame him after a hell of a
fight in the cramped space. I kept out of it in
the cockpit. There isn't really enough light left
for writing as we only have one lamp that
works now. The kerosene is running low. Soon
we'll be in total darkness.

Maybe they were arguing over whether it had been a mistake to sit tight, instead of following Count von Mantauffel. The storm and cold were so severe when we landed that you couldn't stand up outside, though von Mantauffel didn't let that hinder him. Our attempts to force the door off its hinges are in vain. The plane will be our tomb and I suppose that fact has started to come home to us all. We're slowly dying inside a coffin made of metal and ice.

We've lost track of time. It could be two or three days since we landed. Maybe longer. Hunger is becoming an increasing problem. There's nothing to eat and the air in the cabin is very stale; I suppose the oxygen's not being replaced quickly enough. The Germans are dozing. They haven't taken any notice of me since the crash. At the time they were mad at me, yelling until von Mantauffel ordered them to shut up. I wish I understood more German. I would have liked to know what this mission is about. I know it's important, otherwise you wouldn't have sent me, but what's it all about? Why are we collaborating with the Germans? Aren't they our enemies any more?

Ratoff's reading was interrupted.

'Phone call from Carr, sir,' a soldier called into his tent. Ratoff trod the same short walk back to the communications tent and took the receiver.

'The Icelandic government are coming under increasing pressure over the military exercises on the glacier,' Carr began, without preamble. He was speaking from the base in Keflavík where, twenty minutes earlier, his plane had landed and taken off again immediately after refuelling. Carr himself planned to personally accompany the Junkers back across the Atlantic in the C-17. He had had a brief meeting with the admiral who had told him of the Icelanders' mounting anger at the presence of the army on Vatnajökull. The lie about the volcanic eruption alert would not work for long. Time was running out and the situation was deteriorating with every passing minute. He was afraid of being stranded here with the German plane and the bodies and the secret connected to them. The Icelandic government was growing ever more impatient and a diplomatic catastrophe loomed which would send shockwaves around the world.

'We'll be gone from here in no time, sir,' Ratoff reassured him. 'We're just waiting for the choppers.'

'We don't want any more bodies,' Carr said. 'We don't want any more disappearances. Get yourselves off that glacier and vanish into thin air. Is any of that unclear?'

340

'None, sir,' Ratoff replied. He avoided any mention of the rescue team or Kristín.

'Good.'

Ratoff handed the phone to the communications officer and stepped outside. In the distance he heard the massive rotors of the Pave Hawk helicopters beating as they came powering in from the west, two pricks of light growing larger in the darkness. His men had prepared a landing site on the ice with two rings of torches, and launched four powerful flares that hung in the air like lanterns and blazed for several minutes, throwing a bright orange-yellow light over the entire scene. The Pave Hawks flew into the glow cast by the flares and hovered for a moment above the tents before settling with infinite care on the ice like gigantic steel insects, the noise deafening, clouds of snow whipping up all round. The men on the ground took cover until the engines had died and the blades finally stopped turning, their whine fading in the cold air. When the doors opened and the crews clambered out, they were directed straight to Ratoff's tent. Soon all was quiet again.

The pilots looked around in astonishment at the floodlit scene: the city of tents pitched in a semicircle around the plane, evidence of its excavation from the ice, the swastika instantly identifiable below the cockpit, the camouflage paint flaking off to reveal the gunmetal grey beneath, the special forces personnel swarming all round and over the wreckage. The fuselage had been cut in half but they were unable to see inside because plastic sheeting had been fitted over the yawning mouth of the exposed cabin. They glanced at one another and back at the wreckage. They had been given no reason for their summons in the middle of the night to Vatnajökull; their orders were simply to airlift some heavy equipment off the ice cap and ask no questions, their destination the C-17 transport that had been on standby at Keflavík Airport for three nights.

Ratoff greeted the helicopter crew members. There were four men, two per machine, aged between twenty-five and fifty and clad in the grey-green uniform of the US Air Force. They had already removed the thickly lined leather jackets and helmets they wore on top when they entered Ratoff's tent. They did not recognise the operation director and plainly had no idea what was happening on the glacier. They looked from Ratoff to one another, exchanging puzzled glances.

Ratoff studied the pilots. He could tell

from their expressions that they had had minimal briefing on the purpose of the mission. They seemed unsure of themselves, shifting from foot to foot and looking about uncomfortably, but he had no intention of putting them at their ease.

'We're going to airlift the wreckage of an old plane from the glacier to Keflavík Airport,' he announced.

'What plane is that, sir?' one of the pilots asked.

'A souvenir,' Ratoff replied. 'Don't worry about it. We've cut it in two, so the helicopters can take one half each. We're grateful for your assistance but the operation should be straightforward. I recommend you stay put in the tent as it would be best for everyone if you avoided compromising your plausible deniability. Is that understood?'

'Compromising our what?' one of the pilots queried, looking at the others to see if he was alone in being baffled by these instructions. 'May I ask what's going on here?'

'That's precisely what I mean,' Ratoff said. 'The less you know, the better. Thank you, gentlemen,' he concluded, indicating that the conversation was over. But the pilot was not satisfied.

'Is it the German plane, sir?' he asked

hesitantly.

Ratoff stared at him, amazed that this man sought to question him. Had he not been adequately clear?

'What do you mean, "the German plane"?' he asked.

'The German plane on Vatnajökull,' the pilot answered. He was young, fresh-faced, and his lack of guile made him hard for Ratoff to read. 'I've heard about it before. I saw the swastika.'

'And just what have you heard about this German plane?' Ratoff asked, moving closer.

'In connection with the astronauts, sir.'

'What astronauts?'

'Armstrong, sir. Neil Armstrong. He went looking for it in the sixties. Or so the story goes. It's supposed to have a bomb on board — a hydrogen bomb. If that's the case, if I'm going to be flying with it strapped to me, I'd like to know about it. From an operational point of view, of course, sir.'

'Is that the rumour on the base?' Ratoff mused. 'Nazis, Armstrong and a hydrogen bomb?'

'So is there a bomb? Can we see inside the plane? Regulations mean I need to verify what we're going to be transporting, sir.'

'I'm afraid you'll just have to trust me, Flight Lieutenant, when I tell you that there is no bomb in the plane. The aircraft is German, obviously, and dates from World War II, but it's completely safe. This is the first I've heard of Armstrong looking for it and certainly the first I've heard of any Nazi bomb. We haven't found anything of the sort. Satisfied?'

'I guess so, sir,' the pilot said uncertainly.

'If it's so harmless,' another pilot asked, 'why can't we watch, sir? Why do we have to stay cooped up in the tent?'

'Jesus Christ,' Ratoff exclaimed under his breath. He sighed. 'How many different ways can I put this, gentlemen? I am not required to give you any explanations.' He went outside and beckoned three soldiers into the tent. 'Shoot anyone who tries to leave,' he ordered.

The pilots stood in a huddle, shuffling together like stunned livestock, utterly baffled by this latest development. Brought to the middle of nowhere, witness to some inexplicable excavation, bound to secrecy and now held hostage by their own side, they stared speechlessly at one another and at their captor.

'What's the meaning of this?' demanded their leader at last. 'What kind of treatment do you call this? How dare you? Who'll fly the helicopters now?'

'We have people for that. You're surplus to requirements,' Ratoff said and stalked out of the tent. A man stood waiting to join him as he walked down to the plane.

'How was the flight?'

'Like a dream,' Bateman answered with a grin.

31

Kristín was met by an extraordinary, utterly surreal sight, a scene from science fiction. Perhaps it was the exhaustion that now coursed through her limbs like a dull drug, but all at once she felt she was losing her grip and succumbing to an overpowering sense of helplessness. Everything that had happened to her was reduced to a jumble of hallucinations, a long, intense nightmare in which she was on the run but could never move fast enough. Was she in fact still lying at home on the sofa? The sight that met her eyes made it hard to put the events in any sort of context, hard to distinguish between this outlandish reality and her own delirious imaginings.

She saw the Pave Hawk helicopters perched side by side, their immensely long rotor-blades extending in all directions.

About thirty tents of varying sizes were arranged in a semicircle; snowmobiles, tracked vehicles, trailers carrying oil-driven engines and portable generators, floodlights and satellite dishes and a host of other equipment she could not put a name to littered the area. Scores if not hundreds of personnel were milling around on the ice. Some, she now noticed, had begun to take down the tents — they were starting to clear up after themselves. She understood. They were finished here. Soon there would be no trace of them: the snow would obliterate their tracks. Deep down the realisation struck her, triggering a warning bell that gradually restored her wandering wits: they were leaving the glacier.

Only then did she see the plane. It lay, cut in half, in a shallow depression in the ice. Two groups of people were busy fixing strong, thick slings around each half, attached to cables which extended in the direction of the helicopters. Evidently the helicopters were there to remove the plane wreckage and after that it would not take the soldiers long to disappear too.

It was very still, several degrees below zero. The black vault of the night sky arched over the area, reflecting the glow of the powerful floodlights. The journey had been uneventful; she and Steve had been forced to ride pillion on the snowmobiles behind their captors, who maintained radio contact with the camp throughout. After fifteen or twenty minutes they had ascended a small ridge and the tents had come into view below them. The vehicles careered down the ridge and into the camp, stopping by one of the larger tents. She and Steve were shown inside, past two soldiers who stood guard either side of the opening.

'Are you okay, Kristín?' Steve asked once they were at the back of the tent, as far from the guards as possible.

'Yes, and you? Are you all right?'

As she looked at him, her thoughts strayed to what had happened between them at Jón's farm. For a brief moment her present surroundings faded and she pictured a future with him.

'Could be better,' Steve said. 'Could be at home watching basketball. There's a big game on tonight, Lakers against the Bulls.'

'It could hardly beat this,' Kristín said. Neither of them smiled. Looking at Steve, she saw her own anxiety reflected in his face.

She surveyed their canvas cell with a sudden sense of hopelessness. On the table sat a large gas lamp which lit up the tent and emitted a faint heat, but otherwise it was freezing inside. There were also four camp chairs and, at the back of the tent, close to where they were standing, they noticed several heavy canvas sheets spread out over the ice. She glanced towards the tent opening where the soldiers stood watching them.

'I want to speak to Ratoff,' Kristín called out but received no reaction.

'Shouldn't your rescue team be here by now?' Steve asked under his breath, the worry just audible in his voice. 'And the Coast Guard, or whatever it's called? And the police and reporters and TV crews? Where's CNN? Where's the cavalry?'

'I know,' Kristín said. 'Something must start happening soon. Look, let's think for a minute. How can we get out of here? What is this tent anyway? What are they using it for?'

She looked down at the sheets of canvas.

'What's this?' she asked in a low voice, backing further into the tent. Steve moved unobtrusively towards her. Distracted by the commotion outside, the guards had lost interest and gone back to watching the spectacle of a small army erasing all trace of itself. From under one of the tarpaulins, the corner of a grey body-bag could be glimpsed.

'What have they got here?' Steve whispered.

Kristín stepped on the corner of the canvas and drew it quietly towards her, then repeated the movement. Her legs were stiff from the walk up to the glacier and weak from lack of food; it took all her concentration to stop the muscles in her thigh from going into spasm. The canvas shifted and she continued dragging her foot until she had partially uncovered what lay beneath. The body-bag was open at the top, the heavy-duty zip which joined the bag's shiny grey folds drawn back perhaps ten inches. A peaked cap met their eyes, bearing the eagle and swastika insignia. When Kristín tugged with her foot a little more, a face appeared beneath the cap. They stared speechlessly at the body. It was a middle-aged man whose deathly pallor was almost as translucent as the ice. Kristín could hardly grasp what she was seeing; she stood in silent wonder, her attention riveted on this new discovery.

Her heart nearly stopped when a hoarse voice spoke behind them.

'Pretty sight, don't you think? As if he'd died no more than a week ago.'

Ratoff had entered the tent, with Bateman at his heel. Kristín instantly recognised the man who had twice tried to murder her;

she also knew in her bones that she was finally standing face to face with Ratoff. She had formed an image of him which in no way fitted the man before her. He was so short that she almost burst out laughing. She had imagined a man well over six feet tall, yet here he was, a man with no physical presence whatsoever; in spite of his padded ski-suit, she could tell that he was nothing but skin and bone. For a moment it crossed her mind that he might be suffering from some incurable disease. His features looked vaguely Slavonic: a bony face, the cheek-bones and chin jutting through the taut skin, a narrow, dead straight nose, and small, sharp, deep-set eyes. As he came closer she noticed that he had white rings round his pupils that made his eyes appear eerily bright. His ears were small and grew close to his head, and his mouth seemed to underline the cruelty above, but her atten-tion was drawn irresistibly to the scar under his left eye. She could not stop staring at it. It was round like a little sun, radiating tiny grooves down his cheek.

'You're not the first,' Ratoff said in his odd, rasping voice, noting the direction of her gaze: 'She did her best.' He scratched the raised purple outline of the old scar with one finger.

'I hope it hurt,' Kristín replied.

'An accident,' Ratoff said. 'The bullet went right through my face and out behind my ear. I lost part of my voice, nothing else.'

'Pity she didn't kill you,' Kristín retorted.

'She came close.' He smiled. 'Are you looking for your little brother, Kristín? I fear it may be too late to save him now.'

'Don't be so sure. He was alive the last I heard. It was a close call but if a shit like you can survive being hit point-blank, there's still hope for him.'

Ratoff considered this.

'Icelandic women,' he said at last, sliding his gaze over to Steve. 'I've read about them. They are fond of sleeping with foreigners. Are you, Kristín?'

'Fuck you,' Kristín growled.

The thin line of Ratoff's mouth twitched almost imperceptibly.

'It doesn't matter,' he said. 'We're finished. And the best of it is that we were never here.'

'Everyone knows. We've told everyone we could about you and the plane on Vatnajökull. It's only a question of time before the glacier is crawling with well-informed observers and you won't be able to throw all of them down a crevasse.'

'That's why we have to make haste. A pity I can't spend a little more time with you two first. Bateman would especially enjoy that.'

'So the asshole has a name,' Kristín exclaimed.

Bateman did not stir but Ratoff walked right up to Kristín, causing her to take an involuntary step backwards. His face touched hers. Looking deep into the small eyes, she saw nothing but cold revulsion. She breathed in his stale, sour smell.

'You look like you have more guts than your little brother,' he hissed from between his thin lips. 'How he could howl. How he screamed and cried. First when I put his friend's eyes out, then when I started on him. Whined and whined for his big sister. I thought he'd never stop. But she didn't hear him. She was too busy fucking an American. You should have heard him. Very moving, it was.'

He did not flinch, even when the saliva landed on his forehead and dribbled into his eye, just carried on in the same low, hoarse voice.

' "Kristín" he moaned, but his big sister never came.'

A special forces soldier appeared at the tent flap.

'They're ready with the choppers, sir,' he called.

Ratoff turned, wiping the saliva from his face. He glanced at Bateman and nodded.

'Load the body bags into the plane,' he ordered and started to walk away. He was halfway out of the tent when Kristín shouted at his back:

'I know about Napoleon!'

Ratoff stopped dead, then turned round.

'I said I know all about Napoleon,' Kristín repeated.

'You have no idea what you are talking about,' Ratoff said, entering the tent again.

'I know about the Napoleon documents,' Kristín continued, in a blind rage. 'Or Operation Napoleon, as it was known.'

'Tell me, Kristín. What exactly do you know about it? Or is it just a word you have heard? I'm afraid that's not much of a card to play,' Ratoff sneered.

'Everything. What the Germans were up to,' Kristín said, feeling her way blindly. 'I know what your precious plane is hiding. A secret in a briefcase. No bomb, no gold, no virus. Just papers.'

'Well, well. Let's imagine you do. Who else knows about Napoleon?' Ratoff asked, standing right in front of her again. His soulless eyes searched hers. He repeated his question and Kristín realised that she had touched a nerve but had no idea how to press her advantage. Her mind was blank. Under his gaze she felt paper-thin, transparent, exposed.

'Who have you told about Napoleon?' Ratoff asked, and Kristín saw a sudden flash of steel in his hand.

32

Vytautas Carr stood in the doorway of hangar 11 at Keflavík Airport, gazing out into the night, his mind preoccupied, his nerves frayed. Although he could not see the C-17 in the darkness, he knew it was being prepared for take-off. The two halves of the plane would be airlifted from the glacier imminently, and if all went according to plan, they would have left Icelandic soil within three hours. Then it would be over.

The Icelandic authorities were becoming increasingly agitated. More importantly, they were confident that they had legitimate grounds for protest and any hint of subservience in their relations with US officials had long been cast aside. The US embassy in Reykjavík had been questioned by the media in connection with the pub shooting

357

and also what the press described as the military operations on Vatnajökull. As if that were not enough, the Reykjavík police had learnt of troop movements on the glacier; someone in the force knew Ratoff's name and had been asking questions both of the embassy and also of the army authorities in Keflavík. A Coast Guard helicopter had been dispatched to pick up two men who were reported to have had an accident on the glacier. The Coast Guard were, moreover, aware that the Defense Force had failed to respond to a mayday from the men's teammates. Meanwhile Reykjavík air traffic-control had been tracking the movements of the Pave Hawk helicopters. It would not be long before this information leaked out and people began to connect it with the fabricated volcanic eruption alert that had been broadcast earlier on the radio; they would draw their own conclusions. By then it would no longer be possible to suppress the affair.

He had long reflected on the possible consequences if the purpose of the operation were exposed; not just the international outrage but also the consequences for him personally. It was his responsibility to ensure that the story of the plane never got out; he was in charge of the mission that had already cost two lives; it was he who had illegally deployed US special forces troops in the territory of a friendly nation and instigated a web of lies, fabrications and manipulation. The buck would stop with him. A few days ago he had been happily planning his retirement; now he was filled with trepidation about the future.

The first priority was to secure the plane wreckage and what it contained. What happened after that did not really matter. The remaining soldiers would return to the base and the admiral would invent some halfway convincing untruth to account for the presence of his men on the glacier. They would bombard the Icelanders with misinformation until any news about the army came to be regarded as suspect. The process had already begun. They could expect public anger, condemnation and hostility, but it would all be for show, since Iceland still could not decide whether it wanted the American army in its territory or not. Carr was not losing any sleep over the public reaction. Economic considerations would prevail in the end. In a week or two nobody would give a damn about US military manoeuvres on Vatnajökull.

The only real danger of exposure came from that woman, Kristín, but who would give her the time of day once the plane had left the country? Who would believe her crazed talk about a German World War II plane that had been buried in Vatnajökull for half a century, concealing something dangerous, incomprehensible, preposterous? Carr felt certain that she was ignorant of the real secret. How could she know? They had tracked her movements minutely and knew who she had spoken to before she went to the glacier; no, there was nothing to indicate that she knew or understood the reality. No lasting damage had been done. Carr kept telling himself this, willing it to be true.

His thoughts strayed to the director of the operation and he wondered if he had put his faith in the wrong man when he chose Ratoff. Ratoff could be trusted to get things done but he exacted a high price in human lives in the process. Back in the early seventies, Carr had personally recruited him as a military intelligence agent; he had proved his worth but no one who worked with Ratoff felt any warmth towards him. He was a man people would rather not know, would rather turn a blind eye to. Eventually he became a type of invisible operative within the service, the subject of unconfirmed rumours that most preferred to ignore.

Carr's knowledge about his background before he joined the organisation was better than most, but still sketchy. He had signed up to the marines in 1968 and served in Vietnam for two consecutive tours of duty. By the time he came from Vietnam to meet Carr he already had the scar. Ratoff had a simple explanation: an unfortunate accident; his rifle had caught between the door and door-frame in his barracks, firing a bullet into his face. The doctors had described it as a miracle that he did not hit an artery, his brain or spine, escaping with nothing more serious than damaged vocal cords. Carr, however, had sent a man to check up on his story who questioned the men in Ratoff's platoon and heard various different accounts: Ratoff was a sadist who could always be trusted to go further than anyone else in trying to extract information from the enemy, even when there was no information to be had; he had maimed and killed to his heart's content and it was said, though never confirmed, that he collected body parts from his victims as trophies. He would not have been the only marine to sport a necklace of human ears but Carr's stomach turned at the thought. What was common to their stories was that Ratoff got his wound when a young Vietnamese woman managed to seize his gun and force him down on his knees in front of her, shooting him in the face. She had shot herself dead immediately afterwards.

However distasteful his reported conduct, Ratoff had proved valuable to army intelligence in South America in the early seventies. He served in El Salvador and Nicaragua, then Chile and Guatemala, involving himself with the troops that the government sent in to support dictators. When the US government later cut back on its support for right-wing dictatorships following vociferous protests at home, Ratoff was relocated to the Middle East. There he continued with his old habits, gathering information by means that Carr preferred to remain ignorant of. He was stationed in Lebanon, serving for a period with Mossad. By this time Ratoff did not officially exist. His intelligence records had been taken out of ordinary circulation and Carr had become one of only a handful of senior officials who knew of his existence. That was another qualification to lead this operation. No one would miss him.

A piercing wind blew about Carr as he stood by the hangar, wondering what kind of race could endure living in such perpetual cold and dark. He did not hear the serviceman approach or speak, remaining sunk in his thoughts and unaware of him until the newcomer took the liberty of touching his heavy woollen overcoat. Carr started.

'There's a man here asking to speak to you, sir,' said the serviceman, who was dressed in air force uniform. Carr did not recognise him.

'He's come over from the States to find you, sir,' the man repeated.

'To find me?'

'Landed fifteen minutes ago, sir,' the man said. 'On a civilian flight. I was sent to inform you.'

'Who is he?' Carr asked.

'Name of Miller, sir,' the man said. 'A Colonel Miller. He landed at Keflavík Airport fifteen minutes ago, on a civilian flight.'

'Miller? Where is he?'

'He was in a hurry to see you, so we brought him here, to the hangar, sir,' the man said, looking over his shoulder. Turning, Carr saw a door open and Miller enter. He was wearing a thick green anorak with a fur-lined hood that almost completely obscured his gaunt, white face. Carr strode hurriedly over. This was the last thing he had expected; they had not discussed Miller's further involvement, indeed he had not heard from him since their previous meeting and he was completely wrong-footed by his sudden presence in the hangar.

'What's going on?' he called while he was still ten yards away. 'What's the meaning of this? What are you doing here?'

'Same pure, fresh air,' Miller remarked. 'I've never been able to forget it.'

'What's going on?' Carr repeated. He glanced at the men who had brought Miller to him, three intelligence agents in civilian dress who accompanied Carr wherever he went.

'Relax, Vytautus,' Miller said. 'I've always wanted to visit Iceland again. Always wanted to breathe this cold pure oxygen.'

'Oxygen? What are you talking about?'

'Would you be so good as to step aside with me,' Miller said. 'Just the two of us. The others can wait here.'

Carr walked slowly over to the hangar doors, each one a steel construction the size of a tennis court. They stopped in the opening where an overhead heater was struggling to keep the bitter cold at bay.

'The first time I came to this country,' Miller said, 'a lifetime ago now, at the end of the war, it was to meet my brother. I sent him on that mission and I intended to be there to meet him when he made a stopover with the Germans to refuel in Reykjavík. I was going to fly back with them. That was the plan. I know it's absurd, but I blame myself for what happened to him. It was selfish of me to put him in that position. I took him off the battlefield. Well, I was punished for that. He lost his life here in the Arctic instead. Died in the crash or froze to death afterwards — we never did find out which. Or I never found out. All because of that preposterous operation that should never have been set in motion.'

'What's your point?' asked Carr impatiently.

'I haven't heard anything from you. What have you found up there? Are there any bodies and what sort of state are they in? Do you know what happened? Tell me something. It's all I ask.'

Carr regarded his former commanding officer. He understood what motivated Miller; knew he had been waiting for the greater part of his life to find out what had happened to the plane. There was a light in his eyes now that Carr had never seen before, a gleam of hope that Miller was trying but failing to disguise.

'Most of them are intact,' he said. 'Your brother too. They've been preserved in the ice. Apparently the landing wasn't that bad.

They must have had to cope with a fire but nothing major. As you know, the weather conditions were severe when they crashed and they would have been buried by snow in no time and trapped in the plane. It's irrelevant, anyway. They couldn't have survived the cold even if they had dug themselves out of the ice. There are no signs of violence. It's as if they simply passed away, one after the other. They were all carrying passports and only one appears to be missing: Von Mantauffel wasn't on board or in the vicinity of the plane.'

'Which means?'

'Which might mean that he tried to reach help. Tried to get to civilisation.'

'But never made it.'

'No. I don't think we need worry about him.'

'Good God. He must have frozen to death.'

'Indeed.'

'Any personal documents on board?'

'Nothing that Ratoff has reported. Do you mean a message from your brother?'

'We exchanged weekly letters throughout the war. We were close. It was a habit we got into — a way, I suppose, of explaining to ourselves everything we were witnessing. I thought he might perhaps have written something down, a few words or thoughts, if he survived the crash. His regrets.'

'I'm afraid not, no.'

'And the documents?'

'Ratoff has them.'

Neither man spoke.

'You're complicating things,' Carr said. 'You know that.'

Miller turned and started to walk away. 'I don't want to lose him again,' he replied over his shoulder.

33

Kristín was transfixed by Ratoff, as a snake before a charmer. He had brought his face close to hers and was running the awl playfully up her throat, chin and cheek to her eye. She did not have a clue how to answer him about Napoleon but she had to say something — anything — to stall him; something he wanted to hear. It did not matter what. She had a sudden intuition that she was now in the same situation her brother had been in and understood how he must have felt, understood his terror of this man, his terror of dying. Understood what it was like to be this close to a maniac. Was it really such a short time ago? Yesterday evening? The day before yesterday?

What could she say?

'Kristín, your attempts to delay us are delightful. But pointless,' Ratoff said.

Kristín had retreated to a pole at the back of the tent. The two guards were restraining Steve. Bateman held a gun levelled at them.

'You think the place will fill with rescue teams,' Ratoff continued, 'that you'll be saved and the whole world will find out what's going on here. Well, I regret that this is the real world. No one can touch us here. We have the government in our pocket and the rescue team has been intercepted. What are you going to do, Kristín? We're leaving the glacier and after that no one will know a thing. Why is it your self-appointed duty to save the world? Can't you see how ridiculous you are? Now tell me from the beginning . . .'

'The choppers are taking off,' a soldier called into the tent.

'. . . how you found out about Napoleon.'

They heard the helicopter engines growl then roar into life outside and the rising whine of the rotor-blades that magnified as they spun faster.

'It was a retired pilot from the base who told us about Napoleon,' Steve shouted. 'And she's not the one who knows what it means, I am.'

'He's lying,' Kristín said.

'How touching,' Ratoff whispered.

Kristín did not realise immediately that he

369

had stabbed her — it felt more like a pinch. In one deft movement he had thrust the awl into her side just below her ribs, through her snowsuit and clothes, the steel penetrating several centimetres into her flesh. She felt a searing pain and blood seeping inside her clothes. He held the awl in the wound.

She cried out in agony and tried to spit at him again but her mouth was too dry. He twisted the awl and her eyes bulged as a spasm of pain racked her body, forcing a shriek from her lips. Out of the corner of her eye she saw Steve shouting and struggling in the grip of the guards.

'Who else knows about Napoleon?' Ratoff repeated, observing Kristín's reaction to the pain with scientific detachment. She stood on tiptoe, looming over him.

'Everyone,' she groaned.

'Who's everyone?'

'The government, police, media. Everyone.'

'I think you're lying to me, aren't you?'

'No,' she said in Icelandic. 'No.'

'In that case you can tell me what Napoleon is.'

He twisted the awl.

Kristín did not answer. The pain was unendurable. The wound must be ten centimetres deep. She thought she was going to faint; her mind was clouding over, making it hard to concentrate, hard to come up with the right answers to play him along, to keep stalling.

'What is Napoleon?' Ratoff repeated.

Kristín was silent.

'Have you asked yourself what they did to Napoleon?'

'Constantly,' she replied.

'And what can you tell me about that?'

'Plenty.'

'So what's Napoleon?'

'You know what he was famous for,' she groaned.

'A great emperor,' Ratoff said. 'A great general.'

'No, no, not that,' Kristín said.

'What then?'

'He was small. A midget like you.'

She prepared for another wave of agony. It did not come. Ratoff jerked the awl out of the wound and the tool vanished as mysteriously as it had appeared.

'Never mind,' he said, pulling out a revolver. Kristín had just long enough to register how small and neat it was, the sort of weapon she imagined might be designed for a handbag.

'I'm going to leave you with a beautiful memory. It didn't have to be like this. You could have saved him. Think about that on cold nights when you are alone. This is your fault.'

Without the slightest warning he half-turned and fired a single shot into Steve's face. A small, puckered hole appeared under Steve's right eye as his skull exploded and an ugly splatter coated the wall of the tent. He dropped instantly to the ground, eyes open, a look of bafflement fixed on his face. Kristín watched as if in a daze. The gunshot rang deafeningly in her ears; for a moment time seemed to slow down; she could not grasp what had happened. Ratoff was standing unmoving, observing her; the attention of the men in the tent was focused on Steve as the bullet hit home. She saw him fall on to the ice, his head striking the frozen ground with a thud, his dead eyes fixed on her face. She saw the obscene red streak on the tent wall, the ice under his head soaking up the blood.

Bile rushed up into her mouth. She dropped on to the ground, retching, her body shuddering. Then she blacked out.

The last thing she saw was Steve's empty eyes. But the last thing she heard was Ratoff's voice.

'This is your fault, Kristín.'

34

Vatnajökull Glacier,
Saturday 30 January, 2330 GMT

The team had settled down, some inside the two tracked vehicles, others alongside them, to wait and see what would happen. No one dared make a move against the soldiers or give them the slightest provocation to use their rifles again. After the soldiers had halted the rescue team, they had confiscated all communications equipment and conducted a thorough search of both people and vehicles, until they were confident that they had removed every flare, radio and mobile phone, before withdrawing to their original position. They seemed content to have impeded the team's progress and simply stood next to their snowmobiles, holding their ground and ensuring that the Icelanders could not proceed.

Júlíus climbed into the back of the second vehicle, taking care to sit beside a door.

After they had been waiting for some time he cautiously opened the door and slid out. The stand-off had calmed down and he sensed that their guards had relaxed. He lay for a long while in the snow underneath the vehicle, not moving a muscle. The chill gradually crept up his legs despite his thick ski-suit; his toes were agonisingly cold, his hands growing dangerously numb. He would have to move soon, if only to generate some warmth.

He heard the soldiers talking but could not make out what they were saying. After about ten minutes he crawled away from the vehicle, between two snowmobiles and away into the darkness. When he believed he was safe, he rose to his knees, peered behind him and saw that no one had spotted his departure. Rising to his feet, he set off in a wide detour around the soldiers, taking care to keep far enough away to be hidden by the night.

He seethed with fury; he was not going to let any bloody Yanks from the base threaten him, search him and rob him, abuse and attack his friends, or ban him from moving about in his own country. Besides, Kristín was relying on him. If he could support her account of the army's activities on the glacier, he would at least have achieved something. The shame and guilt of almost losing Elías burned in his chest; it was too much to bear that Kristín might also be in physical danger. Try as he might to rid his mind of these thoughts, he was haunted by the prospect of being responsible for both siblings coming to harm.

Soon the soldiers were behind him and, driven by a mixture of anger and distress, he broke into a run over the ice towards the glow which lit up the sky about three kilometres away. He knew the Americans would be monitoring the glacier closely and that he could expect soldiers to appear out of the darkness at any moment to arrest him — maybe even to use their weapons.

Júlíus was extremely fit and covered the distance rapidly, the freezing air burning invigoratingly in his lungs. At once, the flood of light ahead grew brighter and he heard a roar approaching; from behind him, helicopters swooped in and landed in the midst of the pool of light. He heard the drone of the rotor-blades diminishing until all was quiet again. Quickening his pace, he reached the margin of the lit-up area. There he slowed down and finally threw himself panting on the ice, before crawling the last stretch up a small rise which afforded him a good view of the area.

He had not known what to expect but what he saw was staggering. The two Pave Hawk helicopters, the wreck of an old plane cut into halves which were now being covered with tarpaulins. Soldiers swarming everywhere. Tents. Equipment. It defied explanation. He noticed the helicopter pilots being escorted to one of the tents and not long afterwards saw a woman being taken into another tent. He had never set eyes on Kristín, let alone the man who was roughly frogmarched in after her, but it was clear that they were captives of the soldiers.

At that moment he heard the snow creak beside him and, turning, encountered a pair of shiny, black boots. Following them upwards he discovered three men aiming guns at him. Like the soldiers who had intercepted the rescue team, they were wearing white camouflage, skiing goggles obscuring their faces and scarves bound over their mouths to keep out the cold.

Júlíus climbed warily to his feet and, not knowing what else to do, raised his hands in the air. The soldiers seemed content with this submission and, without a word, gestured with their rifles towards the camp. They had followed Júlíus from the moment he had appeared as a dot on their radar screens, approaching the prohibited zone by infinitesimal degrees.

All the way he made desperate efforts to memorise what he saw. He noticed that the soldiers were beginning to take down their tents and collect up equipment and tools, as if their work on the glacier, whatever it was, would soon be at an end.

On reaching the ragged, makeshift encampment he was brought before another man. This one was clearly an officer of some sort. There was no one else in the tent. He stared at the Icelander as if he had come from another planet, and it crossed Júlíus's mind that this was not far from the truth. When asked, he explained to the officer how he had slipped away from his team and made his way here under cover of darkness. He made sure to claim that there were other Icelanders in the area, lying that his men had received a message from Reykjavík before the soldiers had confiscated his team's radios that other rescue teams were at this moment on their way to the glacier, together with the police and members of the Coast Guard.

The officer listened, nodding and went on asking his monotonous questions:

'Has anyone else escaped from the guards?'

'No,' Júlíus replied. 'Is this an

interrogation?'

'Are you sure?'

'Why are you interrogating me?'

'Please answer the question.'

'I protest in the strongest terms about your treatment of an Icelandic rescue team. What on earth do you think you're doing? Who are you?'

'Are you alone?' the officer persisted, ignoring Július's outburst.

'Don't think this is over. I'm looking forward to telling the press exactly what's going on here; how you're jackbooting around in Icelandic territory, putting Icelandic lives in danger.'

They heard a whine, rising to a crescendo as one of the helicopters started up.

'Don't move,' the officer ordered. He walked over to the door of the tent where he saw Ratoff's back disappearing into the helicopter. With an even greater commotion, it gradually rose to hover thirty or forty feet above the ice. The noise was deafening and the helicopter whipped up so much snow that it could barely be seen. Below it, the dangling thick steel cables tautened and soon the fuselage of the old plane began to shift, inch by inch, off the ice, swinging in the glare of the floodlights. Higher and higher it rose, the helicopter then rotating itself westwards before setting off on its course and slowly melting into the darkness. The other would be minutes behind it.

When the officer turned back into the tent he was met by nothing but a man-high slit in the canvas wall. He leapt through it but Júlíus was nowhere to be seen.

Júlíus was fairly sure which tent he had seen Kristín being taken into and sprinted over to it. Without a moment's hesitation he slashed the canvas from top to bottom and stepped through the opening. He was met by a horrific scene. In the middle of the floor a man lay face down. One of the tent's walls had been spattered with blood and there was a gaping hole in the back of the man's head. A short way from him a young woman was prone on the ice, apparently unconscious. His heart lurched. Who else could these be but Kristín and Steve?

Júlíus stooped over Kristín's slack body and slapped her cheek repeatedly. Her skin was tinged with blue and cold to the touch. To his surprise, she opened her eyes after a few seconds and stared at him. Quickly he forced his hand over her mouth and laid his own face close to her ear.

'It's Júlíus,' he said. 'I'm alone.'

35

Vatnajökull Glacier,
Sunday 31 January

It was a close call: the helicopter nearly failed to lift the wreckage off the ice and for a moment it appeared as if it would plunge back to the glacier. It seemed that this half of the German aircraft had not been loosened sufficiently and the attention of the men standing around was fixed on the helicopter's battle with its cargo.

Ratoff had found himself a seat in the hold of the Pave Hawk and sat, hunched tensely at a small porthole, trying to get a glimpse of the steel cables and their load. The helicopter rose with infinite slowness, jerking slightly and stopping its ascent momentarily as it took up the full weight of the Junkers' fuselage. Little by little the wreckage rose from its icy tomb until it was free. Then the helicopter accelerated away and Ratoff watched the blur of the camp recede steadily into the surrounding night.

The noise in the cabin was mind-numbing but Ratoff was wearing earphones and could communicate with the two pilots in the cockpit via a helmet radio. They proceeded at a sedate pace, at an altitude of five thousand feet, the load dangling from three thick steel cables; this was the front half of the German plane. Before long the second helicopter would lift off the tail section, containing the bodies from the wreck. Both halves had been removed from the ice with their contents untouched and the openings sealed with heavy-duty plastic sheeting. He heaved a sigh of relief; the mission was in its final stages and had been largely successful, despite the inconvenience caused by Kristín and the rescue team. The plane had been safely excavated and he was on his way home. Soon it would be over, or this episode at least.

Ratoff was the only passenger. He tried to prepare his mind for what lay ahead while listening to the radio traffic between the pilots and air traffic control at the Keflavík base. The scheduled arrival time at Keflavík was in just over twenty-five minutes. Flying conditions were ideal — cold but windless — and the journey passed without incident. The helicopter would fly directly to the

C-17 and set down its load on a special pallet where each half of the German aircraft would be loaded on to the transport plane. The air force referred to it as the Keiko plane, after a killer whale which, with the world's animal lovers watching, had recently been flown to Iceland from Newport, Oregon. To save time and prevent discomfort to its unusual passenger, the C-17 had refuelled in mid-air and would do the same during the present mission. Very soon, the C-17 would take off and the Icelandic phase of the operation would be over. What followed would be a flight halfway round the world.

But the other half of his mind was elsewhere. Ratoff was working on the assumption that they would leave him alone until they reached their final destination, but he could not count on this. He considered why Carr had chosen him for the job. It had been Carr who had originally recruited him to the organisation but over the years the general had become increasingly remote until he no longer seemed willing to recognise his existence. Ratoff was reconciled to this fact. Though he was by no means his own master, he was able to decide his own movements and enjoyed a certain amount of freedom within the service, although he knew people disliked him. No doubt he troubled their consciences. After all, Ratoff did their dirty work; he gathered information. How he did it was his own business. The less the service knew about it, the less Carr knew, the better.

He had come to the conclusion while still on the glacier that the reason Carr had chosen him to lead the mission was because he regarded him as expendable. It would be a simple matter to make him disappear. He was an embarrassment, a relic from an era that no one wanted reminding of. Ratoff assumed that Carr knew precisely what the plane contained, along, no doubt, with a handful of other senior military intelligence officers. What he could not know was if anyone else was in on the secret. He was not even sure if anyone outside the army realised what was happening. For the first time he could remember in recent years, Ratoff was threatened, and the sensation awakened every animal instinct in him.

Where had that damned girl found out about Napoleon? The pathetic jerk with her had mentioned something about a pilot on the base but Ratoff knew that had been nothing but a desperate ploy. He could have extracted the information from her had there been time. No matter: Bateman would take over the interrogation, after which both she and her friend would disappear once and for all.

He recalled what he had read in one of the briefing documents from the dossier in the plane, a yellowing typewritten sheet, with a British War Cabinet Office letterhead.

. . . following the meeting in Yalta that Stalin would have excessive power in Eastern Europe and would no doubt fail to keep the terms of the treaties. The British War Cabinet has therefore drafted a plan for an Allied attack on Stalin's government in Moscow, which would result in the elimination of Russia. The plan has been assigned the codename 'Operation Unthinkable'. The war in the European theatre will be brought to an end by means of a treaty with the Germans, according to the terms of which approximately one hundred thousand German soldiers will join the Allies in the attack on Stalin, to be deployed in the front line of the first wave of the invasion. It is considered advisable to launch the eastward attack from north Germany, near Dresden. A second attack, to be launched from the Baltic, cannot be ruled out. It is assumed that the Russians will respond by invading Turkey, Greece, and even Norway from the north. It is also likely that they will attempt to secure oil reserves in Iraq and Iran.

The idea is not a new one and has been debated in the innermost circles where it initially met with overwhelming opposition. Its fiercest opponents regard negotiation with Germany as tantamount to entering into an alliance with the Nazis, who initiated the war that has laid waste to Europe. Recent discoveries in Eastern Europe have also confirmed suspicions about the organised extermination of the Jews. Another credible argument against Unthinkable is that the Russians more than any other nation have changed the course of the war, helping to secure an Allied victory at enormous cost to themselves.

Notwithstanding, there are those who believe they can shorten the war by several months, thus minimising further loss of life. They are looking to the future and fear how the world will appear if Unthinkable is not put into action. There is serious concern about what will follow the end of the war when the Yalta Treaty authorises Stalin control over almost half of Europe as well as the Baltic States. It is already clear that he cannot be trusted to keep the terms of the treaty. His policy of expansionism, this thinking suggests, will threaten the newly won peace in future years. The Prime Minister has referred in private talks to an 'iron curtain' . . .

Ratoff remembered something he had seen in the pilot's diary. The writing was almost illegible towards the end until only fragments could be made out, only the odd sentence, of which Ratoff could make little. Disconnected snatches about his parents, his brother, death. He remembered one sentence in particular. *I'm almost sure I saw Guderian at the meeting.* Guderian, Hitler's chief of staff towards the end of the war.

Ratoff started out of his reverie. The pilots had been trying to attract his attention over the radio and finally one of them shouted his name.

'A message from the glacier, sir, from someone called Bateman,' he said when Ratoff asked what was going on.

'What message?'

'He says she's vanished, sir.'

'Who?'

'Some woman. He won't say over the

radio. Doesn't trust us. The message is: she's disappeared from the camp.'

He ordered them to put him through; his earpiece filled with crackling static and radio distortion as they searched for the correct channel, then he heard Bateman's voice.

'It's incomprehensible, totally incomprehensible, sir,' Ratoff heard him say.

'Go after her,' Ratoff shouted. 'She must be moving away from the camp. She should show up on the radar.'

'No, she isn't. It's as if she's vanished into thin air. The surveillance system doesn't show her anywhere near the camp and we've turned the whole place upside down but she's nowhere to be found. Vanished into thin air. And we're dismantling the system so we won't be able to use it any more.'

A cold tremor of alarm went through Ratoff. He could not afford any more mistakes. They had fumbled their way through this operation and were on the point of getting out intact and now this infernal woman was once again jeopardising his success.

'There's another thing, sir,' Bateman said. 'We found a man in the tent in her place. He claims he's the leader of the rescue team. His name's Júlíus. He evaded our guards and it's obvious that he must have helped her. What do you want us to do with him?'

'Why wasn't I told about this man?' Ratoff snarled.

'There wasn't time, sir,' Bateman answered.

Ratoff looked into the dark oblivion beyond the helicopter's porthole.

'He knows where she is. Get it out of him.'

'There's no time for that. We're almost ready to move out. The first group will be setting off in a matter of minutes.'

The helicopter pilots were listening to the conversation with interest.

'Take him with you,' Ratoff ordered. 'Take him with you and for Christ's sake make sure he doesn't escape.' He would have to deal with him later.

36

The helicopters took off ten minutes apart but the second made better progress and had narrowed the gap by the time they reached Keflavík Airport. They flew straight to the C-17 at the end of runway seven, where each half of the German aircraft was lowered on to a special pallet which was then rolled into the transport plane. There would be no other cargo on this trip. It took no more than half an hour to load the old Junkers into the hold where it was swallowed up by the cavernous interior.

Ratoff strode hurriedly down the runway towards the C-17. He knew Carr was waiting for him on board but no other passengers would be crossing the Atlantic with them. The Delta Force operators would report back to the base over the next fifteen hours, bringing their equipment and vehicles, and the C-17 would make a return journey to fetch them.

By the time Ratoff reached the C-17, the rear section of the German aircraft was in the process of being loaded. He followed in its wake up the ramp and into a hold half the size of a football pitch, lit by powerful strip-lights. The Junkers' front section was already on board, looking tiny in the belly of the machine. Ratoff stopped to watch the manoeuvres, breathing in the stench of metal, oil and high-octane fuel.

'Everything went according to plan, I hope,' said a voice behind him. Turning, he came face to face with Carr. The general had aged since the last time they met, his ashen face was withered and his uniform hung loosely on his frame despite his imposing height. His eyes looked dull and weary behind his glasses and his shoulders sagged.

'For the most part, sir,' Ratoff replied.

'For the most part?' Carr queried.

'That girl is unbelievable. She managed to escape from the camp after we caught her, but it's irrelevant now. She won't be able to expose this,' Ratoff said, jerking his head in the direction of the Junkers.

'Has she found anything out, do you know?'

Ratoff thought.

'She's gotten hold of the name Napoleon,' he said eventually, 'but I don't think she knows its significance.'

'But you do?'

'Yes, sir.' Ratoff's gaze was steady.

'You've read the documents.'

'It couldn't be avoided, as I believe you anticipated, sir.'

Carr ignored this.

'Where on earth can she have heard the name linked to the plane?'

'Maybe someone on the base told her their suspicions. I didn't have time to interrogate her properly but I gather that she and her companion, Steve, had visited a retired pilot who fed them some half-baked gossip. When she mentioned Napoleon, it was a last-ditch attempt to play for time. I don't believe she knows what the name in the documents signifies.'

'She was lucky to get away from you alive. Not many do.'

'You knew what you were doing when you put me in charge of the operation, sir.'

'And what do you think of Operation Napoleon?'

'I haven't formed an opinion as such, but I do have the information,' Ratoff said, holding up the briefcase, 'and hope that we can come to an agreement.'

'An agreement?'

'Yes, an agreement, sir.'

'I'm afraid there's no question of any agreement, Ratoff. I thought you understood that.'

Three men suddenly materialised from the shadows and formed a ring around Ratoff. He did not react. As he watched them, he noticed that the other personnel had melted away and they were the only ones left in the hold. The only aspect that took him by surprise was how quickly Carr had acted. The general extended a hand for the briefcase and Ratoff passed it over without resistance.

Carr opened the case, took out some papers and examined them. They were blank, every page of them. He looked back in the case. Nothing.

'As I say, I hope we can come to an agreement,' Ratoff repeated.

'Search him,' Carr ordered, and two of the men held Ratoff while the third frisked him from head to toe. He found nothing.

'I prepared an insurance policy for myself,' Ratoff said. 'I don't know if the operation mentioned in the files was actually carried out — I don't have a clue about that, but I know about the operation and I'm guessing that knowledge is dangerous — as you've just confirmed. All that fuss: satellite images, expeditions to the glacier. The rumours about gold, a virus, a bomb, German scientists. All designed to mislead people over a few old papers. You must have known that I would read them, Carr. I knew as soon as I'd looked through them that I was in danger, so I have taken precautions to insure myself against whatever you have planned for me.'

'What do you want?' Carr asked.

'Why, to get out alive, of course,' Ratoff said, laughing drily, 'and hopefully somewhat richer.'

'Money? You want money?'

'Why don't we make ourselves more comfortable and discuss this?' Ratoff asked, eyeing the men surrounding him. 'I've been looking for a way to retire and I believe I may have found it.'

Carr made a final attempt.

'What are you going to do with those papers? As you say, the operation was never carried out. It was only an idea. A crazy idea, one among many, formulated during the dying days of the war. It has no relevance today. None at all. Why should anyone be interested? We can easily deny the whole affair as an unholy blend of rumour and demented conspiracy theory.'

'The papers name the island,' Ratoff said. 'Imagine a live broadcast from the island.'

'Even if we did pay you,' Carr said, 'and left you in peace, what guarantee would we have that you would leave it at that? That you're not concealing copies?'

'What guarantee do I have that you won't hunt me down and pay me a visit one day?' Ratoff asked. 'And how could I have made copies? We didn't take any photocopiers with us to the glacier and I don't carry a camera.'

Carr looked even wearier. He had predicted this scenario. After considering the negligible range of alternatives, he nodded at the three men. He did not have time for games, nor any intention of making a deal. Besides, he had never been able to tolerate insubordination, let alone this kind of subterfuge and betrayal. With the mission this close to completion, Ratoff's conduct seemed, if anything, pitiable.

'You're right,' Carr said, his patience audibly exhausted. He addressed the soldiers: 'Take him and find out what he's done with the documents.'

For the first time, Ratoff looked momentarily unsure of himself. Skittering across his unattractive face was the ghost of something that might have been fear.

'If I don't make contact by a designated time to confirm that I'm safe, the papers will automatically be released,' he said quickly.

'Then get to work fast,' Carr told the three men and turned on his heel. He did not hear Ratoff's protests of surprise and alarm because the aircraft's tail-ramp had begun to lift, sealing the aft door.

37

C-17 Transport Plane, Atlantic Air Space,
Sunday 31 January, 0500 GMT

At precisely three in the morning the C-17 took off and, after an hour's flight due west over the Atlantic, changed course, swinging in a smooth curve southwards. It was cruising at an altitude of 35,000 feet, making steady progress in perfect conditions, the thunderous drone of its engines filling the hold which stood empty but for the wreck of the German aircraft.

A heavy steel door connected the flight cabin to the hold. About two hours into the flight, the door opened and Miller appeared. He stepped forwards, closing the door carefully behind him. From where he stood, he could see that the floor of the hold consisted of dozens of rows of thick, mechanised steel rollers that worked like conveyor belts, over which military equipment and armaments could be moved. He was aware that CCTV cameras lining the hold made it possible to monitor the cargo from the flight deck but he would have to take that risk.

The temperature inside was several degrees below freezing and small fluorescent strips provided only a dim illumination. Miller shuffled carefully over to the German aircraft, his breath clouding around him, and began to loosen the tarpaulin from one of the sections, on the side where he believed the fuselage was open. He cut through the ties but, unable to pull the heavy sheeting from the wreckage, resorted to hacking at the plastic until he had made a hole large enough to crawl through. Groping his way forwards, with the aid of a powerful torch which he now switched on, he discovered that he was in the front half of the plane. He did not know which section they had stowed the bodies in. The roof was much lower than he had expected, the cabin surprisingly narrow. Once he reached the cockpit, he panned his torch around, taking in the broken windows, the old instrument deck with its switches and cracked dials, the joystick and levers with which the pilot had once flown the plane. His thoughts strayed to the young man who had last handled those controls and he pictured again, as he had countless times before, the moment of the plane's impact with the ice. After lingering briefly he turned and retraced his steps.

He tackled the ties and plastic sheeting on the other half of the wreck in a similar manner, not caring if anyone discovered that he had entered it. Being already surplus to requirements lent him a recklessness that he was oddly pleased to discover within himself. A lifetime's waiting was now at an end. Nor could he persuade himself to wait until they reached their destination; after all, he had no guarantee that Carr would keep his word — that he would be able to keep his word.

Carr had been minded to send him straight home to the States but he had managed to talk him round. Miller knew Carr of old: he had selected him to be his successor, a man of incredible resourcefulness and daring, utterly lacking in sentimentality. Carr had eyed him for a long time as they stood there in the draughty hangar before accepting that Miller could come along for the ride. Miller had no right to be there, even as former chief of the organisation, no right to interfere, no right to make any demands, and he knew it. But he also knew, as did Carr, that the circumstances were highly unusual; they were beyond protocol.

The unrelenting din of the C-17's engines had taken its toll on Miller by the time he finally succeeded in hacking a hole in the sheeting covering the rear half of the plane. Crawling inside, his head throbbing, he switched on his torch again, shone its beam into the tail-end and immediately spotted the unmistakable outline of the body-bags in the gloom. There were several, each two and a half metres long and the width of a man's shoulders, fastened with zips running their length. They had been set on the floor of the aircraft. The bags were unmarked, so Miller got down on the floor and began to struggle with the zip on the nearest.

He was met by the blue-white face of a middle-aged man in German uniform. His eyes were closed, his lips black and frostbitten, his nose straight and sharp, a thick mop of hair on his head. Miller half expected the figure to come alive and felt a renewed trepidation at the thought of finding his brother. He dreaded seeing the face he had known so many years ago, lifeless, bloodless, deep frozen.

Hesitantly, he opened the second bag but it was another stranger. By the time he reached the third he was beginning to have doubts — perhaps his brother's body was still lost in the wastes of the glacier, undiscovered and now surely destined to remain so for ever? He balanced the torch so as to illuminate the bag and, steeling himself, tried to unfasten the zip but it proved to be jammed. It was not completely closed though: a fairly large opening had been left. Not enough to enable him to see inside but enough to push his hands through and grip the sides of the bag. Tugging at the zip with all his might, he managed to haul it up, but when he tried to pull it down again, it jammed. He wrenched again and again until finally the zip gave way.

He was met by a face so different from the first two that his heart lurched. In the dim light of the torch and with his mind ablaze with memories, he believed for an instant that he was seeing his brother as he had been half a century ago. His lips were red, his cheeks ruddy, his skin pale pink. For an instant Miller was gripped by this unnerving illusion. Then it occurred to him that his brother must have grown his hair since their final meeting. This mouth, this nose, the shape of the face — it was all unfamiliar. In fact, he did not remember these features at all.

Miller reeled back, losing his balance, as the corpse, to his stunned amazement, opened its eyes and glared at him. He sprawled on the freezing metal floor of the hold.

'Who the fuck are you?' Kristín spat, rearing up out of the bag.

38

C-17 Transport Plane, Atlantic Air Space,
Sunday 31 January, 0515 GMT

She had kept up her ceaseless struggle with
the zip ever since she had been left alone,
but in vain. Now and then her mind drifted
back to the stomach-turning noise of a rifle
butt making contact with Júlíus's face, followed by the dull thud of his body landing
on the ice. More soldiers had entered the
tent and soon she had felt herself being
picked up and carried outside.

She had heard Ratoff telling Bateman that
the body-bags were to be placed in the
wreckage of the German aircraft and taken
away by the choppers. For a brief moment
no one was watching them in the tent as
the helicopters were taking off. Júlíus tried
to tear her away from Steve but he was not
strong enough. He yelled in her ear but she
behaved as if he did not exist. Bending
down, he struck her hard on the face and

she finally broke off her howling. He prised Steve's body out of her grasp and laid him gently on the snow. Kristín came to her senses and started frantically looking for a way out and saw some empty body-bags by the wall in the corner where the corpses were laid out. Júlíus did not understand when she indicated the body-bags to him; he merely tried to drag her out of the tent again. Still resisting, she pointed to herself and then to the body-bags, put her mouth to his ear and shouted:

'Help me into one of the bags.'

He stared at her, dumbfounded, then shook his head.

'No way,' he shouted back.

Tearing herself away from him, she ran to the bags by the wall and started opening the first one she reached. Júlíus knew their time had run out. His only thought was to save Kristín. Running over, he helped her unzip the bag and climb inside, then zipped it up again, leaving only a small gap. He laid the bag against the wall beside the other bodies just before the soldiers arrived.

The body-bag was very roomy, with handles at each corner. Four soldiers lifted it easily. She lay on her back, trying to keep still, making herself as rigid and inflexible as possible, regardless of what happened. Through the zip that Júlíus had left slightly open a tiny ray of light entered. She glimpsed the starry sky overhead.

The bag was dumped roughly on the floor of the plane and before long the light disappeared from the zip opening. She heard the noise of a helicopter again, this time directly above her head. There was an abrupt jerk as the wreckage began to lift away from the ice, then swung in the air beneath the helicopter as it set off on its westerly course.

She tried to open the zip and managed to force it down a few centimetres before it jammed. After that, no matter how hard she tried, she could budge it no further. Although she had sufficient oxygen to breathe, she was enveloped in impenetrable blackness.

She hardly felt the impact when the helicopter gently laid down the rear half of the plane on the C-17 transport pallet at Keflavík Airport, nor when it was driven into the yawning hold of the freight plane. She tried to envisage what could be happening, only guessing that she was on board a plane when the C-17 took off and she experienced that hollow sensation in the pit of her stomach that she always felt when she travelled by air. Her ears popped and the bass roar of the engines warned her that she was embarking on a much longer journey than she had imagined. She was still wearing the thick winter snowsuit but, although better than nothing, it provided limited protection against the cold that now penetrated the body-bag.

The damn zip was still stuck fast and she was beginning to doubt she would ever get out of the bag. At this rate, she thought to herself grimly, she would indeed end up in a mortuary, ready-wrapped. Her fingers were bloody from her battle and she was growing afraid that she would freeze to death from the cold when suddenly she heard a rustling sound from within the cabin of the German plane. Someone was close by. She saw a small beam of light through the gap in the bag. Could it be Ratoff?

She heard asthmatic wheezing and groans as if someone were struggling with something nearby, then all of a sudden there was fumbling at her bag. Ham-fisted attempts were being made to unfasten the zip. When it finally gave, Kristín closed her eyes and held her breath until she thought her chest would burst. As she opened her eyes at last, it was to find Miller leaning over her with a look of utter bewilderment on his face.

'Jesus Christ!' Miller cried, starting back, his eyes fixed on Kristín as she reared up out of the body-bag. Corpses coming to life — it was enough to kill a man.

'Who the fuck are you?' Kristín demanded, before he could gather his wits. 'Where am I? Where are you taking the plane?'

'Who are you?' Miller asked, stunned. 'And what are you doing here?'

She had climbed out of the body-bag and was on her feet, looming over the old man who had fallen back on to the floor.

'Your people killed my friend on the glacier,' Kristín said accusingly. 'My brother is hardly expected to live. I would like to know exactly what is going on.' Her voice rose: 'What's happening, for Christ's sake? What's so important about this plane that you're prepared to kill for it?'

She came close to kicking the old man in her desperation, her foot drawn back and her thigh tensed, but thought better of it just before she allowed herself the release of lashing out. Miller, prone and vulnerable on the ground, did not dare move a muscle. She was glaring at him as if demented and long moments passed before she regained control of herself, her features softened and

406

some of the tension left her.

Miller had recovered a little from his shock and sat up on one of the two crates of gold that were on board the plane. She glimpsed the outline of a swastika on the box.

'For God's sake, tell me why this plane is so important to you,' she begged Miller, then abruptly her mood seemed to change to alarm. 'Who are you? Where are we?'

'We're on board a US army C-17 transport plane on our way across the Atlantic,' Miller said in a level, soothing tone. 'You have nothing to fear from me. Try to calm down.'

'Don't tell me to calm down. Who are you?'

'My name's Miller.'

'Miller?' Kristín repeated. A memory stirred. 'Are you the man Jón talked about?'

'Jón?'

'The farmer, Jón. The brothers from the farm at the foot of the glacier.'

'Of course. Yes, I'm that Miller. You've met Jón?'

'He told us about you. Steve and me.' Her voice quavered but she bit her lip, forcing the repugnant image of Steve sprawled across the ice from her mind, and continued: 'You were in the first expedition. You had a brother on board the plane. Is that right?'

'I was looking for him when you . . .'

'You're looking for your brother?'

Miller did not speak.

He could not imagine who this dishevelled stowaway could be. But judging by her appearance and her troubled state of mind, he understood that he must be direct and polite, do whatever he could to reassure her. He had no idea who she was, did not know the ordeal she had endured, her flight from paid assassins, her search for answers, but little by little he managed to elicit her story.

There was something reassuring about this weary-looking old man, something trustworthy that Kristín responded to. He had said he was looking for his brother, just as she was — they had something in common — and she sensed that he genuinely wanted to hear her story, to know who she was and how on earth she came to be hiding in a body-bag in the wreck of the German aircraft. He listened patiently as she recounted the barely credible series of events, culminating in the tale of how Ratoff had killed Steve in front of her. She was to blame for Steve's death. He was gone because of her — her impetuosity, her selfish, pig-headed pursuit. Only now could she begin to absorb this awful truth. Her tale told, she hung her head, sunk in despair.

Miller sat and studied her. He believed her. She had been through an indescribable ordeal and he had no reason to doubt that she was telling the truth. She was obviously near the end of her endurance, yet she seemed calmer now and had taken a seat opposite him on another box. He shook his head over the absurdity of their situation.

'This Steve, did he work at the base?'

'Yes.'

'But they shot him anyway?'

'It was because of me. It was personal somehow. It didn't make sense. Ratoff said he would leave me something to remember him by. Then he shot Steve. He didn't need to. He just did it to torment me. Steve was nothing to him. Tell me, please, what's going on? I need answers. And where is Ratoff? Is he here?' she asked, looking distractedly around the dark recesses of the fuselage.

'You needn't worry about Ratoff any more. And as for the rest, you don't want to know,' Miller said after a pause. 'You won't gain anything by knowing. I assure you, you won't be any better off.'

'That's for me to judge. I haven't come this far to give up now. Do you even know what it's about?'

'Some of it. My brother lost his life because of an operation that was set in motion during the Second World War, an operation that has always been denied. In fact it's imperative that no one should know about it. No one needs to. Not you, not anybody.'

'How can you be so sure?'

'Believe me. I'll see that you get home to Iceland. I'll see that nothing happens to you but it'd be better for everyone, and for you too, if you stopped looking for answers. Try to forget what you've been through. I'm asking a lot, I know, but you have to trust me.'

'And Ratoff too? What about him?'

'Ratoff's an exception. Men like him are sometimes necessary but they can never be fully controlled.'

Kristín considered Miller's words. There was no way she could forget all she had been through; it was inconceivable that she should abandon the search now, after coming this far. She owed it to Elías to carry on, owed it to Steve to find out the truth once and for all. She would not give up, her conscience would not allow her to.

'When you said earlier that you were looking for him when I surprised you, did you mean your brother? Is he in one of these body-bags?'

'He flew the plane,' Miller said, as if to himself. 'We sent him to Germany, all the way to Berlin to fly the damn plane. I sent him myself. We were going to meet up in Reykjavík and travel across the Atlantic together, all the way to Argentina. The gold in these boxes was supposed to oil the wheels of the negotiations. They were to get more later. All of it Jewish gold. For bribing the government in Buenos Aires.'

Kristín studied him for a while; she saw nothing to fear in him, he was simply an old man searching for answers, just as she was. After a moment's pause, she continued with her probing.

'What was Napoleon?' she asked warily. 'Or who was Napoleon? And what was Operation Napoleon?'

'Where did you hear about Napoleon?' Miller asked, unable to conceal his surprise.

'I caught sight of some documents Ratoff had on the glacier,' Kristín lied. 'Saw the name there. I assumed that they'd come from the plane. That they'd belonged to the Germans.'

'I don't know all of it,' Miller said. His manner was an unreadable blend of studied vagueness and what looked to Kristín like genuine distraction, as if his real concern was far from whatever plots were at the

411

heart of this complex knot stretching back over fifty years of lies and deceptions.

'Let's look for your brother,' Kristín suggested, making a great effort to curb her temper. She would have liked to seize Miller and shake him; force him to tell her what he knew about the plane, the Germans, Napoleon. But she would have to handle him carefully, extract the story piece by precious piece. She was too close to the truth now to jeopardise it with more impatience; she swallowed a bitter taste at the thought of what that had cost her already. And yet time was so very short. Ratoff must be nearby, and other soldiers with him; she was trapped in an aeroplane somewhere over the Atlantic with no prospect of escape. The old man held the key to the riddle, tantalisingly, right here in front of her. She had to win his trust, give him more time. Though she placed little faith in his claim that he could protect her, he had about him the air of another outsider, of another person whose place in this scheme was suspect and perhaps unwanted, and this gave her some meagre hope.

Miller nodded, and they stooped down to inspect the body-bags. He found his brother in the last one. Kristín lowered the zip, revealing the face of a man who must have been in his twenties. She stepped aside for Miller, handing him the torch. He bowed over the body of his brother, scrutinising his face.

'At last,' Miller whispered.

Kristín studied the brothers, the man breathing beside her and the still, silent boy in the bag, and marvelled at how well the body had been preserved. The glacier had been gentle with it; not a scratch was visible. The face was utterly drained of colour, the taut skin like thin white paper. The young man had strong features: a high forehead, finely drawn brows and prominent cheekbones. His eyes were closed and his face, though she wished there were some other way of expressing it, looked at peace. It reminded Kristín of a book she had at home containing photographs of dead children. They looked like china dolls: immaculate, frozen, cold. This face too appeared cast from porcelain.

A tear fell, shattering on the hard shell of the cheek. She looked from one face to the other.

'He's only twenty-three,' Miller said.

39

Kristín listened in silence. She no longer felt the cold; her mind was too preoccupied. Her side ached where Ratoff had stabbed her but it seemed he had not injured her seriously. The wound had bled quite heavily at first but it was a compact puncture, if deep, and gradually the bleeding had slowed until it stopped altogether.

Miller was lost in reminiscence. He and his brother had both joined up in December 1941 in the immediate wake of Pearl Harbor but had no say where they were posted. Miller had been appointed to army intelligence HQ in Washington, while his brother was assigned to the air force and sent all over Europe, to Reykjavík among other places. During his time there he had flown over Iceland and Greenland, and later also flew missions from bases in Britain and Italy.

They had kept in touch as far as circumstances allowed. His brother saw more action than he ever did and Miller was dogged by worry about him. They met only twice during the war, once in London, and again in Paris, when Miller gave his brother his assignment. They would write, however, keeping up to date with each other's movements, and looked forward to being reunited after the war.

The assignment required a pilot from the Allied forces, one familiar with the route, who could make the necessary contact with the Allied air traffic control centres. The mission was to fly to Iceland and then to cross the Atlantic. His brother by this stage could have flown it blindfolded so Miller had put forward his name as pilot. The war was in its final phase and he had believed that he had his brother's best interests at heart; they would meet up in Reykjavík and fly on to South America, far from enemy planes and anti-aircraft defences, where they could enjoy a few days' leave. It was a straightforward mission, a safe way of ticking off another precious parcel of time survived before the war ground to its inevitable end.

Miller was kept ignorant of where the idea had originated and who was behind its implementation. He did not even know which division of the army had formulated it. All personnel involved were given only partial information, with no more than a handful of senior officers aware of its ultimate purpose. Miller was merely following orders, conducting his part of the operation as efficiently as possible. He did not know the details, did not know the agenda of the Allied–German talks, or the identities of those who attended the meeting in Paris. All that was revealed later. At first the plan had been for the Germans to provide an Allied plane that they had in their possession, but this course was abandoned and they instead decided to paint a Junkers Ju 52 in Allied colours.

Miller had arrived in Iceland with two other intelligence agents two days before his brother was scheduled to fly the German delegation over from Berlin. The agents took rooms at Hotel Borg. Reykjavík was packed with US servicemen but they avoided company, kept a low profile and checked the facilities at the aerodrome the British had built within the city limits at Vatnsmýri. The plane would have a three-hour stopover in Reykjavík to take on provisions and refuel before continuing its journey west. For the next two days the weather forecast was fine;

after that the outlook was less clear, but there was an inevitable degree of uncertainty at this time of year.

The meeting in Berlin had dragged on. Miller did not know why. They had been issued with a rigid schedule from which they were not to deviate under any circumstances, but it was no good. By the time his brother took off, a deep low-pressure weather system had formed to the south of Iceland and was moving steadily towards the north-east of the country and the barometer was plunging at an alarming rate. Snow and low visibility were now forecast. Air traffic control in Prestwick, Scotland, was the last to make contact with the plane four hours after it left Berlin. By then it was north of the Scottish coast but still within their airspace. After that, whether its radio had stopped working or not, no further news was received until the brothers turned up in the village of Höfn to report that they had seen a plane flying so low that it must have crashed on the glacier.

Miller was informed as soon as it became clear that contact with the plane had been lost; somehow he knew instantly that it had crashed. He sensed it. He waited in a hangar on the airfield, hoping in vain to hear from his brother. Days passed and the storm that had raged in the south-east of the country now passed over Reykjavík, trapping people indoors for days on end. It was Miller's belief that the plane had either crashed into the sea or that his brother had turned back to Scotland when the conditions deteriorated and gone down there. He clung to the forlorn hope that his brother might have survived the crash-landing and would eventually turn up, staggering out of one wilderness or another to some outpost of civilisation. But it was not to be.

When news of a plane sighting in the vicinity of Vatnajökull reached the occupying force in Reykjavík, Miller was appointed leader of the rescue mission. He had spent the entire time since the plane lost contact wandering between Hotel Borg and the aerodrome on Vatnsmýri, preoccupied with potential explanations and scenarios, unable to go anywhere or do anything. The intelligence officers were scheduled to leave Iceland shortly and return to Washington but Miller could not bear the prospect of never learning his brother's fate. When the report came in from Höfn, he felt as if he had received a cold electric shock. He knew his brother was found. He might even be alive, though no one appreciated better than Miller how remote a possibility this was. At the very least he would be able to take his body home with him.

What he did not know were the particular difficulties of the wintry land he found himself in. It was impossible to fly in the storm that had now blown up and he was dismayed to discover that driving to Höfn along the south coast was made impossible by wide, unbridgeable rivers that flowed from the ice cap over vast glacial outwash plains to the sea. The northern route was the only alternative, despite its many challenges. Major General Cortlandt Parker, commander of the US occupying force in Iceland, provided him with two hundred of his best men, some of whom had taken part in exercises on the Eiríksjökull glacier earlier that winter. Few had experience in searching in snow, however. They followed rough winter tracks around the country, at times digging the convoy of vehicles out of snowdrifts as high as a man's head. The days wasted on the northern route were hard to endure for Miller.

Their luck improved, however, and they had good weather and reasonable conditions for their drive south through the East Fjords, finally reaching Höfn on the fourth day. Miller headed directly to the foot of the glacier to find the two brothers who had been the last to sight the plane; they were eager to help. They told him about the glacier and warned him against high expectations. Miller was surprised to find how easy it was to approach the ice cap from their farm, despite the heavy snowfall over the last few days. Pointing him and his men in the direction they believed the plane had taken, the brothers accompanied him to the glacier, lent him horses and assisted in any way they could. They ended up becoming friends.

But it was all in vain. Miller had seen it in the brothers' faces the first time he explained his mission. Saw the glances they exchanged. The soldiers carried out a painstaking search, dividing the glacier systematically into sections and combing the ice in long lines, inserting slender three-metre-long poles into the snow. But without success. All they found was the plane's nose wheel. Every other fragment and trace had been consumed by the glacier.

The day Miller gave orders to abandon the hunt, he walked out further on to the ice sheet than before, far beyond the outer limit of their earlier searches, scanning the surroundings for hours on end before finally heading back, defeated, to his company. The weather had turned fine and the storm now seemed a distant memory. The sun shone high in a clear blue sky and there was not a cloud to be seen in the perfect stillness. The glacier stretched out, a pristine white expanse, as far as the eye could see. Miller could not help but be struck by its magnificent desolation, and would later think of this moment of solitude, cold and calm when recalling Iceland.

But beneath this awareness of the beauty of his surroundings ran the churning, appalling feeling that somewhere below his feet, in the ice, at this very moment, his brother was trapped inside the plane, dying of cold and hunger.

40

Kristín studied the brothers, now reunited after all these years, one so young, the other stamped by conflict and old age.

'So you were looking for your brother as much as Napoleon,' she said eventually, trying to feel her way, to encourage Miller to continue his story. Every utterance was now calculated to lead him to believe that she knew more than he had suspected. Miller raised his eyes from his brother to Kristín's face and stared at her. At last, he seemed to come to a decision.

'Napoleon wasn't on board the plane,' he said in the same quiet voice. Kristín could not hide her excitement.

'Where was he then?' she asked.

'I don't know,' Miller said, his eyes returning to his brother. 'And I don't know where he is now. I'm not sure anyone does any longer.'

He fell silent and Kristín waited.

'You have to understand that only a tightly controlled number of people within the army knew about Operation Napoleon,' Miller continued at last. 'Even I never knew exactly what it entailed, what the documents contained. I only knew the contents by hearsay. I was nothing but a pawn, an errand boy, assigned to solve a specific problem. My brother too.'

He trailed off again.

'I believe it was conceived and planned by a handful of generals based in Europe — American generals, that is. I don't know where the idea came from or who took the initiative, but however it came about, talks were entered into with the Germans. Ever since it had become clear that the Germans were going to lose the war there had been discussions about how Europe would be split into Allied- and Russian-occupied territories. By the time the end was approaching and the Russians were pouring into Eastern Europe, people were beginning to talk in earnest about whether we should invade Russia and finish off what the Germans had failed to do; arrange an armistice with the Germans, prior to tackling the Red Army. The only person to float the idea openly was General Patton but no one took him seriously. People were tired of war. They wanted peace. Understandably.'

'But what's the point of all this?' Kristín asked impatiently. 'This is all common knowledge. Even I've heard of it. There was an article in the British papers recently saying that Churchill had drawn up plans to invade Russia as soon as Germany had surrendered.'

'Operation Unthinkable was its name,' Miller replied.

'Exactly. That can hardly be the secret your people are prepared to torture and kill for. It's old news.'

'As a matter of fact, it's quite a big question, in the light of history,' Miller said. 'The division of Europe. The Cold War. The nuclear threat. The Vietnam War. Could we have avoided all that? We defeated the Japanese and today they're an economic superpower. Might the same have happened in Russia?'

Now he's just wasting time, Kristín thought. Can't he see that we have no time? I have to have answers now.

Vytautas Carr was sitting in the flight cabin. Since he could no longer hear Ratoff's screams above the noise of the engines, he concluded that he must have given in. They all did in the end, even the Ratoffs of this world. It was merely a question of when. He did not know what they had done to him, did not want to know; the sordid details were irrelevant. They were short of time and Ratoff had been shown no mercy. It was futile to withstand the pincer movement of drugs and physical horrors; and no one understood that better than Ratoff himself.

Carr looked out into the night. He would retire when all this was over. It was his last assignment and he felt as if he had spent his whole life waiting to be able to close this chapter. To be able to draw a line under this little footnote left over from the war years, one which the world had forgotten and no one cared about any more.

One of Carr's men materialised beside him and bent to his ear.

'We have it, sir.'

'Is he still alive?' Carr asked.

'Just about, sir,' the man answered.

'Have you made arrangements to retrieve the documents?'

'It won't be a problem, sir. They're on their way to the base at Keflavík. We've arranged to have the convoy intercepted and the documents destroyed. As you asked.'

'Right.'

'What should we do with Ratoff, sir?'

'We have no further need of him. Just do whatever's necessary. And don't tell me about it.'

'Understood. There's nothing further, sir.'

'One thing — the bags. Have you checked the body-bags since we took off?'

'No, sir.'

'It's probably unnecessary. The temperature back there should be low enough to preserve the bodies. Not that it matters. Except perhaps to Miller.'

Carr paused.

'Where is Miller?' he asked.

'No idea, sir. I thought he was with you.'

'He was here not long ago. Find him and bring him back.'

'Yes, sir. By the way, I checked on the bags when the two halves of the plane were loaded and all seven were present.'

Carr was silent. He looked again through the cockpit window at the blackness beyond. The man was turning away.

'Seven? You mean six,' Carr corrected him.

'No, sir. There are seven bags.'

'No, there were only six bodies on the glacier. There should have been seven but one of them was missing. There are six bags.'

'There are seven bags, sir.'

'Don't be ridiculous. Why seven? That can't be right.'

'Sir, I couldn't say. But I definitely counted seven bags.'

'It was the second round of talks with the Nazis,' Miller went on, his eyes on his brother's face. 'We were testing the flight route and the plane, at the same time as transporting the gold and some of the Nazis in the negotiating committee. These two crates were meant as an appetiser. They still had to agree on a final destination in Argentina.'

'Who?'

'The Nazis.'

'Were they escaping?'

'Of course. They all wanted to escape. Cowardly assholes, the whole damn lot of them.'

'Lots of them escaped to South America,' Kristín said, willing him to continue. Since the old man appeared to offer no threat to her, she had temporarily forgotten the danger she was in. At the forefront of her mind was the insistent conviction that she had to fish for more information, that any scrap she could glean might prove crucial. She was in the endgame now, and though she dimly expected some final confrontation, she knew that she would need to gather everything she had if she was to evade the trap which was closing around her. 'Adolf Eichmann,' she added. 'He was caught in Argentina.'

'I believe we let them have Eichmann,' Miller replied.

'What do you mean?'

'We led them to Eichmann.'

'You did what?'

'Besides being ruthless, Mossad are tireless. Like bloodhounds. You can't keep anything hidden from them indefinitely. When the Israelis had sniffed out too much, we arranged things to look as if the trail led to Eichmann. They were satisfied and took the bait. But they would never have found him without our intelligence.'

Kristín had the sensation of being in freefall. Her mind was at once quite empty and yet overwhelmed with trying to take in the implications of Miller's revelation. The individual words were barely registering as sounds but the sense of what he was saying seemed to penetrate her mind obscurely. Her face betrayed no emotion, no great astonishment as Miller went on. She had, it might have looked to Miller, entered a state of suspended animation.

'The Germans were in no position to lay

down conditions for a ceasefire. They were defeated; it was only a question of time before the war ended. They were so terrified the Reds would reach Berlin first that many of them were prepared to join us in the final months if we could be trusted to turn on the Russians.'

'The trail to Eichmann?' Kristín said, as if to herself. 'Whose trail were they on then?'

'A Swedish count acted as intermediary between us and the Nazis,' Miller continued, ignoring her question. 'It may have been his idea, put to a handful of people. Or the Nazis may have raised it first. Himmler wanted to do a deal with the Allies over fighting the Communists; he counted on becoming the new head of government. Meanwhile Churchill drafted a plan to attack Russia with German support and I believe the idea was hatched after that. The Nazis couldn't dictate conditions but they could put in a request. I don't think the plan originated with the US generals but once they considered it, the idea didn't seem so preposterous. After all, there was a historical precedent. There was Napoleon.'

'What's Napoleon got to do with all this? Why Napoleon?'

But to Kristín's horror, Miller appeared to catch himself, to come out of the mist of recollection and confession into which he had drifted, and to regain some measure of control.

'I can't tell you anything else. I've already said more than enough.'

'You haven't said anything.'

'That's because I don't know anything for certain. I never saw the documents.'

'What are you talking about?'

'The Operation Napoleon papers. I never saw them. Never saw what the final plan looked like.'

'Who drafted it?'

'I can't tell you any more. And you don't want to know any more. Believe me. You don't want to know. No one wants to know. It doesn't matter any more. It's irrelevant. It's all buried and forgotten.'

'What?'

Miller looked down at his brother without speaking, and Kristín saw tears welling up in his eyes. She did not understand what he was insinuating and was fast losing patience with his evasions; here he was, perched on the precipice of giving up whatever precious information he had guarded so jealously for so long. She fought back the instinct to shake the last shreds out of him.

'Ask yourself what became of Napoleon,' Miller said abruptly.

'What became of him? He died in exile on St Helena. Everyone knows that.'

'Well, they did the same thing.'

Kristín stared at the old man, forgetting to breathe.

'That's why they called it Operation Napoleon.'

'And Napoleon?'

'He was to be allowed to take his dog with him. A German shepherd called Blondi. Nothing else. I've wondered about this all my life but never had any confirmation. I don't know if the suggestion that his life should be spared originated as part of the negotiations with the German war cabinet, or if he was handed over to the Allies to smooth the way for negotiations, or if the British and Americans were competing with the Russians to get to him first. Perhaps there was another, more obscure reason. The Germans' last hope was to drive a wedge between the Allies, to encourage friction between them. After all, they knew Churchill was no friend of the Russians.'

Miller paused.

'My brother was supposed to fly him,' he said eventually.

'Your brother?' Kristín said, her eyes on the body-bag.

'He didn't know. Didn't know the real

purpose of the journey, I mean. I was going to tell him when we met but I never got the chance.'

'But this is absurd!' Kristín said.

'Yes, absurd,' Miller agreed. 'That's the word for it. Can you imagine what would have happened if news had got out that the Americans had helped him to escape and kept him in detention?'

'But the Russians got him.'

'No. Somewhere near the bunker, in the chaos and wreckage of Berlin, the Russians found the burnt body of a man who could have been anybody. It suited them, and us, and everybody else to make certain assumptions, to draw conclusions. In any case they later mislaid the remains. That made proving his identity impossible and allowed the space for what were always written off as crackpot conspiracy theories to flourish.'

'So where is he?'

'I haven't read the documents. I hardly know anything, really. It was only a plan.'

'Do you mean they never followed it through?'

'I haven't a clue. I don't know if they did. I don't think any one person was in charge. People were involved on a need-to-know basis.'

'But you mentioned Eichmann. You said

432

the Americans had directed the Israelis to Eichmann when they stumbled across the trail.'

'I'm only inferring,' Miller said and Kristín could see that he was belatedly trying to backtrack, regretting having said so much. He had become wary now, unwilling to compromise himself any further. He looked vaguely ashamed of himself, somehow childlike. Even though the genie was out of the bottle, long-held habits of discretion were vainly doing battle with this newer taste for confession.

'Where is Napoleon?'

'I don't know. I'm telling you the truth. I don't know.'

'They put him on an island?'

But Miller had come to the end. His shoulders slumped, his head bowed, he looked physically smaller and more fragile, a husk of a man finally overcome by burdens of grief and concealment.

'Which island?'

Silence.

'After all these years, what are you scared of? Can't you see it's over?'

Before he could answer, if he ever meant to, the dim light of his flickering torch went out and they were plunged into darkness.

41

C-17 Transport Plane, Atlantic Air Space,
Sunday 31 January, 0615 GMT

From the sudden popping of their ears they sensed that the plane was losing altitude. Surely it was too soon for them to be beginning their descent? They waited, listening. After a while a new noise began above the drone of the engines but neither recognised it. Kristín crawled cautiously through the wreckage of the Junkers' fuselage to the gap that Miller had cut in the sheeting. Inch by inch, her chest hammering, she craned her head out to see the vast ramp which formed the aft door of the plane slowly lowering. The night was moonlit outside and in the blue-white radiance she saw the silhouettes of figures standing by the opening. For a few seconds she feared she would be sucked into the black void before she realised that the cargo hold was not pressurised.

She squeezed through the gap and down

on to the floor of the hold, stealing along the fuselage towards the men. There were three of them but trying to hear a word they were saying was hopeless; a freezing wind blew in violent gusts and the noise of the plane reached an ear-splitting level as the view of the night sky grew larger. Her back pressed against the struts of the fuselage, she crept along the left-hand wall, hidden among the shadows. The men were standing only a few feet in front of her. Now that she could make out their faces, she realised they were strangers. She was certain neither Bateman nor Ratoff was among them. She took care to keep at a safe distance, and was about to return to Miller when she saw a pallet emerge from deep within the dark bowels of the plane.

As it became more distinct she realised that there was a figure lying on top of it. He was flat on his back, lashed down, his arms splayed and his legs bound together, as if he were being crucified. His eyes were fixed on the opening which was slowly but inexorably drawing closer. It was Ratoff. Kristín saw that he was stripped to the waist; his torso smeared in blood, his face criss-crossed by lacerations. He approached the void at a snail's pace, struggling with all his might to free himself, straining at the bonds that tied him down, straining to sit up. But his cries of terror were drowned out by the overwhelming din of the engines and the boiling turbulence of the air, and his bucking, screaming progress was reduced to a mesmerising dumb show.

The three men completely ignored him, paying him no more attention than an item of freight. As the aft door completed its slow yawning, Kristín watched them take refuge at a point further inside the plane. She gazed and gazed, watching Ratoff rolling closer to the lip of the mechanised rollers, savouring the loathing which blazed up inside her. She felt once again the ache in her side where her flesh had been punctured, saw Elías in his clutches begging for mercy, saw Steve collapsing with a bullet in his face.

As Ratoff drew near, she rose up, forgetting herself so far as to step out of her hiding place and walk to meet the pallet. She could not take her eyes off the monster who had shot Steve without the slightest provocation; she was drawn to him as if magnetised.

A bone-chilling gust of wind battered and tore at her, the air frozen and thin, but she did not hesitate as she made her way to Ratoff and looked down at him while he writhed and struggled to free himself from his bonds. With horrified fascination she took in the ingenious cruelties they had inflicted on him: his fingers bloody at the ends where the nails had been extracted, both thumbs missing, his nose broken and black holes where several teeth had been kicked in, a patch of skin flayed from his chest. She felt not a single twinge of compassion. The rollers screeched relentlessly onwards.

Ratoff was staring at the approaching void in agonised horror when Kristín reached him. Seeming to sense her presence, he reluctantly tore his eyes from the door. His face twisted in a grimace. Disbelief, confusion and desperation could be read in his eyes. He jerked and winced as his body was racked by a spasm of pain, then seemed almost to laugh, before bursting into a trembling, shaking fit of coughing.

'Never cross Carr,' Ratoff whispered when she bent over him. Blood bubbled through his split lips. 'Take it from me. Do I look convincing? Never cross Carr.'

Kristín did not speak. The pallet crawled on as she watched.

'I must . . . Kristín, isn't that your name? I must say, you're . . .'

Kristín did not hear how the sentence

ended. The noise was deafening now and Ratoff writhed in yet another hopeless attempt to break free.

'Help me!' he croaked at her. 'For Christ's sake, untie me.'

She looked down at him, followed him a little further, then stopped. She no longer felt anger or hatred towards him. She felt nothing. She was drained of all emotion. The pallet continued its measured progress, as a coffin might pass through a curtain, and she watched it tilt, pause, then fall as Ratoff vanished into the black void. When the aft door began to close again, Kristín remained standing as if rooted to the spot. Her strength had run out, she was on the point of collapse, overwhelmed by the full weight of all the nights without sleep, all the horrors she had witnessed. She no longer cared about anything any more and she flirted briefly with the idea of simply disappearing, of stepping into the black eternity while the opportunity presented itself. It would be so easy to let herself fall, to put an end to her ordeal, to the pain and exhaustion and guilt over Steve, to silence the accusing voices in her head, telling her over and over that it was her fault he had died.

The feeling passed.

A great stillness and quiet fell again inside the hold once the aft door had closed. Asking herself how much of this scene she should tell Miller, Kristín turned, only to find herself face to face with a tall, imposing, elderly man, wearing the uniform of a US general. Behind him stood three other men, the same three that she had just seen shepherd Ratoff out of the aft door. Miller too was standing beside the tall man, who now held out his hand to her.

'Kristín, I presume,' Carr said.

42

Carr took a seat with Kristín and Miller in the C-17's cramped flight cabin. Kristín did not know what had become of the other men, nor how many other people were on board. No one had been introduced, nobody had a name; she felt she was in a world of nameless shadows.

A cup of coffee was handed to her. She could not remember when she had last eaten — perhaps at Jón's farm, perhaps not. She had no idea what day it was, what week or month, nor how long she had been awake. All she knew was that she was on a plane somewhere over the Atlantic. And Steve was dead.

'Colonel Miller's trying to convince me that you know nothing about the sensitive contents of this German plane which we have gone to great lengths to retrieve,' Carr

said. 'He says there aren't enough Icelanders in the world.'

'Who are you?' Kristín asked. She was too
shattered and depressed to take in much
about this man. He was just another in the
string of shadowy figures she had encountered over the last forty-eight hours.

'That's of no importance.'

Never cross Carr, Kristín thought. Behind
her eyelids burned the image of Ratoff
lashed to the pallet.

'Are you Carr?' she asked.

'As far as we're concerned, the mission's
over. We just need to tie up a few loose ends
and . . .'

A man appeared at the door, entered the
cabin and bent to whisper a few words in
Carr's ear. Carr nodded and the man went
out again.

'You shit,' Kristín muttered in a low voice.

'Excuse me?' Carr said.

'You fucking American shit.'

His grey eyes appraised her coolly from
behind his glasses. She read nothing in his
gaze — neither amusement nor offence. 'I
can understand how you feel,' he said.

'Understand?' she laughed. 'How could
you understand anything?' As Kristín's
indignation rose, she caught the look of
alarm on Miller's face. He tried to caution

441

her but Carr silenced him.

'You are murderers. You have violated every law and standard of decency. You disgust me — so don't claim to understand how I feel,' Kristín went on.

Carr waited patiently until she was finished. 'For what it is worth, I regret what was done to your brother and his friend,' Carr said. 'It should never have happened.'

Kristín moved faster than Carr had expected but it was all over in seconds: she sprang out of her chair and struck him in the face so hard that his head rocked back. Miller shouted at her — she had no idea what — and two men materialised behind her and forced her down into her seat. Carr rubbed his cheek, which was already turning a mottled red.

'You saw what became of Ratoff, I assume,' he said calmly.

'Is that supposed to appease me? Seeing that sadist wheeled out of the plane?'

'He overestimated his usefulness and was punished. I didn't see you trying to help him.'

'You shit!'

'Don't, Kristín,' Miller warned. 'That's enough.'

'We'll see you get back,' Carr said. 'We'll send you home to Iceland. Of course, we'll

442

have to wait until all our personnel have left with their equipment but after that you'll be free of us and we'll be free of you. You can say what you like: you can talk to the authorities and the press, to your family and friends, but I doubt anyone will believe you. We've already begun disseminating misinformation about the purpose of the mission. At the end of the day no one knows anything and that's for the best. Incidentally, there's a man on his way to Keflavík with the troops. His name's Júlíus. A friend of yours, I believe. Leader of the rescue team on the glacier. He's perfectly safe and will be set down outside the gates of the base. He'll be able to back up your story. And so will your brother — Elías, isn't it? I gather he's safe, by the way, and has been admitted to a Reykjavík hospital.'

'You mean he's . . . alive?' Krístín gasped.

'Yes,' Carr replied, 'to the best of my knowledge.'

'You're not just playing with me?'

'Certainly not.'

The relief was overwhelming. It did not matter that the news had been delivered by a stranger, a man who, from what she could tell, bore the chief responsibility for what had happened to her. She had been unable to face up to the possibility that, despite all her efforts, Elías might die. Now, however, here was the confirmation that she had managed to save his life and suddenly all she could think of was that it was Steve who had paid the ultimate price. She ground her teeth in frustration.

'We can always send people after the three of you. It's up to you to make that clear to the others. And I do urge you to take me seriously, Kristín. Go ahead and tell who you like, but if Júlíus were to go missing one day, you'll know why.'

'All because of . . .' Kristín began.

'An old plane,' Miller interrupted. 'All because of an old plane.'

'All I want to know is what's happening. What's going on? What's the truth?'

'Kristín, Kristín, you ask too much,' Carr said. 'Truth and lies are nothing but a means to an end. I make no distinction between them. You could say we are historians, trying to correct some of the mistakes made during a century that is now coming to its close. This has nothing to do with any truth, and anyway what's in the past is irrelevant now. We reinvent history for our own purposes. The astronaut Neil Armstrong once visited Iceland — we know that. But who can say for sure whether he ever landed on the moon? Who knows? We saw

444

the pictures but what proof do we have that they weren't staged in a US air force hangar? Is that the truth? Who shot Kennedy? Why did we fight the Vietnam War? Did Stalin really kill forty million? Who knows the truth?'

Carr stopped.

'There's no such thing as truth, Kristín, if ever there was,' he continued. 'No one knows the answers any more and few even care enough to ask the questions.'

It was the last thing Kristín heard.

She felt a pinch on her neck. She had not noticed anyone behind her and never saw the needle. All of a sudden she went limp, a feeling of utter tranquillity spread through her body and everything turned black.

43

Tómasarhagi, Reykjavík

Who was Ratoff? A name in her head.

She was lying on the sofa in her living room at home in Tómasarhagi. She felt unable to move, as if pole-axed. Slowly, gradually, she resurfaced from the depths of unconsciousness. She was vaguely troubled by the thought that the shop might have closed, but sleep still held her in a powerful grip. She must have overslept. She usually drank her coffee with hot milk but had forgotten to buy any when she came home from work. The name kept resurfacing in her mind, like a cork bobbing in a stream. It frightened her somehow. She pondered this but still could not summon any energy. All she wanted was to go back to sleep. She had got up far too early that morning.

But she had to buy some milk, she must not forget. That was the first thing she remembered.

That and Ratoff.

Slowly she opened her eyes. Their lids felt heavy as lead. It was pitch dark in the flat. She just wanted to lie there, letting the tiredness flow out of her body. A jumble of unconnected thoughts swam through her mind but she made no attempt to lend them any order. She was too comfortable; she did not want to spoil it. She had not felt so well in ages. God, she was tired.

For the first time in as long as she could remember she thought about her parents and her ex-boyfriend the lawyer, and about Steve — she had always regretted dropping him the way she did. One day she would have to put that right. She would like to see him again. In fact, she felt a powerful urge to talk to him. Her thoughts drifted to that madman Runólfur and her colleagues at work, and she wondered idly if it might not be time to look for another job. Perhaps open her own legal practice with a friend. They had discussed the idea. She did not particularly enjoy working at the ministry and now that people had started threatening her it was even less appealing. The thoughts flitted through her mind without her being able to fix on any of them, fleeting, gone in a flash, snapping at her unconscious.

She had been lying on the sofa for half an hour before she tried to move and only then did she become aware of the throbbing ache in her side. She gave a startled cry as the pain lanced through her, and slumped back, waiting for the spasm to pass. Her overalls were filthy but she did not even stop to wonder why she was wearing outdoor clothes. Undoing the zip, she pulled up her jumper and found a dressing below her ribs. She stared blankly at the plasters and gauze, then gently lowered the jumper over the dressing again. When had she hurt herself? She could not remember going to hospital to have the wound dressed, nor did she know where the injury had come from, but clearly she must have been to hospital.

She made another attempt to sit up and this time managed, in spite of the stabbing pain. She did not have a clue what time it was but assumed that all the shops must be shut by now. When she glanced around the flat, the little she could see of it, everything looked normal, yet she could have sworn she had left the kitchen light on when she lay down. And where had the injury come from? It must have been serious because the dressing was quite large and her whole side was bruised dark blue.

Rising to her feet with difficulty, she

limped into the kitchen, turned on the light, went over to the fridge and fetched a can of Coke. She was dying of thirst. She gulped it down where she was standing by the open fridge, and having emptied the can, went to the sink, ran the cold water for a while and drank greedily straight from the tap. It was stiflingly hot in the flat. She went to the big kitchen window and opened it, breathing in the cold winter air.

Her briefcase was in its place and the papers she had brought home from work lay untouched on the kitchen table. She looked at the clock; it was just past seven. She had slept far too long — for a whole hour — and missed the shop. She swore under her breath. Groggy, devoid of energy, she slumped into a chair and stared into space. Something had happened, something terrible, but every detail of it was shrouded in an impenetrable fog in her mind.

Ratoff?

Kristín jumped as the phone started to ring, the sudden noise splitting the silence. She stared at it dumbly, as if she had no idea what to do with it. It rang and rang. Her first reaction was not to answer it. What if it was Runólfur? Then she remembered that Elías was going to call from the glacier. But had he not called already? Was there not also something wrong with Elías?

She stood up, went slowly over to the phone and lifted the receiver. The voice was foreign, the words English, the speaker almost certainly American. Could it be Steve? But no, this man sounded older.

'Never cross Carr,' said the voice on the phone, then hung up. The receiver was not slammed down but replaced gently, as if the caller was in no hurry.

'Hello?' Kristín said, but could hear only the dialling tone. She set the receiver down. *Never cross Carr.* Meaningless. Must have been a wrong number.

God, she felt lethargic, as if she were coming down with something — flu, maybe. It was rampant at this time of year. She went back into the living room, the sentence spoken over the phone still echoing in her head.

Never cross Carr. Never cross Carr. Never cross Carr.

What did it mean? She stood in the middle of the living room, alone in the gloom, in dirty outdoor clothing, the sentence lodged in her head. Then she remembered something rather odd; an absurd incident — something she had surely dreamt. Holding her side, she peered into the hall. She stood quite still before moving closer to the door.

It felt so vivid, so genuine, as if she had experienced it for real. She stood hesitantly by the door, before opening it and peering cautiously out into the dark entrance hall. Then she turned on the light and examined her door.

Her gaze fell on a small, neat black hole, unmistakably made by a bullet. She raised her finger to it, touching it gently, and the tears welled up in her eyes. All at once she knew the truth — that it was not a dream, nor was this the day she had believed she had woken up on. It was much later, far too late. It was all over.

She remembered Ratoff. Remembered Steve. Understood the voice on the phone.

Never cross Carr.

Kristín closed the door. A mirror hung in the hall and when she caught sight of her reflection in the glass on her way back to the living room, she did not recognise the figure in it: a gaunt-faced stranger with dark circles under her eyes and dirty hair, matted around her ear which was now red with fresh blood where the wound had reopened. She was wearing the thick snowsuit which was still stained with Steve's blood. She did not know this woman. Did not know where she had come from. She stared at her, shaking her head with incomprehension.

Steve. She remembered Steve.

And then she watched the woman in the mirror crumple as she broke down in tears, felled by an overwhelming grief.

44

Tómasarhagi, Reykjavík

That first half hour while her senses were returning was a blizzard of memories flooding back. She understood the phone call only too well now. Remembered Ratoff's words on the plane and all that Miller had said. Remembered the body-bags, and Steve, and Jón, the old farmer who lived at the foot of the glacier, the shooting outside the pub, being hunted all over the US base. The Jehovah's Witnesses, and Elías calling her from the glacier. Oh God, Elías!

There were two major hospitals in the Reykjavík area, the National and the City Hospital. She rang the National Hospital, the larger of the two, and was put through to the information desk where she asked about her brother and after a short wait was told that there was no one by that name among the patients. Next she called the City Hospital, told them her brother's name and waited, holding her breath, while the girl who answered checked the admissions list.

'Yes,' came the confirmation at last. 'He's here.'

It transpired that he was in intensive care but off the critical list and would soon return to a general ward. She could visit him whenever she liked.

'Though it's unusual for visitors to come this early,' the nurse remarked.

'Early?' Kristín said.

'So early in the morning.'

'Sorry, what day is it?'

'It's Tuesday, madam.'

Kristín hung up. It had been Friday when the Jehovah's Witnesses tried to kill her. Only four days ago. A whole lifetime compressed into four short days. Pulling on a coat, she ran out of the flat, then on second thoughts turned back and called a cab to come to the house.

'To the City Hospital,' she said, once she was in the back seat.

The city was coming to life. People were getting up, seeing to their children, leaving for work. Large flakes of snow spun lazily to earth. She felt oddly disconnected, as if she were detached, watching herself from outside; as if this was not her world and her normal life were going on peacefully in some other parallel dimension. As she paid for the taxi she had a strong intuition that she should not be using her debit card. Why, she did not know.

The nurse who took her to see Elías handed her a mask and made her don a paper robe and blue plastic shoe-covers. They walked down a long, brightly lit corridor and entered a dark room where a man lay motionless, connected to a mass of tubes which in turn were attached to a variety of machines that hummed or beeped at regular intervals. His face was obscured by an oxygen mask but Kristín knew that it was Elías. She stopped beside his bed and at last rested her eyes on him, unable to hold back the tears. Only his head was visible above the covers and she noticed that he had a bandage over one eye.

'Elías,' she said quietly.

'Elías?' she repeated slightly louder. He did not move.

She longed to gather him up in her arms but held back, inhibited by all the tubes. The tears spilled over and ran down her face, her body trembled and shook. Elías was alive. He would live. He would recover and before long he would be able to come home. She remembered being in the same position when he was hit by a car all those years ago: but she no longer felt guilty. That at least had gone. She knew she could not be held responsible for Elías's life — or anyone else's. It was beyond her power to decide life or death.

'Are you Kristín?' asked a weary voice. Flinching, she half-turned. A man had arrived unnoticed and was quietly watching her. He was tall, with a thin face and body, and a thick mane of black hair that he combed straight back off a high forehead. There was a bandage round his head.

'Are you Kristín?' the man repeated slowly.

'Who are you?' she asked.

'You can't be expected to recognise me with this turban,' the man said, squinting up at it. 'But we've met once before. My name's Júlíus.'

'Júlíus!' she said quietly, as if to herself. 'My God, are you Júlíus?'

Going over, she put her arms round him and they exchanged a fierce embrace. She gripped him as if he were the one fixed point in her existence. Eventually, he took hold of her shoulders and loosened her clasp.

'They released me yesterday and I came straight to the hospital,' he said. 'Elías is going to make it. They told me they managed to save his eye.'

'His eye?'

'One of his eyes was badly damaged but they managed to save his sight.'

Kristín looked at Elías. He breathed calmly, his machines pulsing and humming reassuringly.

'What happened to you?' she asked.

'More to the point, what happened to you?' he said.

'I don't know. I mean I don't know how they did it. I think they must have drugged me — there's a mark on my neck, here — and delivered me home. I woke up about an hour ago to find myself in my flat. I've been getting clearer and clearer flashbacks since then but I think there's a lot still missing. What about you?'

'Well, they took me prisoner and forced me to go with them when they decamped from the glacier. The man who cracked my skull kept asking me where you were. He couldn't understand how you could have vanished but I pretended not to know anything. When we got down from the glacier there were trucks waiting to transport all the equipment and I was put in one of them. I don't know how long it took but he was constantly in my face, making threats. He even threatened me with a knife.'

'That must have been Bateman.'

'If you say so. I don't know what he was called but the weird thing was that the truck suddenly stopped and some soldiers burst in and from what I could tell arrested him. They dragged him out of the truck, frisked him, and confiscated some papers he was carrying. I didn't see him again after that.'

The wheels of her addled memory turned slowly. 'Confiscated some papers?'

'Yes. He had them in his pocket.'

'And what happened to the papers?'

'Someone set fire to them in front of his nose, without so much as looking at them. The ash blew away. They left me alone after that.'

'Where did they let you go?'

'Outside the gates of the US base. I watched the convoy disappear inside. It was dark when we left the glacier and dark when we reached Keflavík so I've no idea how long it took. I got myself to town and made contact with the team on the glacier. The Americans prevented us from coming to join you. They shot at us.'

Júlíus handed her a newspaper, pointing to the headline: RESCUE TEAM ATTACKED BY MILITARY. The article was accompanied by photos of the team's bullet-riddled vehicle. He handed her another paper: SHOTS FIRED AT REYKJAVÍK RESCUE TEAM.

'We contacted the media the moment we were released,' he continued. 'The Americans have issued an apology. Army spokesmen have been busy on the TV and radio, parroting a story about conventional winter exercises involving Dutch and Belgian NATO forces in collaboration with the US army, and claiming that it was never their intention to obstruct us. They deeply regret that certain soldiers overreacted to a perceived threat and fired at us. They promise that they'll be holding an inquiry and that compensation will be offered. But they disclaim all knowledge of Elías and Jóhann's fate. Deny categorically that it had anything to do with them, or that they know anything about you.'

'And what do the Yanks say about the plane?'

'They have no knowledge of any German aircraft on the glacier. The radio news reported that the soldiers were searching for satellite-tracking equipment that had been lost several years ago by a plane crossing the glacier. The TV news, on the other hand, was saying the soldiers had been rehearsing a rescue mission involving a staged air crash, using bits of an old DC-8. And the evening paper mentioned a hunt for lost gold reserves. You see what we're up against.

They've been thorough, all right.'

Kristín took a deep breath and thought about what Júlíus had said. 'And Steve?'

For the first time since he arrived Júlíus looked awkward, his authority deserting him. 'They say he's missing, Kristín. They claim they're trying to track him down but expect it to take time.'

'I see.'

Júlíus searched her face for a reaction but it was unreadable.

'How have the Icelandic government played it?' she asked.

'By saying that they granted permission for the exercises.'

'Nothing about the plane or Steve?'

'I told them about the plane and Steve's murder and that you were missing and probably being held against your will by the Americans. It's all in the paper, but the army won't discuss it. They dismiss it all as "unfounded allegations". But you've turned up now, and soon Elías will come round and there'll be three of us. People must believe us. They'll have to, don't you think? The three of us together?'

Kristín looked from Júlíus to Elías and back again.

'They threatened me, Júlíus,' she said quietly. 'And I'm scared. I've had enough.

They threatened to harm Elías, and you too. I want it to stop, I've had enough.'

It was beyond her to explain her feelings about the ordeal she had been through or the effect it had had on her. She felt as if she were alone in the world with no one to turn to. Perhaps she would tell Júlíus what had happened once she had had some rest and recovered a little but right now all she wanted was to be left in peace.

'But we can't give in now,' he protested. 'Where were you? What was the plane on the glacier carrying? We owe it to the others'

'I saw how they treated the man who did this to Elías and killed Steve. I think I was meant to see it. As a demonstration. As if they had held a court martial, found him guilty and sentenced him, and that that ought to satisfy me. If I pursue it, they know where to find me. That was the message I got.'

Júlíus had no answer to this.

'Come on,' Kristín said, coming to a sudden decision. 'Let's go into the waiting room and talk there.'

They left Elías and walked along the corridor to a waiting room with three chairs, a table and some out-of-date magazines on a shelf. They sat down and Kristín described everything that had happened to her since

461

they parted. She repeated what Miller had told her about Operation Napoleon, and the threats made by the man, almost certainly Carr, who appeared to have been in charge. She could remember nothing at all between talking to him on board the transport plane and waking up in her own living room that morning.

Júlíus had a hard time taking in the implications of the operation. 'That's incredible, unbelievable! Who on earth could have come up with such an idea? Do you really believe it? About Napoleon, I mean,' he asked. 'Do you believe they moved him from Berlin?'

'I think they've behaved exactly as one would expect them to if they wanted to prevent the story from leaking. If the plane was carrying information that sensitive, they would want to know what happened to it, establish whether it had emerged from the ice and make sure that no one discovered its secret, whether or not the operation the papers mapped out was ever followed through. They'd send soldiers to the glacier to remove the plane and all it contained, as far as possible without attracting any media attention. You can imagine what would happen if it was found to be true.'

'And if we take our conspiracy theory to

the press . . .'

'We'll be a laughing stock, Júlíus. Nothing more.'

Neither of them spoke. They sat there in the blandly impersonal surroundings of the hospital lounge with its synthetic flowers, quietly contemplating their separate fates.

45

Reykjavík, August

The days passed, turning into weeks and months, and the media furore caused by the US army opening fire on an Icelandic rescue team gradually died down. Kristín spent much of her time at the hospital with Elías who soon regained consciousness and was able to tell her about his encounter with Ratoff. His recovery was slow but steady. Their father returned from abroad and learnt about Elías's condition, but he did not seem particularly interested in hearing the details.

'All this bloody messing about on snowmobiles,' he said. 'It's time you grew up.' Four days later he was off on another trip.

Kristín broke the news to Elías about his friend Jóhann. To her surprise, Jóhann's parents were satisfied with the explanation that the two men had fallen into a crevasse.

Kristín and Elías debated whether to tell them the truth and finally decided they would. Once Elías was stronger, they asked Jóhann's parents to the hospital and told them about the circumstances of their son's death and the eventual fate of his murderer. They chose not to mention anything relating to the German plane. Although Elías had witnessed the incident, Kristín pointed out, it was obvious that the army would not admit to any kind of violence, let alone murder, and no witnesses would come forward from among its ranks to support their statement.

Jóhann's parents, however, a wealthy, middle-aged couple, were determined to find out the truth. They called on Elías, Kristín and Júlíus as witnesses but as Kristín had suspected, the charges they submitted to the public prosecutor's office and the subsequent investigation failed to yield any results and their case was not considered strong enough to mount a prosecution. The army spokesmen declared themselves astonished by the accusation that they were harbouring a killer in their ranks; they disclaimed all knowledge of the presence of Delta Force operators or a C-17 plane in the country. The legal proceedings dragged on, the media whipped themselves into a new feeding frenzy, but this too ultimately fizzled out.

Runólfur's murder remained unsolved. Kristín was summoned again and again by the police for cross-examination but stubbornly insisted on her innocence. After an exhaustive investigation, the police concluded that there were no grounds for prosecution. The decision was taken on the recommendation of the two detectives handling the case, one of whom was the sympathetic man that Kristín had talked to on the phone while at Jón's farm. The case ended up deadlocked between the Icelandic police and the Defense Force in Keflavík.

It was announced that Steve had been found not far from the Andrews movie theatre on the base, shot in the head by an unidentified gunman, and his body was repatriated to the States for burial.

During all the legal proceedings in which she was involved over the following years Kristín never once spoke of the plane's secret, but in her spare time she read up on the history of Nazi Germany and the fall of the Third Reich. To her surprise, she discovered that many different theories had surfaced over the years as to Adolf Hitler's fate. She knew he had left orders for his remains to be burnt in the Berlin bunker when the Russians took the city. After the war, however, many doubted that this had truly been his fate. She learnt that the doctor's report on his remains, published by the Russians some time after his death on 30 April 1945, concluded that the body was probably that of Hitler; they also claimed immediately after the war ended that they had compared the skull to his dental records and had confirmed that it was Hitler's. Yet before long rumours began to circulate that he was being held prisoner in the British-occupied sector of Berlin, while at the summit meeting in Potsdam in July of 1945, Stalin announced that the Russians were ignorant of his fate; they had not found his body, and Stalin even hinted that he might be hiding in Spain or South America. This gave birth to a host of wild conjectures that he was staying in a Spanish monastery or on a South American ranch. Kristín came across yet another theory that the British had put him on board a submarine and taken him to a remote island. Indeed, towards the end of the war Stalin had suspected the British of engaging in secret talks with the Germans.

She also read that Hitler had been quoted as saying that in the end he would have only two friends — Eva Braun and his dog, Blondi.

One summer's evening, about six months after the traumatic events, she was sitting in the kitchen after a simple supper, her thoughts wandering, as so often before, back to the glacier and what had happened there, when she remembered the piece of paper she had found in the pocket of her overalls. She had emptied them before throwing away the bloodstained clothing and put the bits and pieces she found in a kitchen drawer where they had been sitting untouched ever since. Rising, she went over, opened the drawer and rummaged in the accumulated junk until she found the folded scrap of paper. Opening it, she read again the words OPERATION NAPOLEON. It was a fragment of the document that Jón had found on the body of the German officer. She placed it under a bright light and set about trying to decipher the rest of the typewritten text.

She could only read the odd word here and there but she wrote these down, along with any letters she could make out from the illegible words. Having copied down everything she could, she took her notes to a friend at the foreign ministry who had been a diplomat in Germany, and asked him to translate the text into Icelandic and, if possible, fill in the blanks to the best of his ability. She declined to tell him what it was about, where she had acquired the text or what it was part of. As she watched over his shoulder, he did his best to translate it and make some sort of sense of the whole, though he could make no suggestion as to what it added up to:

> . . . put ashore on a remote island off the southernmost tip of Argentina. There is a small uninhabited archipelago which might provide a suitable location. Although inhabited in earlier centuries, the islands were long ago abandoned on account of their harsh climate and barren terrain. The island we have in mind is known as Borne in the local language. It is the final option. The other two locations proposed for OPERATION NAPOLEON . . .

That was as far as it went. Kristín took the notes home with her, along with the translation. She told no one of her discovery, not even Elías or Júlíus, just tried to put the knowledge out of her mind. But it was no good: she had been beginning to find her feet when she came across the document but now she was once again possessed by memories of the glacier, of Steve, of Miller's story. After studying it, however, she found that she was still none the wiser about what to do, so she put the piece of paper in a drawer and locked it.

■ ■ ■ ■

2005

■ ■ ■ ■

On the day of her departure she woke up in the early hours, as she had every morning since her escape from the glacier, feeling cold and empty, as if something inside her had died.

She had neither heard nor seen anything of Carr or his henchmen since her conversation with him on board the plane in the last year of the old millennium, but there were times when she was assailed by an overwhelming conviction that she was being followed or that someone had been in the flat or rifled through her files at the office. That she was not alone. She had no idea who Carr and Miller were, or what organisation they belonged to, and made no attempt to find out. Indeed she was careful to do nothing that could risk connecting her to the plane on the glacier.

An intense paranoia filled her. She was convinced now that there had been a link between her turning on the light in her flat the morning she woke up on the sofa and the phone call she had received with the warning not to cross Carr. Someone, or more than one person, had been watching her windows and knew when she woke up and switched on the light. Sometimes when she entered her flat she sensed a presence that made her profoundly uneasy. Yet she never received another phone call.

She adopted a new way of life. She never left the city and abandoned foreign travel. Any relationships were short-lived, never intended to last. She did not have children. Not even among her tiny circle of friends did she confide in anyone about what had really happened on the glacier. Shortly after the millennium her father died, going to his grave with nothing but the vaguest idea of what his children had gone through. As she had planned, she left the ministry to open her own practice, and led a quiet, solitary sort of existence, though she and Elías remained close and Júlíus was a frequent visitor. They spent hours discussing what had happened on the glacier, but never more than that.

Hardly a day passed when she did not recall the camp, the plane, the swastika, the bodies in the tent, Ratoff, or the secret

474

knowledge she possessed. The years passed, but however hard she tried she could not quite forget the island called Borne off the southern tip of Argentina. She tried to block the memory, to convince herself that the matter was over and had nothing to do with her, but it had its claws in her and in fact it developed into a mild obsession as time went by. As if the affair were somehow unfinished.

What convinced her was the thought that Steve had died because of this knowledge. He was in her mind every day and she relived his death over and over again, during her waking hours or in her dreams. He had left a void in her life that would never heal, nor would she have it any other way. But if the matter ended like this, he would have lost his life for nothing, and that she found unbearable.

It was a ship's captain who first made her consider the possibility seriously. He engaged her to handle his divorce and a sort of friendship had developed between them. He was captain of a merchant vessel and once confided in Kristín that he had helped a young Icelandic woman flee her husband with her two children by smuggling her from Portugal to Iceland. Kristín could have chosen an easier way and flown to Argentina via Spain or Italy, but she did not dare. Did not dare risk the surveillance cameras, the passenger lists, passport control.

Even after taking the decision she did nothing precipitate. She tried as far as possible always to use cash, never credit or debit cards for transactions, to avoid places with CCTV, including some streets in the city centre where the police had installed cameras, and never used the internet at home. She fled from every aspect of the surveillance society.

She went about it as if she were organising a long holiday. The island existed, after all; she had located it with the help of the British Royal Geographical Society, whose website she visited at the National Library. Their information about the island was mainly of geographical interest, although it included a brief description of its history and the coordinates for its exact location. She considered flying to South America via Europe, or travelling there via a variety of other routes but none of these had the same attraction of invisibility.

When her friend the captain told her one day that he would shortly be sailing to Mexico to deliver an Icelandic trawler to its new owner, she decided to enlist his help. Initially he refused because she would not explain why she wanted to stow away on board his ship and slip ashore unseen in Mexico. The captain was not unaccustomed to taking passengers — there were always people who were afraid of flying and preferred to sail on merchant ships — but he wanted nothing to do with anything illegal.

She never knew why he changed his mind but one day he came and agreed he would help her, if that was what she wanted. She had asked it as a favour of a friend, he said, and who was he to deny her?

Until the very last minute she dithered about whether to go. In the end, however, she reasoned that she was approaching forty and would never make the trip if not now. The only person she told was her brother Elías. She did not want to get Júlíus involved, the way she had with Steve. She could manage her brother, but Júlíus was another matter.

The ship sailed early in the morning. She stood on deck, watching the land sink below the horizon. It was summer and her face was warmed by the sun which had already been up for several hours. The voyage was uneventful and when the ship docked at a small town on the east coast of Mexico, she managed to slip ashore without passing through customs or immigration. She had enjoyed long conversations with the captain during the voyage and they parted on good terms.

She selected a reliable car, paid for it in cash, and drove south through Mexico like any other tourist, sleeping at motels, seeing the historical sites, lingering here and there to enjoy the scenery, to savour the national cuisine and hospitality. During the journey she felt more relaxed than she had allowed herself to feel in a long time. It was delightful to be abroad again.

Several days later she reached Buenos Aires. Evening had fallen by the time she drove into the capital city. She found herself a room at a reasonably priced hotel and purchased a detailed road map on which she marked out the route south. She was confident that she was not being followed, that she had managed to make it to Argentina unremarked.

Two days later she set off from Buenos Aires. She sold the car and made the first leg of the journey by plane, landing that afternoon at Comodoro Rívadavía in the middle of Patagonia. There she bought a bus ticket and calculated that the journey to the south of the country would take a further three days. The route ran for the most part along the coast. She stayed the first night at Caleta Olivia, travelling the next day through the farming settlements of Fitzroy and Jaramillo, from where she headed due south across the Rio Chico and by ferry across the Magellan Straits to the town of San Sebastián in Puerto Harberton, a town of about 15,000 people just north of the Chilean border.

She arrived towards evening and took a room at a small hotel. The following day she walked down to the harbour and found a sailor who spoke a little English. He was in his fifties, bearded and toothless, and reminded her pleasingly of an Icelandic fisherman. She asked about the island and he nodded, waving his arm in a wide arc. It was a long way out, she gathered. They negotiated a fee and agreed to meet early next morning to sail out to the island.

She spent the day strolling around the town, browsing the shops and the market. Noticing other tourists, she did her best to mingle. Although it was out of season, she had met countless travellers on her journey through the country; no matter how small the backwater, they could be found examining wares and lounging in cafés.

The fisherman was waiting for her down by the harbour next morning and as they sailed out in his little boat the day was perfectly calm, the air warm on her skin. She paid half the fare in advance; he would get the rest when they returned, as they had agreed. She tried to question him about the island's history but he seemed completely uninterested, saying dismissively that he knew nothing about Borne, that there was nothing to know.

They chugged along at a comfortable speed past rocks, islets and archipelagos for about five hours until finally he nudged her and pointed ahead. She watched the island rise out of the sea, surrounded by a few smaller skerries. It reminded Kristín of the rugged Icelandic island of Drangey, not as high but at least three times larger, an inhospitable rock supporting some vegetation but no bird life at all. It was enveloped by silence. They sailed round the island until the fisherman thought he spied a place where Kristín could clamber up the cliffs. He intended to stay behind in the boat.

In the event it was not a difficult climb; a gravel path led from the beach to the cliffs where there was a fairly easy incline to the top. On reaching the plateau, she saw some ruins in the middle of the island and headed that way. As she got closer she observed tumbledown wooden walls, a beaten-earth floor and a doorstep. She made a circuit of them, noticing something that reminded her of an old kitchen hearth. The island had indeed been occupied in earlier centuries.

She walked among the remains, searching carefully for any clue that might support her suspicions. But in vain; there was simply nothing there. She was surprised to find that this prompted no sense of disappointment in her, despite the journey halfway round the world. Afterwards she walked the length of the island to the brink of the precipice and gazed at the waves breaking on the cliffs while the sea breeze caressed her face. For the first time in years she felt a weight lift off her chest.

Turning round, she retraced her steps through the ruins. A short distance beyond them, on the way back to the waiting boat, she tripped on a rock lying buried in the long grass. She glanced down and was about to carry on — the fisherman would be wanting to leave — when she noticed its shape. It was no ordinary rock. It was thin, about half a metre long, square at the bottom and rounded at the top. She looked down at it in puzzlement, before crouching and trying to turn it over. It was heavy but with some effort she managed to raise it on its edge, then let it fall back on to the other side.

Squinting down at the stone, and rubbing at the accumulated dirt with her finger, she made out a crude carved inscription:

BLONDI
1947

ABOUT THE AUTHOR

Arnaldur Indriðason won the CWA Gold Dagger Award for *Silence of the Grave* and is the only author to win the Glass Key Award for Best Nordic Crime Novel two years in a row, for *Jar City* and *Silence of the Grave.* The film of *Jar City,* now available on DVD, was Iceland's entry for the 2008 Academy Award for Best Foreign Film, and the film of his next book, *Silence of the Grave,* is currently in production with the same director. He lives in Iceland.